ASSASSIN'S CREED
THE DESERT THREAT

The flash of two blades interrupted his thoughts. He'd barely stepped into the forest when the two hidden guards leapt out on either side, attempting to skewer him. They'd been ordered to check their victim's identity, but the darkness and rain had driven them to accomplish their task as quickly as possible. Used to working together, they'd intended to make quick work of the brazen individual who had dared to follow their captain. No one could stand against their Xinchun sabers, short-bladed weapons that were easy to maneuver.

But instead of slicing flesh, their blades met nothing but empty air.

The two men spun around, incredulous, their astoundment quickly turning into fear. Captain Hu had only ordered them to wait for an hour. Even better, he didn't necessarily expect them to bring back a body. And since the young man had vanished, they could say that they hadn't seen anyone. That was much better than trying to face a ghost.

MORE ASSASSIN'S CREED® FROM ACONYTE

Assassin's Creed: The Ming Storm by Yan Leisheng
Assassin's Creed: The Magus Conspiracy by Kate Heartfield

Assassin's Creed Valhalla: Geirmund's Saga by Matthew J Kirby
Assassin's Creed Valhalla: Sword of the White Horse by Elsa Sjunneson

ASSASSIN'S CREED®

The DESERT THREAT

YAN LEISHENG

Translation by
Nikki Kopelman

ACONYTE

UBISOFT

First published by Aconyte Books in 2022.

ISBN 978 1 83908 172 9

Ebook ISBN 978 1 83908 173 6

Cover art by Simon Goinard

Distributed in North America by Simon & Schuster Inc, New York, USA
Printed in the United States of America
9 8 7 6 5 4 3 2 1

ACONYTE BOOKS

An imprint of Asmodee Entertainment Ltd

Mercury House, Shipstones Business Centre

North Gate, Nottingham NG7 7FN, UK

aconytebooks.com // twitter.com/aconytebooks

PROLOGUE

Sharp fangs of reef occasionally burst through the surface of the oily sea, threatening to pierce any unwary ship. The danger was well known to local fishers, and this area had been off limits for years; only pirates and a few daring merchant ships dared enter. And yet, a small boat was anchored a respectful distance from the reef, carrying two women dressed in men's clothes and a surprisingly mature-seeming young boy. The latter sat in the prow of the boat, carefully scanning the waves.

His prolonged silence worried the younger passenger, in her twenties, A-Qian, who turned her dark-skinned face towards her slightly older companion. Unshakable of demeanor since the beginning of their journey, the elder passenger, Shao Jun, nodded calmly. If the boy wasn't reacting, it was simply because there was nothing to get excited about. But just then, the lad in the prow turned towards them and exclaimed, "I feel it!"

Relief shone in Shao Jun's eyes.

"What is it, Xiao Gui?" she asked, using the affectionate "xiao" to put him at ease.

"There's a hollow mound under the surface... and two towers standing inside it!"

Even he seemed amazed.

"Describe it for me."

"They're made of metal, and very tall... but they've collapsed in places, like they've melted somehow," he added, gesturing as he spoke.

"Are you sure, little sister?" Shao Jun eagerly asked her young friend A-Qian.

"Yes, it is close," she replied quietly after a moment of thought.

Several years ago, Dai Yu Island stood on that spot, until the eruption of its volcano wiped away the last traces of its mysterious hidden past. Even Shao Jun, who had seen those fantastic towers for herself, couldn't recall what they looked like, not even in her dreams. But Bai Gui's brief description quickly brought it all flooding back.

While she didn't show it, Shao Jun was filled with an excitement she hadn't felt for an age. Bai Gui was able to feel the presence of the remnants of the Precursors. Incredibly courageous and intelligent, he had a propensity to understand everything, an infinite wisdom that up until now she had only seen in Wang Yangming. The young man had the potential to take up the torch of the venerable master, perhaps even to surpass him.

The Society of the Mind would endure, she was sure of that.

A shot rang out, accompanied by a cloud of blue smoke

that rose into the sky several miles away. The passengers on the small boat would never have seen these warning signals had the sea been rough. Since only clandestine ships braved these treacherous waters, if one of them had cause to resort to their guns, it was best not to linger.

"Raise the sails!" Shao Jun ordered as she began to haul up their makeshift anchor, a simple rope knotted around a large stone.

Born on the coast, A-Qian had spent more time at sea than on land, so boats of this type were nothing new to her. Seeing her struggle to raise the heavy sails, Bai Gui rushed to her aid.

"Let me help you, big sister!"

"Don't talk to me like that," she retorted.

"A-Qian..." He hesitated for a moment before adding "Aunt Qian", his reluctance making the young woman smile.

"'You do know that if names be not correct, language is not in accordance with the truth of things, do you not?'"[1]

Glancing at Shao Jun out of the corner of his eye, the young man began to recite the relevant *Analects* passage from Confucius:

"'If names be not correct, language is not in accordance with the truth of things. If language be not in accordance with the truth of things, affairs cannot be carried on to success. When affairs cannot be carried on to success, proprieties and music will not flourish. When proprieties and music do not flourish...'"[2]

---

[1] Translation from the Chinese taken from *The Analects of Confucius*, Book 13, Verse 3 (James R Ware, translated in 1980)

[2] Translation from the Chinese taken from *The Analects of Confucius*, Book 13, Verse 3 (James R Ware, translated in 1980)

"You don't need to recite the whole thing, I can see that you've learned your lesson!" she cut him off, slightly embarrassed that she wasn't quite so well learned. "But don't forget to call me Aunt Qian, please?"

"Yes, Aunt Qian."

The adolescent's docile response and his clear lack of understanding drew a smile from A-Qian. But as they spoke, her rope became tangled with the pulley, leaving the sail only half-unfurled. Used to this kind of problem, she climbed the mast to untangle the rope; as she completed her task, another shot boomed in the distance. Shading her eyes with her hand, she squinted in the direction of the battling ships, then suddenly jumped onto the deck.

Having just finished pulling up the anchor, Shao Jun quickly noticed her agitated demeanor.

"What is it, A-Qian?"

"Big sister, that ship… It's my brother's!"

"Tiexin?"

A-Qian nodded vigorously.

Her brother, Huan Wangquan, was nicknamed Tiexin, meaning "heart of fire". He had begun his career as a trader of semi-legal goods off the Sino-Japanese coast, then become a pirate due to a change of circumstance when the empire had declared these waters off limits. Shao Jun had met him through Yangming, who had persuaded him to help destroy Zhang Yong's base on Dai Yu Island, but he had abandoned his sister to certain death when faced with its sheer horrors.

After risking her own life to rescue Shao Jun, A-Qian had remained at her big sister's side and hadn't seen her brother since. Despite the years, her feelings towards him were still complicated. Some bonds are not so easily broken.

Now at the prow, Shao Jun could now make out the colors of the two ships as they fought. The flag on the most distant ship bore the five mountains of Wufeng, Tiexin's fisher clan. And the other...

"It's the blue moon banner!" she couldn't help but shout.

"You know it, big sister?"

"Yes, it belongs to an old friend!"

Shao Jun silently contemplated the ships until A-Qian, bursting to find out more, dared disturb her.

"Would my big sister consider helping my brother?" she asked.

Tiexin had initially hoped that the small boat spotted earlier might be inclined to help, given their shared hatred of the maritime authorities, but the closer he got, the more convinced he was that he was not dealing with pirates. He moaned in disappointment.

"I don't recognize that boat," murmured his sworn brother Ye Zongman at his side.

The day before, they had thought they might have a chance at an easy target, an imposing merchant ship from Korea or the Ryukyu islands, full of exotic goods and run by a crew inexperienced in combat. In short, a pirate's dream. But as soon as they began to board, they realized their error: the ship was in fact a battleship in the local navy. They quickly changed course to head straight towards their hideout, not even waiting for those of their number who had already begun to mount the opposing deck. Later, much later, Japanese associates would help Tiexin obtain a Dutch ship that would rival any of the navy's, but for now, on board his fleeing junk that was incredibly vulnerable to artillery fire, he was no match for the battleship.

While the navy ship hadn't been able to match their speed, they could pursue them relentlessly without losing distance, which they had done throughout the night and following morning. Judging by their controlled shots, their aim seemed to be to capture their prey alive rather than to sink the pirate ship. But just then, a cannonball hit, destroying a large part of the stern.

Sensing imminent defeat, the entire crew grew restless. Ye Zongman had a strong relationship with the captain, and their familiarity allowed them to act as one. But after their fateful boarding attempt, they were now equally powerless to escape this predicament. With fleeing or fighting both doomed to failure, what other choice did they have?

"Brother Tiexin," shouted Xu Weixue, another of his sworn brothers, "those filthy curs are going to wipe us out!"

"Set course for that tiny skiff," Tiexin declared simply.

"And if they don't take the bait?" Ye Zongman breathed.

He'd guessed the intentions of his companion, who answered him with a nervous smile.

"Then we'll make sure it costs them dearly!"

While he usually avoided getting innocent civilians mixed up in his business, Tiexin was planning a desperate gamble: taking the small boat's passengers hostage to force the imperial patrol ship to turn back. But even so, there was no guarantee that the battleship's captain would let them go. Whoever these unidentified intruders were, and whatever their nationality, they were violating the law and may be deemed unworthy of clemency.

Xu Weixue nodded his head.

"Understood, big brother Tie, I ..."

"Huh? What are they doing?" interrupted Ye Zongman.

Instead of fleeing, the modest sailboat was sailing straight toward their pursuers. But this was only the first of several surprises, as Xu Weixue quickly discovered when he was able to make out the passengers.

"There! Is that... A-Qian?"

At the time she left, the brilliant young woman had been the beloved of the outlaw band, including the captain's sworn brothers. Most of the Eight Celestial Kings had died or been injured during the assault on Dai Yu Island, while Tiexin's sister, in all likelihood, had been swallowed by the waves. Despite his iron heart, the pirate captain had felt responsible for her death and wept mightily over the loss of his younger sister. Now he bent eagerly over the railing to try to spot her for himself. And there she was! He immediately recognized A-Qian underneath the canvas of the sail, despite her men's clothing. But just as he was about to call out, he suddenly stopped as he recognized the person alongside her.

Shao Jun!

Just as he had feared, she hadn't ended her days as ash on the seabed... What should he expect then from her return? And why was she heading towards the patrol ship? She was anything but a government agent...

Truth be told, the coastguards were more used to people fleeing before them than coming towards them in these prohibited waters, so shared Tiexin's confusion. But given its reduced size and the small number of people on board, it was clear that this boat which had seemed to appear from nowhere posed no threat. As such, no shots were fired in its direction, and when the two hulls came into contact, a soldier appeared at the stern of the imperial ship to throw a suspicious glance over the new arrivals.

"We are the imperial guard!" he shouted. "State your identity and the reason for your presence here!"

"This humble citizen requests to see Captain Hu," Shao Jun answered.

Having mistaken her for a man, the soldier was surprised by her youth, grace, and authoritative tone.

"How do you know Captain Hu?" he asked without aggression, appeased by the mention of his superior by name.

As he spoke, the young woman jumped from one ship to the other, climbing the hull with fluid, nimble gestures, using the blade concealed in the toe of her boot for purchase. The soldier had never seen anything quite so extraordinary. His hand moved reflexively towards the dagger that hung from his belt.

"What the hell are you, friend?" he called with an authority that impressed only himself.

"I recognized your flag. Please tell Captain Hu that an old acquaintance wants to see him."

Having never experienced such an attitude, the soldier was baffled by the mysterious stranger's calm, confident indifference. Lost, he was unable to do anything but stammer and nod before slipping away. While the patrol ship's cannons were pointed at the Wufengs' junk, they hadn't yet received the order to fire. Tiexin contemplated their black mouths and Shao Jun's silhouette from his own deck, consumed with anxiety. What was the little viper playing at? When she was invited to enter a cabin, the pirate felt himself boil with rage.

Captain Hu had earned the trust and admiration of his men through his skills and air of authority rather than from mere rank alone. The fact that he had agreed to meet the intruder had conferred on her the status of guest in the eyes of his crew. This ship had belonged to Yu Dayong when he was commander of the imperial guard, a post he had inherited from his father, Yu Feng, and which he himself had passed down to his favorite nephew, Hu Qianhu, a few years ago. The gold and jade trinkets had been removed, but the cabin was still decorated with representations of the forests and mountains of Yunlin, testament to his old-fashioned yet elegant taste. A man stood near a side-facing window, arms crossed in his sleeves as he looked out at the Wufengs' junk.

"Close the door behind you," he said to Shao Jun, not turning around as she entered.

The young male voice surprised his guest.

"You are not Captain Hu Shangren," she noted respectfully.

"I am Hu Ruzhen, his son. And who do I have the honor of addressing?"

"My name is Shao Jun."

"The imperial concubine…"

Her body betrayed no surprise, but a shock briefly flickered across her eyes before they regained their piercing stare. His fair skin and beardless chin had been clearly visible when he turned.

Wang Yangming had once described Tiexin to Shao Jun as useful but unreliable, and Hu Shangren as reliable but of little use due to his official duties. Originally from Jixi and then posted to Huizhou, he was a captain in the imperial guard, a hereditary post. While he didn't excel, he had been principled enough not to give in to the endemic corruption and brutality that had characterized Zhang Yong's governance; his remarkable integrity had led him to repeatedly refuse to submit to Yu Dayong's evil schemes and had saved the lives of more than one victim of his corruption. His affable character had nevertheless allowed him to remain on cordial terms with both men. On the contrary, he had won their trust enough to receive the rare privilege of his own banner, a blue moon under whose colors he proudly sailed.

While he wasn't a member of the School of Mind, Hu Shangren had had immense respect for Master Yangming, so much so that he had taken his then-teenaged son to Jishan University so he could benefit from the philosopher's advice and teachings. It was due to this sympathy, this manifest ideological closeness, that Shao Jun had thought it reasonable to ask to see him, despite her official status as a wanted criminal. Obviously, she had never expected to meet his son instead. But it would take more than that to make her lose her composure.

"It's been a long time since I was the imperial concubine, young Master Hu."

"And you no longer receive the benefits of that status, true. So why board an imperial battleship?"

"Because Master Yangming believed your father to be wise, and that you would become an extraordinary man… One in a million."

The mention of this precious accolade cooled the anger that had been threatening to engulf the captain. As a youth, he had been profoundly affected by his brief encounter with the venerable scholar whose every lesson had been of immense value to him. He was overwhelmed by the knowledge that the great man he so admired had seen such potential in him. However, he tried not to let his emotion show as he calmly responded.

"Thank you for those words, big sister. I strive to be worthy of the words of Master Yangming."

Relieved that the son was of like mind with his father, Shao Jun bowed.

"Thank you, young master, and–"

"If these pirates agree to give me what I am trying to recover," he interrupted, "I will let them go."

"What is it?"

"Not their heads, I can assure you! Just an iron box."

This box was the real reason why Hu Ruzhen had avoided sending the Wufengs' ship to the bottom of the sea, and his otherwise gentle smile was full of threat: if the bandits refused his offer, this encounter would come to a bloody end.

The young woman couldn't do anything but comply, at least until she knew more.

"I'll pass on your message, but I doubt my opinion means much to them."

"The honor of your intervention is already far more than they deserve, big sister. If they lack the wisdom to take such a generous offer, they will have only themselves to blame, and your conscience is clear. Go!"

At the cabin door, the enthusiastic sailors saluted their captain. The devotion he inspired in them despite his youth was undeniable.

"Are you sure you want to board that ship of vagabonds?" one of them whispered as they reached the ship's prow.

"I have faith in the benevolence of the sky, young master," she answered quietly.

She grabbed a rope hanging from the sail and leapt towards the junk, flying like a swallow several dozen feet above the waves, to the cheers of the onlooking sailors and pirates.

Tiexin was gripped by a deep malaise: he was relieved that he hadn't been sent to the depths, but also concerned by the return of Shao Jun, whom he had betrayed and left for dead two years earlier. And while A-Qian must have interceded on his behalf to offer him the chance to negotiate, her presence did nothing to simplify this delicate situation. What should he expect? Seeing his agitation, Ye Zongman stepped forward to speak in his stead.

"Shao Jun, what a pleasure to see you safe! And your skills are as exceptional as ever!"

The young woman knew that pirates were certainly direct, and so spared them the usual courtesies to convey the message she carried. She did not know then that the pirate captain had wanted this iron box for a long time; it was only after learning that it was on Dai Yu Island that he had agreed to join Wang Yangming in his fight against the Eight Tigers. As a result of the events that took place there, it had taken him two years to find the precious item … and then he had had the bad luck to cross the path of the imperial patrol ship.

"But how does Hu Ruzhen know we have it?" he asked Shao Jun, too shaken to think clearly.

"I don't know, and that's not the question. Will you give it to him, or not?"

It was difficult for him to give up the object that had cost him so much, but as he had just remarked to Ye Zongman, pirates had a clear understanding of the inflexibility of the law of the strongest. Sensitive to the opinion of his sworn brother, Tiexin called out to the patrol ship that he wanted to board, then walked across the narrow planks laid between the ships with the assured step of man accustomed to fighting for survival. Jostled by the swell, he knew there was no chance of turning back now.

Standing firmly, Hu Ruzhen waited for him on deck flanked by his two best men. He gave Shao Jun a nod of recognition before speaking.

"Am I speaking with the honorable Wangquan?"

The question threw Tiexin off balance, unused as he was to being called anything other than his nickname.

"I'm just a common sailor, Lord Hu," he replied with unexpected deference as he offered the box to the other man.

The captain of the patrol ship took it, glanced at the interior without revealing any emotion, then handed it to one of his subordinates.

"Master Wangquan," he continued, "as a mutual acquaintance interceded on your behalf, I'll let you go."

But, seeing that the pirate was content to thank him with a sigh before turning on his heels without asking for anything more, he decided to call him back.

"Wait a moment!"

"What is it, Lord Hu?" Tiexin asked, smoothly turning back around.

"As the hereditary custodian of the post of guard captain in Huizhou, my duty is to protect these seas from bandits.

I would be neglecting my duty if I allowed you to continue your exploits in this area."

"Are you trying to say that you want my head in addition to the box?"

"My initial intention was to have both, yes. But I am not a man to go back on my word. However, know this, it has cost me to allow a pirate to roam free, and our agreement applies to this encounter only. The next time we cross paths, our cannons will do the negotiating. So, I would advise you to go and pursue your business far, far away from the coasts of the empire. For at least twenty years."

Shao Jun relaxed imperceptibly. For a moment she'd worried that the captain would go back on his word. But his menacing tone and ironic smile unsettled Tiexin, who brandished a powerful arm corded with muscle in front of him. He was proud of his fighting skills, and in particular, his mastery of *Celestial drums beating the thunder*, a dazzling series of alternating oblique punches. While few fighters were able to maintain the precise rhythm required for this technique for more than three rounds, the pirate was able to manage eight, earning himself the title of "Eight Celestial Drums".

"I'm touched by your concern, Lord Hu," he replied arrogantly, "but I've known how to stand up for my own interests since I was a child…"

"I see that Mr Wangquan has mastered the fighting style of Mount Kailash…" Hu Ruzhen muttered. "One day however, you will meet someone able to resist your *Celestial drums beating the thunder*, and then all you'll be able to do is cry."

"Bold words, Lord Hu, but do you really think you could survive eight rounds of my technique?"

"While I have no special skill, I would take it if I had to. Would you care to test it out?"

"Are you serious?" Tiexin inquired cautiously, concerned he would quickly be killed by the crew if he injured his opponent too seriously.

"You have my word as a gentleman," Hu Ruzhen calmly confirmed before addressing his men authoritatively. "If I succumb to Mr Wangquan's attacks, it is only because I deserve to do so. You are forbidden from helping me."

"Understood!" chorused his men, the elite of the imperial troops.

Normally, their coordination and discipline ensured their victory against the disorganized pirate hordes they faced. A duel, on the other hand, evened out the odds a little, Tiexin thought to himself, certain he could beat this arrogant captain whose youth was sure to equal his inexperience. If somehow he lost, he would be forced to stay out of imperial waters for twenty years, but a potential victory was just as worrying, as he didn't trust the captain to keep his word.

For Hu Ruzhen, this impromptu combat was a way of resolving his dilemma: as he had said, he couldn't let Tiexin go. The brief time he'd had the iron box in his possession could have been enough for him to learn about the information contained within, perhaps even to memorize it, and even exile wouldn't be enough to prevent this information coming out. The simplest way of course would have been to blow up the junk, but a promise was a promise, and he had given Shao Jun his word, so now it all came down to his own strength and agility. Rather than take off his long coat, he tied it with his belt to avoid it hampering his movements, then moved into a guard position with his left foot back.

"Let's see how brave the young lord is under my flaming fists!" Tiexin growled, moving forwards to deliver a straight punch.

He hit Hu Ruzhen with a resounding thud, forcing him back a step. Having already seen the pirate in action, Shao Jun knew that even Master Yangming himself would have struggled to resist this famous technique, which was unstoppable when executed correctly. She would have stopped the duel if she could, but the conversation between the two men had left no room for an alternative. However, against all odds, the navy captain had merely trembled slightly under the impact, before suddenly freezing.

Fire lotus!

Having been delighted a moment before at meeting the son of one of her master's close friends, the young woman was now overcome with bitterness. She'd recognize that technique anywhere… because it was the same one used by Zhang Yong to kill Wang Yangming. But it was so difficult to master that even Wei Bin, second among the Eight Tigers, had been unable to learn it. So how was it that this young man was able to use it? The implications were clear: he must have a connection with the former captain of the imperial guard. That explained why he seemed so sure he could defeat Tiexin.

The pirate leader was also stunned. Never had he seen his *Celestial drums beating the thunder* so easily thwarted. Such a level of martial skill sent a shiver up his spine, because defensive moves of this caliber hinted at the possibility of a deadly counterattack. He lowered his fists.

"I concede and agree to exile," he declared, smiling to try to hide his resentment. "I'll come back in twenty years and ask you to teach me."

"Thank you, Mr Wangquan. You can be sure I'll be eagerly awaiting your return."

Hu Ruzhen turned towards Shao Jun as the pirate quietly slipped away.

"I'm in your debt for acting as a mediator, Mr Shao," he said. "The fog is lifting; I encourage you to return to shore."

"Mr" Shao? A subtle way of suggesting the young woman keep her identity hidden, both on this ship and within the empire. She was surprised, but it was neither the time nor the place to discuss the details.

"Thank you, young Lord Hu," she simply replied.

As she left, the captain called out one last time.

"One moment, Mr Shao. What did Master Yangming say before he breathed his last?"

"That you were one in a million, destined to become a hero."

She slowly turned towards him as she spoke, her words hitting Ruzhen harder than Tiexin's punches ever could. His admiration for the venerable master was genuine; the young woman clearly owed him for the chance to save the life of A-Qian's brother. Her confusion only increased. How could one of Zhang Yong's associates hold Wang Yangming in such high esteem? The two men's ideologies were completely incompatible.

"Master Yangming really said that…" breathed the captain before bowing, then added, "Thank you. Those words mean more to me than all the gold in the emperor's treasury."

Once again, those words had a double meaning: if the

destructive forces of the empire ever sought to harm Shao Jun, the captain would be on her side rather than theirs. Although to arrive at such extremes, she would first have to go against his previous advice, for example by trying to revive the School of Mind… After spending the last few years immersing herself in poetry, philosophy, and all of Master Yangming's writings, she had become an expert in the subtle art of deciphering insinuations and other hidden meanings. Better still: she was able to create her own.

"Thank you for your warnings, young Lord Hu. Heaven is prosperous; no one can destroy themselves."

With these words, she agreed to avoid the court, the emperor, and the powerful people at his side, but also affirmed to him that if heaven so desired, she would re-establish the Society of the Mind and nothing would stand in her way. This signaled the end of their exchange: Shao Jun leapt off the patrol ship back onto the small boat where A-Qian and Xiao Gui waited. Hu Ruzhen bent over the ship's rail as he watched her leave. Perplexed, the young woman couldn't bring herself to judge him too harshly. Tiexin had fled straight towards the horizon without even having the courage for a last backward glance at his little sister.

"Is everything settled?" A-Qian asked.

"Actually… it's only just beginning!"

Note: According to official historical documents, a pirate named Tiexin marauded along the Chinese and Japanese coasts from year 31 of the Jiaqing era, twenty years later…

Chapter 1

When the region of Baoding in the county of Mancheng experienced a hot period, the clay earth of its roads dried and cracked. With the first rains, the mud that formed bogged down the wheels of carts, exhausting the beasts tasked with pulling them. Such as the large muscular horse heaving with exhaustion while the two passengers from its carriage, wearing hats and oiled coats, scraped at the excess mud with shovels so the vehicle could get underway. A third man followed, walking carefully on the slippery and treacherous ground, dragging a wooden board behind him to erase the evidence of their passage. The man was Hu Ruzhen, holder of the office of captain of the imperial guard at Huizhou. While light, the rain had been falling constantly since the previous evening.

When they arrived at the edge of the woods that their narrow road led them to, two men emerged to greet their superior officer. They must have been waiting there a while.

"Captain," said one, "we've done as instructed!"

"Were you followed?"

"Not to our knowledge."

Hu Ruzhen slid his plank into the cart and looked back to check that the sodden road was as undisturbed as if no one had set foot there.

Satisfied, he handed out his orders:

"We need to get rid of them for good this time. You two, wait here for another hour, then catch up with us if no one comes."

While he still had no idea who was responsible, he had found himself being tracked four days earlier, and everything he had tried so far had failed to throw his skilled pursuer off the scent. But time was short, and he didn't have the luxury of indulging in this game of cat and mouse any longer. At that moment, the rain and cover of night were in his favor. Earlier, at an intersection, he had ordered his two guards to set false trails to shake off the unwanted company, who would waste a least an hour by the time they realized they'd been fooled. And if they had the misfortune to find his trail once more, the two soldiers hidden in the woods would soon take care of them.

"Do you want us to take them alive, captain?"

"There's no point," Hu Ruzhen responded after a moment of thought.

As those two guards accepted his instructions with a curt "Understood," he gestured at the others to stop scraping at the cart's wheels. Now the road entered the forest, the foliage and plants on the ground made for much easier travel. The two weary men needed no further encouragement to climb onto the cart alongside their commander.

"Let's get going, Zhou!" he called to the driver. "We've still got a long way to go before we reach Datong prefecture."

The sound of a whip cracked through the air, and the rustle of dead leaves accompanied the sound of the rain. The two guards at the entrance to the forest had disappeared, and nothing living was visible as far as the eye could see. This long journey would soon be at an end. Nonetheless, one question remained unanswered: who was following them? A disgruntled pirate seeking to take possession of the iron box, perhaps. If that was the case, the bandit would receive no mercy. If it was Shao Jun, however…

The young man's heart sank, as if gripped by the claws of a nameless shadow. He could still hear the poignant regret in his father's voice when he'd spoken of the former imperial concubine, who he simply believed to have taken the wrong path in life. As a high-ranking officer in the imperial guard, Hu Shangren had been opposed to the members of the Central Plains Brotherhood, but he'd ardently hoped they would survive the massacre. After his father, it was the son's turn to become enraptured by her when she reappeared to attack the Eight Tigers, of which his Uncle Zhang was now the last remaining member – because it took someone out of the ordinary to cause so much trouble for the most powerful man in China, and perhaps the entire world. The tales of her fascinating exploits had earned Hu Ruzhen's admiration, and he'd always harbored a secret desire to meet her despite his official allegiances. What a surprise it had been to meet her on his ship! It had been everything he had hoped for: extraordinary.

Add a pair of wings and she would make a perfect phoenix, he smiled to himself.

His thoughts took him back to his eighteenth birthday. Encouraged by his father, his guests had sung "Trading a mink coat for a cup of wine", evoking the debauched life lived by the sons of wealthy families, with which he hated to be associated. Master Yangming's assessment of him as "one in a million", reported to him by Shao Jun, gave him an entirely different view of himself; it placed him above ordinary mortals.

Lifting his head, he felt as if his eyes could pierce the canvas covering his cart to see through to the infinite sky beyond.

He had proven his benevolence by allowing the young woman to leave after their meeting at sea, but if she was the one following him, she might die at the hands of his two hidden guards lying in wait. It all depended on her. And her good fortune. With this thought, Hu Ruzhen's smile quickly disappeared under his men's watchful gaze as they wondered what could possibly be going through their captain's mind.

Half an hour had passed since their departure. The rain was now pouring down.

A young man in a large hat and straw coat strode along the edge of the road in the pelting rain. Despite the low light conditions, his tracking skills had allowed him to follow the mostly obscured tracks that a less experienced eye would have missed. The tracks were recent, indicating that the carriage had passed through around an hour before. Certain it was heading for the capital, he had hidden himself next to the road that led there and been surprised to see it turn in a different direction, towards Datong prefecture. Realizing his mistake, he'd been momentarily stunned. Quick, intelligent, and highly skilled in martial arts, he had been destined to lead the Society of the Mind. But he'd misjudged Hu Ruzhen's intentions and lost his trail as a result. He would find it hard to forgive himself for this mistake.

Of course, a carriage traveled at twenty or thirty lis[3] per hour on average, so the key was figuring out its destination ....

The flash of two blades interrupted his thoughts. He'd barely stepped into the forest when the two hidden guards leapt out on either side, attempting to skewer him. They'd been ordered to check their victim's identity, but the darkness and rain had driven them to accomplish their task as quickly as possible. Used to working together, they'd intended to make quick work of the brazen individual who had dared to follow their captain. No one could stand against their Xinchun sabers, short-bladed weapons that were easy to maneuver.

But instead of slicing flesh, their blades met nothing but empty air.

The two men spun around, incredulous, their astoundment quickly turning into fear: it was going to be tough if this turned into a fight. Standing back to back, they strained their ears to try to pierce the pattering of the rain as they considered their options. Captain Hu had only ordered them to wait for an hour. Even better, he didn't necessarily expect them to bring back a body. And since the young man had vanished, they could say that they hadn't seen anyone. That was much better than trying to face a ghost.

"Shall we go?"

"Let's!"

---

[3] Li: A Chinese measure of length equal to around 500 meters.

Quickly sheathing their swords, they ran at speed and disappeared into the woods in less time than it took to speak.

A few moments later, a silhouette stealthily dropped from the upper branches of a tree. It was the tracker. Looking down at himself, he noted with a grimace that one of the blades had ripped his clothing. Despite his martial prowess, he observed painfully, he'd allowed himself to be surprised by mere soldiers. The path leading to the resurrection of the Society of the Mind had grown even longer.

The darkness of the forest was absolute, and dawn was still a long way off.

Baoding, the prefecture Hu Ruzhen had just passed through, was known for three things: its noodles with fermented soybean paste, its eternal season of spring, and metal balls. While the first two existed elsewhere, the skill required to produce a sphere as perfect as those made by the local craftsmen was rare.

In the Chen workshop, a young apprentice worked his bellows in front of the furnaces while the smith took off his shirt. It had rained all night, but the sky was clear now, and the heat of the sun was beginning to dry the muddy ground. Bare-chested under his apron, the man sent showers of sparks into the air as he hammered a piece of glowing red metal on his anvil, flattening and shaping until it began to resemble a blade. He could have done it with his eyes closed: like his father and his father's father before him, he had repeated these movements thousands of times. Blades made by the Chen family were not among the official treasures of Baoding, but their quality was renowned throughout the region.

In front of the workshop, a young boy, barely twelve years old, couldn't stop staring at a sight which others would consider purely mundane. His clothes, simple but high quality, attested to his privileged position. Intrigued by his presence, the smith called out to him as he quenched his blade in a bucket of water.

"Does my work interest you, boy?"

"Yes, sir!"

"Why?"

"I'd heard the Xi Kang plays the lute like a smith but hadn't really understood the comparison until now. But seeing you wield your hammer with such grace, lightness, and precision to render rigid metal into malleable material, I felt like I was watching Xi Kang's fingers dancing over his instrument."

While he had never heard of Xi Kang, the great poet and musician of the Three Kingdoms period, the smith understood that he was being complimented, and was amazed. It was the first time that a young man from a great family had ever called him "sir", a courtesy that left him dumbstruck.

"You seem educated," he answered with a genuine smile. "I would have liked to learn to read, but I've spent my life selling pieces of metal." He turned towards his apprentice. "Add some charcoal, we've got two more blades to make before we can take a break."

Just as he had placed two lumps of metal into the forge, a woman arrived at a run. Her dark complexion, brisk gait, and unbound feet suggested that she was a servant. Nonetheless, the young boy greeted her with the respect due to elders when she called out to him.

"So, this is where you were hiding, Xiao Gui!"

"I'm sorry, Aunt Qian. Does my mother need me?"

"Yes, she's looking for you. She said you had probably come to watch the smith at work. I can't see what you find so interesting about it..."

While A-Qian secretly rejoiced that he had spontaneously called her "Aunt", Bai Gui shot a last glance towards the smith as he returned to his work with a resounding metallic clang. As his mother often told him, "Nothing is true, everything is permitted". And so it was with iron, an inflexible material that could be shaped into countless forms in the right hands. Watching the shaping and transformation of the metal had helped him understand the meaning of those obscure words. Shao Jun encouraged him to educate himself through real experiences, and he would have certainly learned even more if A-Qian hadn't interrupted... One thing was for sure: he couldn't question the principles of the Society of the Mind.

They entered a large but almost deserted building, then crossed a rear courtyard scattered with dead leaves. There they met two young men, the first handsome and cold, the second small, vigorous, and elegant. They were Tang Yingde and Zhuo Mingke, recommended to Shao Jun by her fellow disciple, Wang Ji, who had taken over the School of Mind after Master Wang Yangming's death, and while he himself eschewed fighting so he could dedicate himself to philosophy, that was not the case for his two students, who had been educated in martial arts since they were young. They had even had the honor of spear training from Yang Yiqing, a close friend of the venerable scholar. Thanks to them, the Society of the Mind now had five members. *It only takes a single flame to ignite an entire meadow.*

At sea, Shao Jun had been intrigued by Hu Ruzhen's determination to gain the iron box in the pirates' possession, as well as by Tiexin's reluctance to part with it. After investigating, she had discovered that its contents would help find medical cargo stolen from a Flemish ship. But on Dai Yu Island, Zhang Yong had created his monstrous inhumans with the help of herbal remedies, obtained through the Portuguese. The Fire Lotus techniques used by the coastguard captain proved his close relationship with the last of the Eight Tigers, and that couldn't be a coincidence.

To avoid being recognized, the young woman had set Tang Yingde, who had almost been killed the day before, onto Hu Ruzhen's trail. Their target appeared to be heading towards Datong, the border prefecture governed by Yang Yiqing. Beyond its frontiers lay the Mongolian steppes, loyal to the Yuan dynasty and thus hostile to the Mings who had deposed them. What business could the Huizhou guard captain have there?

Her two new recruits had just delivered their most recent reports when A-Qian and Bai Gui arrived in the courtyard. While used to the coarse company of pirates, the young woman blushed like a peony and lowered her eyes as she greeted them.

"Hello, brother Zhuo, hello brother Tang."

"Hello big sister Qian!" they replied with a smile.

While she was a member of the Society of the Mind, she hadn't been a direct disciple of Wang Yangming, so she found it disconcerting that they addressed her with the same respect as Shao Jun. But traditional Confucians were sticklers for convention. She gestured to Bai Gui to greet them in turn, which he did, bowing gracefully. It was their first meeting.

"Brother Zhuo, brother Tang, I'm honored to meet you," he said.

"Finally, the young disciple recruited by big sister Shao!" exclaimed Zhuo Mingke, surprised by his maturity. "How old are you?"

"I'm studying as a novice and I would gratefully accept any instruction you are willing to give, big brother."

"You seem exceptionally talented, little brother. You have a promising future."

Tang Yingde contented himself with silently nodding his head. He prided himself on his literary talent and martial skill, but the assured manner of this child, who described himself as a novice at only ten years old, made him uncomfortable. This brief exchange completed, he was relieved to slip away with his companion. A-Qian couldn't tear her eyes away from their backs as they left the courtyard.

"They're gone, Aunt Qian," Bai Gui ventured after a long moment. "And mother is waiting for us."

"What a little devil you are!"

On the day of the young boy's birth, his grandfather dreamt that a white tortoise entered their home, and so had named him after the animal. But his name also sounded like the word for devil, hence the gently mocking wordplay. The subject of the joke accepted it with an amiable smile.

Sitting beneath a gallery, Shao Jun distractedly watched the leaves that occasionally fell from the tall elm opposite.

She clearly couldn't rebuild the Society of the Mind without first dispatching Zhang Yong, former captain of the imperial guard battalions and head of the Eight Tigers.

During their last encounter, they had both committed to a fight to the death, and only a quirk of fate had ensured that they escaped. Certainly, he no longer had as much influence as two years before due to Minister Xie Qian, but his partial retreat from official business would have given him time to regain his strength and train his followers. Men such as Hu Ruzhen, whose fighting style and unorthodox negotiation technique were reminiscent of Master Yangming's murderer.

While she had avoided showing it, she had been surprised to learn that Zhuo Mingke and Tang Yingde had lost his trail. Had the pupil become the master? He had yet to display an equal level of cruelty, but the barely veiled threats he had aimed at Shao Jun suggested that if they ever met again, their meeting would be far from cordial. Underestimating such an individual would be a fatal error, particularly when he was skilled enough to shake off the talented trackers set to follow him. While they had discovered he was traveling towards Datong prefecture, what was more important was to discover what he was doing so close to the border...

She was drawn out of her reverie by the voices of A-Qian and Bai Gui calling her with a "Big sister!" and "Mother!" respectively.

"Gui, have you finished your studies for the day?" she asked.

"Yes, mother!"

This appellation had become the young woman's greatest pride over the last two years.

The young boy's intelligence and literary curiosity constantly surprised every adult he met, and it was already certain that he would pass the imperial examinations. Luckily, there were enough students from Jishan University and direct disciples of Wang Yangming remaining – such as Wang Ji, Zhuo Mingke, and Tang Yingde – to give him an education that equaled his potential. He had the intuition of the Precursors, a completely unique gift... He wasn't perfect, however, and his fighting skills left much to be desired, which still prevented him from being seen as the true heir to the grand master of the Society of the Mind. To catch up – he had barely begun learning the *Way of the Heart* – he needed to spend more time training his body and less time studying.

Satisfied that he had completed his daily studies, Shao Jun challenged him to a game of Go.

She had been introduced to the ancient game by Master Yangming, who had presented it to her as a way to apply one of the foundational principles of the School of Mind: "The universe is my mind, and my mind is the universe." In this context, playing it regularly prepared the mind for all aspects of life, both civil and military. It therefore went without saying that the young woman, who had only come to understand its deeper meaning over the last two years, had made it a core part of her adopted son's education. What's more, this exercise helped develop the ability to make difficult decisions and then react to the consequences. For all his talents, Bai Gui still suffered from a temperament that was far too submissive and timid, a weakness of character which could pass in a scholar, but certainly not in the future grand master of the Society of the Mind.

A-Qian on the other hand found these intellectual contests tiresome, so pretended to go and get some food so she could disappear as the mother and son sat either side of the game board.

Despite being no expert, Shao Jun had achieved an entirely honorable level of skill, yet in the middle of the game the bitter fight she waged against her opponent began to wane. Her black playing pieces became confined to scattered, awkward positions from which her tactical skills couldn't extract them, while the white pieces were incredibly mobile, using every space that opened up. Though Bai Gui had real talent for the game, he felt as if the victory nearly within his grasp was less due to his own merits and more to the weaknesses of his adversary.

"Getting worried, mother?" he finally dared, carefully taking a square.

And so he had grown. Six months earlier, he wouldn't have had the courage to broach such a potentially delicate subject.

"Why do you ask?" the young woman asked him in turn, fixing him with an encouraging smile.

"My last move was a direct attack, but rather than responding with a bold move as you normally do, you let it through. So, I guessed you must have been preoccupied, because it's not like you to be so hesitant."

Shao Jun shivered. With a subtlety worthy of the great Wang Yangming, the young boy had described the delicate situation she found herself in with Hu Ruzhen.

She feared he was working for Zhang Yong, and that he had attacked the pirates at his request. But then why had he let the former imperial concubine go with just a simple warning? She hoped to get the answers to these questions by following him. What concerned her the most however was the ability of the captain general of the twelve battalions of the imperial guard to create new yuxiao, inhuman monsters, to help him realize his terrible designs. Dai Yu Island had been destroyed, but he still had the Precursor box in his possession and access to the knowledge it contained…

"You're right, Gui. But is there still time to fight, do you think? Even halfway through the game?"

"Indecision is the cause of the greatest disasters," he answered as solemnly as a general holding the future of the world in the palm of his hand.

"Aren't you worried about losing?"

The question struck her. After all, what child wouldn't want to win a game?

"Victory or defeat, it's a question of perseverance," he answered.

"Then let's see who wins this game."

Despite the occasional pearls of wisdom he was able to deliver, Bai Gui felt himself turning red as the situation began to turn against him. His intense concentration and quick offensives were unable to get past his mother's defensive positions. When she had been under Wang Yangming's tutelage, she had found herself facing seemingly inevitable defeats on more than one occasion. But seeing her sweating and boiling over with frustration, he had taught her to avoid focusing on the specific threat, and take a step back to see the whole board. This advice could apply to any situation, and so she decided to share with her adopted son the exact words her master had used with her:

"Gui, look at the pieces on the board from above!"

Then, considering her victory complete, she collected her playing pieces to put them away.

"But mother," interrupted Bai Gui, "it's not over yet!"

Shao Jun laughed in surprise. Looking at the around forty options at his disposal, her son had played an unexpected move. One by one, she wiped then replaced her pieces on the board without the slightest mistake.

"Is that correct, Xiao Gui?" she asked after placing the last one.

The young boy's exceptional memory meant he could remember even the most complex configurations.

"No mistakes," he answered, a little dejected.

"A quick solution only provides a temporary benefit."

"Yes, mother."

While he had given in, his expression betrayed his confusion. Even Master Yangming or Wang Ji couldn't have explained the meaning of these words to him in simple terms. And short of perfectly memorizing the concept, Shao Jun would need to have a lengthy conversation to cover all its subtleties. But, just as she was about to explain, A-Qian reappeared with a plate of food. While their lodgings weren't opulent, the food was excellent, and as the slanting beams of late afternoon sunlight suggested, it was time to eat. The young woman sat with the mother and son.

"Big sister," she asked between mouthfuls, "what did you send brothers Zhuo and Tang to do?"

"They're preparing the carriage. We're leaving for Datong."

"Datong?"

"I need to figure out Master Hu's intentions."

According to Wang Yangming, who had been responsible for them, the borders of Jizhou, Liaodong, Wanfu, and Datong were particularly sensitive. If the neighboring Mongols passed through the latter two prefectures, they could easily reach the capital of the Ming empire. Defending these regions was therefore key for those in power, so their garrisons were especially large. Datong's garrison was led by Minister Yang Yiqing, who was also the general of military affairs. This powerful man had been close to Wang Yangming, and Shao Jun hoped to benefit from his protection.

After spending her life at sea and on the coast, A-Qian already considered Baoding prefecture to be far inland and far from home. In comparison, a journey to Datong seemed like an incredible expedition. Usually courageous by nature, she chose to express her concern by projecting it onto others.

"Won't it be too much for the young one, big sister?"

"A good Confucian gains as much by traveling a thousand lis as by reading a thousand books!"

"Alright, alright, but there won't be any inns or places to eat outside of the garrison. Are you prepared to sleep in a tent and eat raw meat, like the Mongols?"

"Come now, Aunt Qian, tests of the body and mind are gifts from the heavens to allow humans to cultivate their skills. I welcome this mission; it will strengthen me. And if you're able to make the journey, then I am too. It's not the first time you've left your home region!"

While the young woman hadn't recognized the words of Mencius, she understood that the boy was both provoking and boasting in the same instance. That said, he had indeed slept under the stars more than once in his wanderings with his mother across the empire, and he hadn't ever complained. On the other hand, his first journey at sea hadn't been without its problems – the waves and a mainly fish-based diet could upset the metabolism of those unused to them. A-Qian had nursed him for the two whole days he spent vomiting on the vessel.

"You boast, Xiao Gui," she replied, "but don't count on me to look after you if you get ill again!"

"There's no need for a boat to get to Datong! Besides, that wouldn't scare me anyway."

This harmless bickering warmed Shao Jun's heart, reminding her of times spent with her masters, Zhu Jiuyuan, then Wang Yangming. Now she was keen to pass on what she had learned from them in the hope that, perhaps, Bai Gui may succeed them someday.

Tests of the body and mind are gifts from the heavens to allow humans to cultivate their skills.

She looked up at the unusually gloomy and cloudy sky. The storm could break at any moment.

CHAPTER 2

Twelve years earlier, a memorial to honor past heroes was erected on the hill at Majuan. Further to the east lay the famous Daoma, or "fallen horse" pass, named for the mortally wounded mount of General Yang Liulang in the Song dynasty. Under the Wei dynasty, this highly strategic choke point helped contain any invasions from the nomads to the north, hence the Great Wall also running through the area. Later, the borders of the empire extended to the north to encompass Lingqiu, then Datong, and new fortifications were built to bring the cities into the fold. Defending the pass was less important than it once was, so its garrison was significantly smaller; therefore it was understandable that its soldiers were less vigilant than their fellows assigned to watch the border.

And so, they had no objection to letting through a small five-person carriage, with two women and one child among its passengers, going toward Datong to visit family.

A dozen lis after the pass, the River Tang led to a dilapidated section of the old, abandoned wall. Two shepherds stood there watching over their sheep and cows as they grazed on the tall grasses between the ruins, with greenery much more luxuriant than their normal pastures at this time of year. The twilight lent the ruined fortifications a gloomy air.

Inspired by the desolate landscape, Tang Yingde, sitting at the front of the cart, began to recite a verse:

Stay at home, and hear the cicadas sing.
Leave, and you know your horse will have a bad back[4].

While Shao Jun wouldn't have admonished him for doing so, he blamed himself for losing the trail of the cart that he had followed, and for failing to confront the hidden soldiers who had attacked him in the forest. He was among Wang Ji's most talented pupils, in which he sometimes took excessive pride, something equaled by how harshly he judged his own failures. Overcome by the inadequacy he had shown in his pursuit of Hu Ruzhen, he had spent the last two days in abject misery.

Zhuo Mingke, who himself had followed a false trail, could at least have a clear conscience.

"Homesick already?" he asked Tang, who held the reins.

"I could never stay home while my enemies still live!"

The coldness of this response spoke volumes about the young man's wounded ego, so his fellow disciple chose to change the subject.

---

[4] Poem by Tang Shunxhi (1505-1560)

"I'm also hoping to pass the imperial exams… I plan to take them when this is all over."

He allowed himself a discreet glance over his shoulder as he spoke. More passionate than his scholarly demeanor would suggest, he had been overwhelmed with feelings for A-Qian since their first meeting. Unfortunately, the young woman only had eyes for Tang Yingde, who was clearly not interested in her at all. He hoped that one day he might yet find the opportunity to engage her in a proper conversation.

Once past the Great Wall, the carriage continued to follow the River Tang, surrounded by mountains for almost a hundred lis. The watercourse snaked through a narrow, uninhabited valley frequented only by shepherds bringing their herds and passing travelers. Its pine trees, rocks, waterfalls, and streams were a source of constant amazement for Bai Gui and A-Qian, who looked all around with wide eyes.

Shao Jun on the other hand was far too absorbed in her own thoughts to spare a thought for the landscape. Would the road they were traveling take them to the Zouwus' base – with seven of the Eight Tigers dead, it seemed more appropriate to call them by their original name – or simply to a direct confrontation with Hu Ruzhen? As for Zhang Yong, if he really was involved, it must have been to create an army of yujing… Knowing that the yuxiao were practically invincible, their improved version could hand whoever controlled enough of them the world on a silver platter. The mere thought of it sent shivers down her spine.

She looked down at the topographic maps of the northeast spread out in front of her. It was almost empty, except for the fortress at Xuanhua. Due to their rugged terrain and the constant wars raging across them it hadn't been easy to map these regions on paper. Between founding the Society of the Mind and its destruction during the Great Rites Controversy, Wang Yangming had had the grand ambition of documenting the entire empire, but he hadn't had the time to complete his work.

It wouldn't be hard to cross Zhili[5] from south to north, but they would no longer be so alone in the prosperous west. Despite the general instability, the region had a large number of merchants come to trade horses and animal skins for porcelain and silk, a profitable trade for both parties in times of peace. The last great city before this transit zone was Lingqiu, located at least three hundred lis from Datong, which owed its wealth to this constantly changing melting pot of transient visitors.

It was there that Shao Jun and her companions stopped for the night. The innkeeper was very welcoming, and reassured them that this time, their destination was free of any major conflict.

Toghan Temour, the emperor driven out of China by the Mings, was a direct descendant of Kubilai Khan, founder of the Yuan dynasty. But when he fled to the steppes, he had to face the hostile descendants of the brother of his glorious ancestor, who had controlled the west of the country for generations. However, he didn't live long enough to pursue this new war, because one of his ministers soon killed him to take his throne... before himself being killed by another

---

[5] Under the Ming and Qing dynasties, Zhili referred to the region administered by Beijing and roughly comprising Hebei, Henan, and Shandong.

minister. Both came from the Oirat tribe, which tore itself apart through these coups. While this was going on, their neighbors didn't hesitate to fan the flames of discord to encourage the tribe's self-destruction. It wasn't until the reign of Zhengtong of the Mings, in the middle of the 15th century, that eastern Mongolia was at peace once more. Several years later, Dayan Khan of the Yuans replaced the Oirat on the throne and finally united the country. At the time he was known as the "little prince", though history remembered him as a wise and brilliant leader. But his accomplishments survived only a short while after him: after the premature death of his grandson and heir, Bodi Alag, tensions between east and west resumed. It would be another of his descendants from the same generation, Altan Khan, who would successfully reestablish apparent peace and resumption of trade with China.

As a result, these border regions were dangerous by nature, but Yang Yiqing had succeeded in ensuring they had a semblance of stability, even if only around the major crossing points. On the roads, however, travelers were often on their own…

In the early hours of the second morning, as she was making the final preparations, Shao Jun asked Tang Yingde to re-read Bai Gui's essay, to ensure that his studies didn't suffer from any interruption.

The main recruitment examination for scholar-officials of the Ming empire was an essay in four parts: definition, analysis, critique, and redefinition of the subject, with each sub-divided into four paragraphs (introduction, development, examples, and conclusion). The exercise itself was as difficult as the format, requiring rigorous referencing, flawless dialectic, and elegant writing to link it all together. Tang Yingde had already been preparing for seven years when he successfully passed aged twenty-two, so he was particularly impressed by the maturity of young Bai Gui's prose. He was even a little jealous. Just how far would this child go? He had a bright future ahead of him.

Meanwhile, Zhuo Mingke was gleaning information from the market stallholders. He learned that a carriage had passed through on the road to Datong early that morning, alone and without an escort. Traders used to the region only traveled in caravans of at least thirty or forty people; it was pure suicide to do otherwise. The route had been beset by bandits for some years, an endemic problem which the authorities made only half-hearted attempts to resolve. It was the hunting grounds of the Zephyrs, a band of thieves as quick and elusive as a fleeting gust of wind, who ruthlessly attacked in groups of twelve to fifteen, leaving mutilated victims and bodies in their wake.

The young man immediately realized that it could have been none other than Hu Ruzhen himself.

Shao Jun and her acolytes set off again after eating. They were alone too. They would be the talk of Lingqiu for days. Leaving at midday, they could hope to cover the three hundred arid lis of steep terrain that lay between them and Datong by the following evening, including camping overnight.

Thanks to the lack of vegetation, sand blew freely in all directions. The passengers drew the canvas over the carriage to protect themselves while the drivers covered the lower half of their faces with scarves.

It would take more than that to stop Zhuo Mingke, who feared boredom more than anything, from talking. Anything and everything, gossip included, were suitable discussion topics to escape the monotony of the road, even if Tang Yingde seemed content to remain silent, contributing only the occasional evasive answer here and there. But he suddenly came to life just as his companion was in the middle of a strange story about a fish which could dig.

"Riders!" he cried.

"Brother Tang, what's happening?" asked A-Qian, having heard his warning and becoming concerned after feeling the carriage stop.

"It's nothing, sister Qian–" Zhuo Mingke began to reassure her before his comrade cut him off.

"I hear hooves!"

"Yes, it's galloping horses!" Shao Jun confirmed.

With visibility cut to less than a hundred paces ahead and the wind constantly blowing, it was amazing that the two had noticed anything at all. It was still impossible to determine the identity or intentions of the unknown riders. Were they simple traders, or were they outlaws? Doubtful, Tang Yingde preferred to rely on the judgment of his elders. Although only two years separated them, she was his hierarchical superior and he respected her as such.

"Big sister, should we stop?" he asked.

"I don't think they're coming towards us. Do you think they're traders?"

"It could be Hu Ruzhen," Zhuo Mingke interrupted. "It might be our chance to catch him!"

"Mingke," the young woman asked, "what did the people

in Lingqiu tell you about the group that came before us?"

"Only that it was led by a young man. Why, big sister?"

"I don't think it's Hu Ruzhen… but let's try to catch them anyway."

"You're right, big sister," replied Tang Yingde. "He wouldn't move so slowly."

With a small shake of the reins, Zhuo Mingke got the carriage moving again and encouraged the horses to increase their speed.

"Mother, what's happening?" Bai Gui whispered.

"Don't worry. Use the journey to review your lessons."

The young woman thought it unlikely that they had already caught up with Hu Ruzhen. They had mostly likely come across either some intrepid traders, or bandits who would quickly regret targeting their group. Apart from her son, the carriage's four occupants were highly skilled fighters to whom even a group of a dozen brutish cutthroats posed no threat.

The reality turned out to be a mix of the two: a single cart was under attack and was fleeing directly towards the acolytes of the Society of the Mind. But the squalls of wind had increased in strength, forcing Zhuo Mingke to pull down his hood to protect against the sand, so that he only became aware of the cart hurtling towards them when its two panicked horses appeared twenty or thirty feet away. Fortunately, he was a skilled driver and changed their direction just in time, while the other driver pulled on their reins, almost strangling their beasts to force them to suddenly stop. Collision barely avoided, the two vehicles stood side-by-side in the middle of the road.

The young man felt the chill of cold sweat sliding down his

back. Pale as a ghost, he almost let out a stream of expletives. He was so relieved that he didn't have time to react when a crossbow bolt flew in his direction.

It had been shot by one of the deputy leaders of the Zephyrs, who couldn't believe his luck at having not one, but two carriages to pillage. A former border guard, he had deserted after killing one of his brothers-in-arms a few years before, then turned to banditry to put his skills to use. He was no scholar, but this elite crossbowman had embodied the meaning of Dai Fu's verse: "To down the man, aim at the horse"[6]. There was nothing more certain to stop a cart escaping. It was Zhuo Mingke's sudden swerve that had accidentally put him in harm's way.

He was saved at the last moment by Tang Yingde, who had seized his short spear and knocked the bolt out of the way a fraction of a second before it would have buried itself in his friend's skull. Both had been the best students of Yang Yiqing's younger brother, Master He, whose teachings they had followed at Chaotian Temple in Nanjing. He had begun living there as a Taoist monk, just one among many, after a series of professional failures had ruined his career as an official. There, he had been inspired by Zen Buddhism to develop his own spear technique, derived from the same spiritual foundations yet different from the *Three Revelations of the baton* that had made his elder brother famous. His own name meant "crane", one of the five animals whose imitation was key to the fundamental styles of kung-fu.

When a new bolt flew towards their animals, it was Zhuo

---

[6] Translation taken from Ballad of the Frontier, *Chinese Poetic Writing* by François Cheng, p. 228

Mingke's turn to break it in midair. While he was pleased to prove himself as capable as his comrade, he had little time to enjoy it, because another projectile, countered by Tang Yingde, was already upon them. They had to admit that the crossbowman was skilled, because it was rare for a shooter to be able to reload their weapon so quickly. But the latter was starting to panic. He thought he was facing scholars, not martial artists. He never missed under normal circumstances.

The bandits had already suffered a serious defeat two days earlier, when a carriage stopped at the side of the road had answered their bolts with gunfire. The brief confrontation had resulted in no casualties for the travelers but had cost the lives of a handful of Zephyrs before their leader ordered them to retreat. An experienced man, he knew how to recognize when a fight was lost… and to learn from his mistakes. And so, when his scouts had told him about this new, solitary carriage, he'd watched it carefully to ensure it posed no threat before attacking. He would never have imagined that they would accidentally run into a group of martial artists as it fled. As the proverb went, "he who rides a tiger is afraid to dismount". He unsheathed his short sword from his saddle to charge at the cart driver, who had dismounted from the vehicle.

Soldiers on the northern frontier had been fighting the nomads from the steppes for centuries. At Yuerhai in 1368, the cavalry of the Ming empire had vanquished the eighty thousand men led by Chief Tamerlane, who had narrowly escaped with only a handful of officials. Aware of the advantage offered by an effective cavalry, the army had long focused on

training its recruits in several mounted techniques designed
to strike an enemy, unhorse them, or drag them by the stirrup.
As they faced a constant turnover of troops and sometimes
without any previous experience, instructors had to go back
to basics to focus on effectiveness, and so they had a saying:
"Fear not a thousand vain sword strokes, fear the man who
wields it." And for good reason, this simple principle, plus a
few riding lessons and well-forged swords, had allowed the
Ming empire to put an end to the Mongols. Though he still
wore the army uniform, the bandit leader was also trained
in *Splitting the wind*, a technique that was easy to learn but
difficult to master. Users charged with their sword held out in
front of them and could easily split their victims in two. Such
was the fate the muscular man intended for Zhuo Mingke as
he galloped towards him.

But as his associate protected him against the steel blade
with his spear of meteoric iron, the young man leapt into the
air over the rider. The balance of power thus reversed, he drew
his knife and thrust down with all his strength.

The two friends' choreographed movements were a
technique called *The crane beats its wings*. It was created at
Master Hu's instigation, when he didn't have any students
skilled enough to face him in a one-on-one fight and asked
them to attack him together in pairs, coordinating their
assault. The resulting synchronized attacks were much more
than the sum of their parts.

The bandit had no intention of allowing himself to be
unhorsed: he grabbed the knife in his left hand with enough
force to stop the blow, and threw Zhuo Mingke to the ground,
breaking his momentum. Though proud of his precision and

reflexes, he had no time to put them to use, because Tang Yingde, making use of the distraction, had jumped onto his back to plant his spear in the bandit's neck. Meanwhile, his compatriot had stood up and leapt up once again to stab their assailant in the heart. During the fraction of a second when his blade was free, the outlaw had almost reacted quickly enough to slice either of the young men in two. It had been a near miss.

Faced with the sudden death of their leader, the Zephyrs descended into panic. Some spun around, others launched into a disorganized charge... None seemed able to realize that the situation had turned against them. As Zhuo Mingke threw the nearest rider to the ground, Tang Yingde rushed screaming at the ones galloping in his direction.

From the carriage, Shao Jun heard him stab their three mounts in a single move, then run his blade through the men on the ground. Her extraordinary hearing allowed her to closely follow the young man's movements, admiring their precision and ferocity. Indeed, he reminded her of the formidable swordsman Xu Pengju, a disciple of Yang Yiqing she had met several years before. He too was much more spirited than his upbringing would suggest.

While Zhuo Mingke began to worry that he could no longer see his friend, who had disappeared in the swirling sand, the young woman was concerned he might not bring back a brigand in any condition for questioning.

"Leave one alive, brother Tang!" she shouted.

One last cry rang out, followed by the young man's voice as he responded.

"Don't worry, big sister, I've got one."

A bandit in a long tunic emerged through the sandy air. Out of reflex, Zhuo Mingke almost attacked him with his knife before noticing the spear pointed at the bandit's back. Tang Yingde ordered his prisoner to kneel with his hands on his head.

"What about the rest?" asked his friend.

"There were eight of them altogether, and I killed five."

"With the one I killed, the leader and this prisoner, that's all of them. But in town they said that the Zephyrs always travel in groups of ten or more." He rested his knife on the brigand's nose. "Are you a member of the Zephyrs? Speak!"

Keenly aware that his life hung by a thread, the brigand blanched pale as the surrounding sand and groaned. He spoke better than his livelihood might have suggested, but the speed at which he spoke was comical.

"You are the masters, and we are just the miserable dogs! I regret that our leader dared attack you and I hope you might spare my miserable life."

"Why were there only eight of you?"

"Seven of us died a few days ago in an attack that went badly…"

"What happened? Who did you attack?" Shao Jun demanded, climbing down from the carriage.

"Travelers armed with guns. Their leader looked barely twenty years old and was a skilled and violent martial artist. Oh, what misfortune to come across two groups of powerful fighters in such a short space of time!"

Zhuo Mingke was having none of the bandit's flattery.

"Shut up!" he shouted. "What was this young man called?"

"I don't know! But his companions called him Master Hu."

Tang Yingde involuntarily jerked in surprise. Looking up at Shao Jun, he saw she was just as shocked as he. So, Hu Ruzhen was two days ahead of them... They had no chance of catching up with him before Datong, where his trail might disappear for good. What should they do? They hardly had time to consider the idea when a booming voice drew them out of their reverie.

"Is that you, Tang Yingde!? You got me out of a tricky situation! What incredible luck!"

It was the merchant they had almost hit head-on, a vigorous young man whose fleshy body suggested that he wasn't adept at fighting. Zhuo Mingke regarded him suspiciously. He'd never seen this person before, and he thought he'd met all of his fellow disciple's acquaintances – they had been inseparable ever since they'd studied together under Wang Ji at Chaotian Temple.

However, Tang Yingde greeted him like a true friend, with a touch of respect, then exchanged a few words with him before turning towards Shao Jun.

"Big sister, allow me to present my friend Luo Hongxian. We took the imperial exams together."

"What? This is the Luo who scored highest on the exam?" exclaimed Zhuo Mingke, stunned.

"Yes, it's him. He wants to travel with us through to Datong."

"What's someone like him hoping to do there?"

"He's traveling to map the region and wants to consult the collection of mathematical works in the residence of the prince of Dai as he passes through. What do you say, big sister?"

"Does he have cartographic skills?" the young woman asked, her interest suddenly piqued.

"It's not his official profession, but yes, he has good skills in that area."

In 1529, year 8 of the reign of Jiajing, when Yang Yiqing was a member of the imperial examinations jury, he had seen two young men full of promise: Tang Yingde and Luo Hongxian.

The first of these was his favorite, and he had summoned Tang five times in the hope of helping him achieve first place. It had been in vain, however, because the young man was too arrogant for his own good and obstinately refused to resort to flattery, which was necessary in this type of circumstance. He'd therefore had to settle for being a good second, which hadn't stopped him from being spotted by the director of the Ministry of Rites. But he had chosen to distance himself from the circles of power when his professor, Zhang Yong, had committed atrocities during the Great Rites Controversy. Ashamed of being associated with such a man, he had returned home to his village to spend three years there mourning his recently deceased mother, as required by tradition. Any pretext was worth it to put an end to his official career, however enviable, which had begun many years earlier with a prestigious first place in the university entrance examination...

The second student noticed by Yang Yiqing was Luo Hongxian, a brilliant man whose success had surprised no one despite being only twenty-five years old. As required by Ming dynasty doctrine, which espoused the application of knowledge, he had complemented his academic studies with martial arts training, although his physique had prevented him from ever excelling in that area... And, thought Zhuo

Mingke, if Tang Yingde and himself hadn't been there to save him, all his study would have been useless in the face of a bandit attack. He did however have many other talents, including traditional cartography, terrain mapping as first practiced under the Yuan dynasty by Zhu Siben. Over two decades spent traveling the empire, the great Taoist monk had drawn a seven-foot-long map that covered a considerable part of the empire. Luo Hongxian had corrected various mistakes and added further details before spending ten years creating the Guang Yutu, an atlas of forty detailed maps featuring explanatory symbols for greater readability.

Strangely, his main weakness was his boundless enthusiasm, which made him blind to the dangers inherent in his travels. He had set out alone on this road against all advice, where he had almost ended up with his throat cut like a sacrificial lamb.

It remained to be seen whether his former classmate and companions would agree to escort him to the next stop on his travels.

"Very well, we'll travel together," Shao Jun answered Tang Yingde. "What did you tell him about me and our journey?"

"I told him that I'm accompanying my cousin to her parents in Datong."

"Good." She lowered her voice. "And what are we going to do with our prisoner?"

"We might as well let him go; we're not going to get anything more from him."

"That's good. Please take care of it."

The young man moved off with the captive.

"Mother," whispered Bai Gui when he was out of sight, "I

know you don't like killing in cold blood but let brother Tang do it. If he lives, that bandit will continue preying on innocent victims on this road."

"Xiao Gui, heaven is merciful to all living things. We must give those who are on the wrong path the chance to get back on the right one. You're too young to be so ruthless."

"Yes, mother. What I said was wrong."

But his eyes, clear and innocent, displayed no shame or remorse. As his teacher, Shao Jun had before been so harsh with this willing, hardworking child. But she felt she had to exercise her authority on this fundamental issue. It was then that she thought of the image of Master Yangming just before his death.

The great sage had long refused to kill Zhang Yong in honor of their past friendship, yet in the end, his old friend had killed him anyway. It was therefore clear that offering the enemy an alternative path sometimes led to a dead end. Of course, the shadow of death hanging over him elicited a sudden surge of remorse in the bandit, but several minutes earlier he wouldn't have hesitated to kill the brave Luo Hongxian, depriving the world of the cultural and scholarly treasures that he held within. What if Bai Gui was right?

A shout rang out across the steppe.

"Big sister!" cried A-Qian. "Is brother Tang in trouble?"

"No, don't worry," Shao Jun answered, having recognized the bandit's voice.

Just then, Tang Yingde reappeared at a run.

"I wounded him in the leg, then I left him with a bandage and water," he announced. "There's no way he'll follow us. And by the time his companions find him, we'll be long gone."

The young woman had nothing to add. The Zephyrs controlled this road, so it was certain that the rest of their journey would now go smoothly.

"Let's go!" she contented herself with saying.

Luo Hongxian let out a long sigh of relief when the ramparts of Datong came into view the following evening.

CHAPTER 3

Yang Yiqing was delighted to see Luo Hongxian again. He congratulated him on his success as a writer at the imperial academy and praised his cartographic enterprise, which would no doubt serve the advancement of future generations as well as his own. He even assigned him an escort to protect him as he traveled.

The young scholar invited Tang Yingde to accompany him to the residence of the prince of Dai to talk and catch up – after all, the prince was known for his hospitality, and he would hardly notice an extra guest – but his companion had to decline: he had more pressing matters to attend to.

It was towards the latter that Yang Yiqing turned as Luo Hongxian departed.

"Sit down, my young friend," he said. "How is your father? It's been a long time since I saw dear Tang Bao…"

"This isn't a social visit, Master Yang. I'm here because I was ordered to be."

The governor of Datong was shocked by the harshness of his response. He should have expected it though, as several years earlier, his efforts to help the impetuous young man to attain first place in the imperial examinations had already been repaid with ingratitude. His devotion to his family, for whom he had sacrificed his career, was however very admirable.

"Master Yang," he continued, pulling a small stone tablet from his sleeve, "my master asked me to show you this."

Yang Yiqing's heart began to race. He gently felt the warm, soft texture of the mutton fat jade that he had recognized at first glance. A long time ago, he had spent an entire night discussing philosophy with his friends Zhang Yong and Wang Yangming, a conversation during which the irreconcilability of their views had seemed as unwavering as the respect they had for one another. As a souvenir of that moment which had marked their lives forever, he had sacrificed one of his prized possessions, a magnificent paperweight from the Yuan dynasty, to create three identical plaques, each bearing the key principles of the introduction to the *Zhongyong*[7]: "What heaven confers is called 'nature'. Accordance with this nature is called the Dao. Cultivating the Dao is called 'education[8]'". Returning the stone to Tang Yingde, he noticed that it bore the inscription *Education*. So, it was Wang Yangming's pendant. Zhang Yong's featured the character *Dao*, and *Nature* was written on the one kept by Yang Yiqing.

"Who is your master?" he asked the young man.

---

[7] The *Zhongyong* or *Doctrine of the Mean* is one of the four classics of Chinese philosophy.

[8] Translation by A Charles Muller taken from http://www.acmuller.net/con-dao/docofmean.html

"I'm about to go and get him, I'm sure he would prefer to introduce himself."

The sage was perplexed. Having no children, one of his deceased friend's pupils must have inherited his jade plaque, but which one? He had trained hundreds, and over the years, he had formed close bonds with many of them. He had met some, but none of them specifically came to mind. In the end, it was a disturbingly beautiful adolescent who bowed before him. It was true that the elderly scholars mixed with the younger generations, but someone this young?

"Excuse my rudeness," Yang Yiqing began, "but I don't believe I know you. What did Master Yangming call you?"

"Look beyond the disguise, master. You'll find his disciple, Shao Jun."

"Shao Jun! How bold! You're still officially under suspicion of treason and are wanted by the imperial guard. Aren't you worried I'll turn you in?"

"Now that would be a strange way to honor my master's memory, would it not?"

"You've got guts! But you're right… Out of respect for my friendship with Wang Yangming, I'll agree to hear you out."

Outside the governor's sumptuous residence, Tang Yingde gazed at a peaceful, prosperous Datong swarming with traders. Now the borders with their bellicose neighbors were sufficiently guarded, the prefecture had grown rapidly; if there hadn't been so many local soldiers present, you might think you were somewhere in the central plains, not somewhere in the extreme northwest of the empire.

With all that, it would be unfair not to recognize the work

of Yang Yiqing, whose skills stretched from civil affairs to military, from great literary theory through to concrete execution. Did he still constantly fear attack by the Mongols? Had he already put in place plans to counter this possibility? Tang Yingde had always wanted to exceed Yang Yiqing, but seeing with his own eyes what had been accomplished, and thinking of the weight which rested on his shoulders inspired a certain humility, a feeling he was unaccustomed to. He almost regretted addressing him with such discourtesy.

Just then, the door opened to reveal the governor and Shao Jun.

"There's no need to accompany me, master," she said.

"Please, stay in the city for several days and enjoy the local area. I'm sure you'll find it very pleasant."

"Thank you, master. The younger generation sometimes lacks manners these days, but not respect."

Yang Yiqing raised his eyebrow imperceptibly as he turned towards Tang Yingde.

"Send your father my regards," he said to him, "and tell him I'll visit him as soon as I can."

The young man, who hadn't missed these allusions, bowed wordlessly. Once outside the residence and far from its occupant, he couldn't help himself anymore and asked:

"So, how did it go?"

"Master Yang will house us. We're going to rest for a little while, then Zhuo Mingke and you will go into the city and see what you can find out."

He smiled in relief. So, Yang Yiqing supported their cause. As minister, governor, and general, he had several sumptuous official residences, but the property he had made available to the small group was much more modest. Set apart from the busier areas of Datong, it had around a dozen rooms. A small sign hung over the entrance, designating it a "private residence".

The young woman and her companions were welcomed by a thin, middle-aged man wearing a steward's uniform.

"Are you Mr Shao?" he asked. "My name is Shen Zhiwei, and Governor Yang has assigned me to serve you for the duration of your stay."

"I am indeed Mr Shao. Thank you, Steward Shen."

He looked at young Bai Gui's pallid face with concern. While the beginning of the journey had gone smoothly for him, the bouncing of the cart had been unbearable once its passengers had pulled across the coverings to protect from the sand. He had been so ill that Zhuo Mingke and Tang Yingde had been forced to slow down to the point that they arrived at their destination an entire day later than planned, something which had greatly irritated Luo Hongxian.

"Is this young man unwell?" the steward inquired.

"He has been travel sick," A-Qian responded.

"An, nothing serious then. Perhaps he should go lie down. We'll bring him some green bean soup and he'll recover in no time."

Despite his homely appearance, Shen Zhiwei was good at his job: he called a groom to unharness the horses before leading the governor's guests to the rooms which had been carefully prepared for them. Zhuo Mingke and Tang Yingde unloaded the cart while Shao Jun put her son to bed, then they informed her that they were going to visit the market. Completely unaware that they were following Hu Ruzhen, the steward found it strange that scholars would mix with the public; but being professional, he refrained from any undiplomatic comments.

If Bai Gui had been born into a family of civil servants, he would have been on his parents' knees rather than recovering from his motion sickness in a strange bed at the edge of the empire. But his father was a scholar who had failed the imperial examinations, and his grandfather had been a guard to Prince Han. Why, then, had he been entrusted to a criminal on the run? Simply in the hope that through her, he could benefit from the teachings of Wang Yangming to, perhaps, have a future better than the one he would otherwise have had. Shao sometimes felt guilty for making him experience the awful uncertainties of her daily life. The young boy already bore the hopes of so many adults on his small shoulders.

Zhuo Mingke, on the other hand, was at home in the tea salons, taverns, and other meeting places of Datong. Frequented by merchants and travelers from all over, these lively and welcoming establishments were the ideal place for fleeting friendships and, at the same time, gleaning useful information on a wide variety of matters. In these northwestern provinces where the twilight was longer than elsewhere, it was never completely dark before the sun set for the day, and, in the orange light of the peaceful evening, the young man attracted the sympathy of an imposing man. Through their conversation he learned that the man, dressed according to the customs of the Ming empire and speaking perfect Mandarin, was actually a Mongol: pacified by Yang Yiqing, the border was somewhat open to commercial trade with others, which benefitted all parties concerned.

Now, even metal items and drugs were allowed through the customs posts, items which previously been prohibited. Zhuo Mingke also learned that a vigorous young man had recently left for the steppes at the head of a cart loaded with medicinal plants...

For Tang Yingde, this discussion was also an opportunity to open his eyes to realities which he had never previously considered. He had always seen the Mongols as rustic, ill-intentioned looters, but this nice man simply wanted to live and work in peace, just like anyone else, and had persuaded him to revise his opinions. He had also learned that Mongolia was not so unified a country as he might have believed, and while half of it was relatively stable, it was the eastern parts that had earned its people's reputation as bandits and looters. Thoughtful and sincere, the man had advised the two companions to avoid traveling through these hostile territories if possible.

When the pair returned to the private residence, they found young Bai Gui copying a calligraphy by Ouyang Xuan. This art was one of the fundamentals of any Confucian education, and they themselves had done just the same for over twenty years. But they were impressed by the balance and distinction of his strokes, by the grace which was so uncommon for someone of his age. A little sleep and a drink of good bean soup had clearly done wonders for his recovery from their journey.

"Carry on quietly," Shao Jun whispered to him.

Zhuo Mingke noted her overly dramatic solemnity.

"Did Master Yang come by, big sister?" he asked.

"Yes..."

"What did he say?"

"That we can stay in the city for a few days, but we need his permission to move. And..." She paused for a moment, aware that her words would have a devastating effect. "And that he won't support us in our fight against Zhang Yong."

"What? Doesn't he want to avenge Master Yangming's death? I thought they were friends!"

"Without proof, he refuses to believe Zhang Yong could have been responsible for his death."

The governor had been quite happy to talk about his old companion at first. But after thinking the question over for a moment, he'd confirmed that as far as he was concerned, Wang Yangming had died of an illness on his return to Sitian, where he had gone to put down a rebellion. As such, he couldn't approve of them following Hu Ruzhen. The longer they talked, the more the former imperial concubine had felt he suspected that she was exploiting the memory of her honorable master to take revenge on Zhang Yong, who was responsible for her expulsion from the imperial palace.

"But how can he be so blind?!" Zhuo Mingke raged.

"There's no point dwelling on it, because it's clear he won't be changing his mind. Now, tell me what you learned in the city."

"Everything I heard suggests Hu Ruzhen crossed the border yesterday."

"Yesterday?"

"Yes, disguised as a trader of medicinal plants."

"Big sister," Tang Yingde interrupted, "if we can't count on Governor Yang's aid, brother Zhuo and I could slip through to the border and find out more on Hu Ruzhen's movements."

"Let's sleep on it and talk about it again tomorrow. It's too important and we should avoid acting hastily."

Shao Jun had been diplomatic to avoid hurting Tang Yingde's fragile ego, but she was mainly concerned about preventing her followers from accidentally making the situation worse.

When they were gone, she lit a candle for Bai Gui to see by. It was unnecessary though, as he had just finished the page which now contained Ouyang Xuan's entire poem. His strokes, energetic and spirited, were far superior to his mother's, who hadn't had the opportunity to start practicing so early in life. He'd even signed his work. Traditionally, the name or surname of the artist was written in very loose cursive, and members of the Society of the Mind often used this technique to communicate. To the uninitiated, it would seem to be a complicated character; the initiated would read a coded message. This was how she had known she had to contact Wang Yangming on her return from Europe.

The hanzi written by Bai Gui was impressively complex. Leaning in, you could see it was composed of several characters and read the phrase "Nothing is true, everything is permitted". Earlier, after Tang Yingde had complimented the quality of his work as the text was in progress, he had been able to concentrate enough to maintain a consistent style as his mother and the governor spoke in the same room. *If only he was just as talented at martial arts!* thought Shao Jun. But he was still struggling to get to grips with the *Way of the Heart*...

"Don't worry too much, mother," the boy ventured as he washed his brushes. "Master Yang hasn't decided yet."

"What?"

"You said he refused to help you, but I watched him closely: he was still considering the question."

"What makes you say that?"

"When you asked for his assistance, he drummed his fingers on his leg twice before refusing."

Separated from him by a table, Shao Jun had had no opportunity to see this for herself. She was more surprised that her disciple had seen and analyzed it, and that he had even managed it while writing such delicate calligraphy.

"Why do you think this detail is so telling?"

"In the *Biography of Study* that you gave me, there is a chapter that says, 'the mind and body act as one' and that the body betrays your emotions. When Master Yang rejected your request, this reaction was a sign of uncertainty."

Bai Gui had just cited a work by Xu Ai, Wang Yangming's first disciple. He died very young at the age of thirty-one, but his *Biography of Study* was a key text for all students of the School of Mind. When she had given her copy to Bai Gui, Shao Jun had had no idea that he would study it so seriously and come to understand it even better than she.

Worried that his mother's silence was disapproving, the young man quietly said:

"But I might be mistaken…"

"Whether you're right or wrong, there's no way I can use this to convince him."

"No… but he invited us to stay in the city for a few days, probably so he has time to try and confirm whether what you said is true."

Once again, he was probably right: if Yang Yiqing hadn't had any doubts, he would have acted immediately rather than risk offering shelter, albeit temporary, to a wanted criminal. On the other hand, if the answers he found in the coming days failed to satisfy him, he would be merciless to those who had dared dirty the name of his friend Zhang Yong. He might spare Tang Yingde out of respect for his father, but a disgraced former imperial concubine would be shown no mercy. So, the important question was: who would the governor speak to? Without finding another witness to Wang Yangming's death – an impossible task – he would have to rely on the opinion of a trusted friend, someone who also knew Shao Jun... Was there such a person?

Her eyes lit up. Yes, of course there was.

The next day, Shen Zhiwei handed her a visiting card decorated with just a single name: *Xu Pengju*.

The young woman found her visitor standing fascinated in the main room as he examined a calligraphy of part of the *List of Masters* by the strategist Zhuge Liang, scribed by Yang Yiqing. After his father's early death, the descendant of the king of Zhongshan had inherited his grandfather's position at a very young age. His title of commander in chief of the troops in Nanjing had been highly coveted, so his mother had entrusted him to Yang Yiqing to protect him from his uncles' influence and ensure he would be ready to take on his duties with the care they required. While the governor's own duties within the empire meant he hadn't always been at his side, Xu Pengju grew up in his orbit and acquired exemplary civil, military, and martial skills, as well as an admirable sense of morality. His master rightly considered him to be the best of his students.

The young man had met Shao Jun a little over two years before, when she was supporting Wang Yangming in his fight against Zhang Yong. He had been forced to be as neutral as possible due to the closeness of the two men to his own master, but he still worked behind the scenes to help and even save the former imperial concubine. She made a strong impression on him when she spent several days at his residence, and he'd never treated her like a criminal.

When he faced her, he recognized her instantly despite her masculine clothing. She noted that he now sported a thin mustache, which gave him a more serious and mature appearance.

"How wonderful to see you again, dear sister!" he said boldly.

"I'm afraid I'm not yet able to repay all the favors I owe you, dear Lord Xu."

"Come now, enough of that, you don't owe me anything! Duty brought me to Datong, but it would have been a shame to miss a chance to see you again. What a coincidence!"

"So, you're here on the emperor's orders?"

"Yes, I'm overseeing the production of the uniforms for the armies on the border."

In reality, the region of Nanjing, and more generally the entire south of Zhili, had many villages of weavers and thus provided the empire with a large quantity of items, and Xu Pengju's presence was not really required in Datong. He had in reality come for the opportunity to visit his master, who was an inexhaustible source of valued teachings and with whom he always enjoyed speaking. Imagine his surprise when the governor asked him to confirm Shao Jun's identity before interrogating him about Wang Yangming's death! Preferring to admit his ignorance rather than lie or speculate, the young man had not been able to enlighten Yang Yiqing about his friend's death, but he had decided to visit the private residence. Once he was there, he found himself speechless, unable to speak about what was really bothering him.

So, he told her about his travels and a sudden flood in Nanjing the previous year, until eventually it was Shao Jun who could no longer stand it, interrupting him mid-flow.

"Lord Xu, do you know if Master Yang will agree to help me?"

"All I can tell you, dear sister, is that he doesn't believe Zhang Yong is responsible for the death of Master Yangming."

Seeing his friend's face grow gloomy, he tried to reassure her.

"But he agreed to let you cross the border... Can I ask what you plan to do in Mongol territory?"

The young woman was relieved. So, Yang Yiqing didn't completely trust Zhang Yong. Deep down, he must know what his esteemed friend was capable of... She told Xu Pengju about her meeting with Hu Ruzhen at sea, and the conclusions she had drawn from it.

"Do you think Zhang Yong is preparing to make more of his demons?"

"I fear so, yes. I'm following Hu Ruzhen to try and get to the bottom of it."

"Very well. I'll try to help as much as I can while I'm in Datong."

The lord of Nanjing burned with curiosity. While he didn't mention it, it was obvious that he would have liked to see for himself one of the formidable creatures once created on Dai Yu Island. Did he have any idea just how dangerous they were? Student of Yang Yiqing or no, his sword would have been nothing against one of the powerful yujing. But the question closest to his heart was something else entirely. A hopeless romantic always surrounded by beautiful women, he had eyes only for Shao Jun, beguiled by her heroism and adventurous spirit. A few moments after he had laid eyes on her for the first time, she had even beaten him in combat – despite being injured at the time! – in a baton duel, winning both his eternal respect and his heart. The years had done nothing to dim his feelings, and he had trembled when he learned she was now accompanied by a child who called her "mother". Either she had taken on a student, because it was common for a master – or, in this instance, a mistress – to adopt their students… or it was a secret child who might be the former emperor's.

There was, as far as he could see, no truly subtle way to approach the subject, so he chose to approach it head on.

"In fact, my master told me in passing that you're traveling with a talented young man…"

"Oh, that's Bai Gui, my disciple! He's ten years old, and I know he has a bright future ahead of him."

"He must truly be remarkable if you hold him in such high esteem."

"Would you mind if he spends time with you during our stay in Datong? He needs to improve his fighting skills."

"It would be my pleasure, sister Jun. Master Yiqing will be terribly busy, but I have enough time. Your disciple won't have a moment's rest!"

The way she spoke with him so freely warmed his heart. He began to hope that she might share his feelings.

He replied with a smile.

"As far as I'm concerned, it is I who would like to learn from you! I've perfected my skills in the *Three Revelations of the baton* over the last two years, and I would like your advice."

"But this house has no courtyard or garden suitable for a duel, dear Lord Xu. We also have no batons."

"You're right, dear sister," he agreed with palpable disappointment. "And it would be too risky for you to go to a military training ground…"

"Wait a minute," she said after a moment's thought, "I might know how we can do this."

As if reading the confusion in his mind, she added: "Like *Dragon dances on a coin.*"

The young woman led her visitor into the office which still held the calligraphy equipment used by Bai Gui the day before. She picked up two brushes, one shorter than the other, and plunged them into the inkwell before handing the longest to Xu Pengju.

"These are our weapons," she said. "My usual sword is two feet seven inches and yours is five feet, so the proportions are the same. I suggest that the first to put a mark on their opponent's hand will be declared the winner of this duel. What say you?"

"Excellent!"

Amused and enthusiastic, the young man took the brush and set himself en garde.

In Zen Buddhism, it is said that law imposes stability, stability allows wisdom, and that wisdom engenders law.

Yang Yiqing had applied these three fundamental ideas when developing his art of the baton, which he had naturally named the *Three Revelations*. Until recently, Xu Pengju had been too undisciplined, because with the impatience of youth, he struggled to practice technique when he should have been focusing on the philosophy in all its depth and complexity. Such was the essence of martial arts as practiced by the great masters: it was as much a question of thought as movement. But his ardor had cooled, and his study of Buddhism had allowed him to make great progress. He had even been able to beat Wei Bin.

His new-found maturity was noticed by Shao Jun, seeing in his movements a man completely different from the one she'd faced two years before. She was impressed by his perseverance. After all, it would have been easy for a young noble swaddled in silks not to pursue the discipline required for martial perfection. Yet here was one who fought as if his life depended on it, wielding his makeshift weapon with three fingers as if it were a real sword.

But in the end he was betrayed by his nature: frustrated at failing to gain the upper hand as easily as he'd hoped, his precision decreased as he gradually gave in to his emotions. After a dozen clashes, Shao Jun's brush split his longer and thicker brush with a dull crack.

"It looks like I've lost again," the young man smiled.

"Your brush broke because it lacked flexibility, and you lacked grace, Lord Xu. *The mind governs the body; the mind engenders knowledge; the mind is the purpose of study. Flexibility and grace are required to link body and mind and the mind to knowledge. Such is the way of perfect harmony.*"

Xu Pengju was a member of a different school of thought, and so Shao Jun should not have revealed the precepts of the School of Mind in such a way. But in a fit of compassion, she had decided to allow herself to bend this rule. The young man realized the significance of her gesture and immediately felt that these precepts would be of great use to him. While he was among the greatest spearmen in the country, he had long been plagued by the feeling that there was something lacking from his education. Perhaps he had finally found it.

"Thank you very much," he responded with gratitude.

All frustration evaporated, his expression was now bright and clear. With his heart light and a smile on his lips, he inwardly repeated the pearl of wisdom that he had just been given.

CHAPTER 4

People said that Mount Matou, whose name means "horse head", was magic. Emperor Qin Shi had wanted the Great Wall to enclose it within the empire, but each night, the ramparts erected during the day collapsed of their own accord, as if the last mountain before the steppe were proclaiming its independence. The desires of man were nothing before the will of nature, and only ruins still bore witness to this fruitless exercise. In any case, the Xiongnu, fierce warriors from the north who once threatened the region, had long been eradicated, and the incessant conflicts with the Mongols had given way to relative calm, the vacuum of war bowing to the benefits of trade.

As a result, the Zhuma Fortress, its five thousand soldiers commanded by the intransigent General Tao Shen, was known to those near the border more as a customs post than as a military structure. While all traders traveling between the two countries were scrupulously checked, passes were easy to obtain, and the usual administrative formalities completed without issue. This was because many people passed through for the large market which had sprung up far from any official supervision at the edge of the steppe. As it grew, violence in the surrounding area decreased, proving that the Mongols desired peace and prosperity just like anyone else. What was the point in fighting when you could earn your living peacefully by trading animal skins for porcelain or fabric? Furs traded could be sold for five times their original price, meaning business conducted there could be very lucrative. After investigating the various stalls selling ceramics, silks, and other fabrics, travelers with any coin left in their pocket could quench their thirst with mare's milk or partake of skewers of meat at any time of day or night. In the center of this bustling, lively gathering, the hardest thing to find was sleep.

But the threatening shadow of politics still loomed over this island of yurts, too autonomous for the powerful men who took a dim view of anything they had no hand in creating. So it was with Khan Bodi Alag, chief of the western Mongolian clans, descendant of the Yuan dynasty and proud member of the Golden Horde, who still nurtured dreams of reconquering the south. It seemed inevitable that one day his tolerance for this symbol of possible peace with his Chinese cousins would run out. His terrible reputation alone was enough to dissuade a number of traders: this season only two thousand had made the journey to the borders of their respective nations, five times fewer than the previous year. Gün Bilig, Bodi Alag's cousin who ruled over the eastern clans, was much more favorably inclined towards a reconciliation, but as long as neither of the two leaders controlled all of Mongolia, the situation was at an impasse.

The travel pass issued to Shao Jun and her group by Yang Yiqing allowed them to pass through Zhuma Fortress unmolested after paying the commercial tax. They soon met a certain Dou Decai, a loquacious merchant whose name, which meant "riches from rags", suited him perfectly. Zhuo Mingke, himself jovial and talkative, chatted with him as they traveled, introducing his companions as traders coming to buy furs. The merchant offered to introduce them to an interpreter he knew named Baoyin, who would allow them to avoid trouble and conduct business smoothly, which was preferable for anyone's first visit to Mongol territory. The old scholars of the Yuan dynasty hadn't worked to maintain Mandarin after the rise of the Mings, and the Mongols spoke only the dialects of the steppes, so it was impossible to get anywhere without a bilingual partner alongside. Rather than admitting that he had no interest in animal skins, Zhuo Mingke subtly changed the subject.

Shao Jun stayed out of the discussion. Lost in thought, she absentmindedly stroked the mutton-fat jade pendant that hung from her neck, considering once more the philosophical divergences that had both separated and united three of the greatest thinkers of their time. Zhang Yong wanted to unite the world by conquering it, Yang Yiqing wanted to let nature take its course, and Wang Yangming… Wang Yangming had believed that salvation could be achieved through education. It was this principle that had driven Bai Gui's parents to entrust the young woman with their child, but at times like this, she wondered if she was really fulfilling her duty. But did she really have any other option? The child had the ability to sense Precursor artifacts and was probably their only chance of finding Zhang Yong and preventing him from carrying out his terrible plans. Like an injured monster hiding in the depths of its lair, he bided his time before returning to the fight. He had lost most of his influence when Minister Xie Qian had formed a new cabinet, but Yang Yiqing had allowed him to retain some of his power at court. Shao Jun was convinced that his only objective at present was the creation of his terrifying, superhuman creatures, probably in a laboratory somewhere in Mongolia, and that Hu Ruzhen must be taking him the medicinal plants required for his experiments.

Once in the market, she sent Tang Yingde and Zhuo Mingke to search for any information they could find while she made her own inquiries. At her side, A-Qian seemed fascinated by the unique place they found themselves in.

"Big sister," she asked, "do you think we have any chance of finding Lord Hu?"

"It's unlikely… But we might find his trail."

They noticed a strange crowd had formed nearby and decided to see what they were gathering around. Shao Jun called out to an elderly man in the crowd:

"Excuse me, what's going on?"

"Oh, you obviously don't come here often!" he responded amicably. "People gather here to see Prince Altan, Gün Bilig's younger brother. He's inspecting the market."

Very curious to see this prestigious individual, the two young women elbowed their way forward to a coveted position at the front of the crowd.

"That barbarian is so handsome!" exclaimed A-Qian when she saw the prince. "As handsome as... as Xiao Gui!"

She'd been trying to compare him to Tang Yingde, who also had fine features and fair skin, but since she had left the sea, she had been trying to act more like a well-bred young woman, which meant hiding her true feelings. On the other hand, as her elder's disapproving glare made obvious, it was inappropriate to refer to the Mongols as "barbarians" within their own lands. Fortunately, no one had noticed.

A familiar voice could be heard above the crowd. It was Dou Decai, whose yells had made him the center of his own small group of spectators.

"These skins are poor, Baoyin!" he cried. "I asked for high quality. And if you dare argue, I'll complain to the prince himself!"

He was facing a man dressed in silk and Suzhou satin. That must be the interpreter he had mentioned to Zhuo Mingke a little earlier.

"We mustn't inconvenience the prince," the interpreter answered. "The product you're holding is worth what you paid, that is all."

"Come, my friend, you're trying to scam me. These skins aren't worth a tael! I insist, let's ask the prince his opinion!"

It was a classic scene: the crafty Chinese trader who wanted to buy high quality items at a rock bottom price and felt swindled when he received goods equal to the value of what he paid. His intermediary, who should have been pleading his case, seemed to be more on the side of the fur seller. As the argument grew more intense, the crowd, always drawn by the scent of scandal, grew to the point that it blocked the prince's path. More used to seeing people clear the way for him, he frowned before whispering a few words into the ear of one of the riders around him, who pushed through the crowd towards the two men.

"Who dares impede Prince Altan's inspection?" he said imperiously in perfect Mandarin.

"Ma Fang, listen!" replied a smooth-talking Baoyin in a pronounced accent. "The sheepskins this trader was asking for are worth between ten and fifty taels, but he was unwilling to pay anywhere near that. And now the transaction is complete, here he comes to complain. That's not honorable!"

"We've seen enough," Shao Jun whispered. "Let's go!"

"No," A-Qian retorted. "The prince is coming; I want to see how he'll settle this dispute."

The former imperial concubine acquiesced. She could use this opportunity to scan the crowd for any strange or unusual behavior.

The prince finally appeared beside the two men.

"So," he asked in Mandarin, "what is the problem here?"

"My prince," replied Dou Decai, "these skins are unusable, and the seller refuses to take them back! Help me!"

"Then refund four-fifths of their purchase price. That seems a reasonable compromise to me."

"The prince is a wise and just man," the merchant declared meekly.

Like the audience, Shao Jun agreed: despite his youth, Prince Altan was already clearly a chief, worthy and able to lead his people to a prosperous future that would likely come to overshadow the Ming empire. Did Bodi Alag, the khan on the left wing of the Mongol clans, have the same intelligence despite his notoriously bellicose character? If so, it would be worrying if he was allied with Zhang Yong, because the consequences of such an alliance would be truly chilling.

The young woman had no idea just how close she was to having answers to her innumerable questions. Unknown to her, Hu Ruzhen was also there at the market. He had also been surprised by this gathering of traders, where he'd found order instead of the chaos he expected. Like any good military man, the captain liked discipline; it was how he had successfully carried out his mission despite his personal concerns.

His conscience gnawed at him. Had he done the right thing? When he had raised his doubts with his master, particularly on the dangers of allying with the three khans of Mongolia, his concerns were waved away. But it would have been wise to consider the possibility of failure and its potential repercussions.

At his side was another commander of the imperial guard whose military division, while smaller in number, was founded at the same time as his own. The young officer, answering to the name of Zhou Chong, had quickly become Hu Ruzhen's right hand, and the captain often found reason to appreciate his clear headedness. But since their arrival in the market, he had been nervous and constantly on his guard, affecting even his abilities as a rider.

He discreetly drew his superior's attention.

"Captain Hu," he whispered, "I think we're being followed."

"Can you see them?"

"No, I'm afraid not."

"Very well. Let's separate and try to surprise them."

Hu Ruzhen was amazed. He was sure someone had been following him in China, but he thought he had lost his pursuers in Mongolia. This time, he swore, he wouldn't hesitate to put them to the sword personally, a right granted him by his rank. He picked up an item to give the impression he was busy shopping and began to walk through the busiest parts of the market. Detouring around a yurt, he pretended to fall for the sales patter of a Mongol trader, who banged a metal pot with a stick to attract passersby to his pottery stall. He studied the people around him out of the corner of his eye but didn't find anyone suspicious.

Could Zhou Chong have been wrong?

Far over the other side of the market, some sort of commotion seemed to have attracted a crowd. He tried to ignore them, all the while having no idea that Shao Jun was among them. He did however think of her in that moment and told himself that if she was the one on his trail, he hoped he could lose her rather than having to face her. Anyone else, on the other hand, would be immediately torn to pieces. While the captain was a man with impeccable manners in polite company, he was ferocious as soon as he unsheathed his weapon. Seized with a sudden taste for blood, he was almost disappointed not to see any familiar or suspect faces around him.

When the commotion died down, everyone went back to their business and the crockery vendor to his loud clanging. At the customs point Hu Ruzhen met Zhou Chong, who was also disappointed to have turned up nothing. Yet his captain, conscious that the most important thing was that their cargo had been delivered, did not hold his apparent failure against him. Besides, once back within the empire's borders, they could return to the calm of their official duties.

Meanwhile, the northern end of the market was whipped into a frenzy by a new disturbance: a horse was arriving at a gallop down the long row of yurts.

"Hey," said A-Qian, "she looks like she's in a rush!"

"Get out of the way," Shao Jun instructed quietly.

As an experienced rider, she had immediately realized that the beautiful young woman in Mongol clothing riding the horse had lost control and that the beast might injure anyone in its path. The rider wasn't to blame, she had simply been the victim of an unfortunate accident: her reins were torn, and only a short piece of leather remained hanging from the bit of her mount. She tried vainly to reach it, stretching out along her horse's neck and gripping the terrified creature's mane as it charged straight towards a trader's stall.

"Big sister, it's going to run the trader over!" cried A-Qian.

Too focused to respond, quick as lighting Shao Jun grabbed the remains of the reins dangling from the beast as soon as it came within reach, forcing it to change direction. But the animal, panicked even more by this sudden movement, snorted and kicked madly to dislodge her She'd be trampled to a pulp if she let go now. But then the thin hand of its rider wrapped around her wrist, giving her the stability she needed in the moment. Her reflexes, surpassing even those of Wang Yangming, allowed her to strike the ground with her foot to turn and then use the stirrup as a platform to land astride the beast's back, just below its neck.

One of Master Ezio's former students in Europe, Shao Jun

had developed her own technique that combined aspects of Eastern and Western martial arts, a technique so effective that it had allowed her to face Zhang Yong head-to-head. In emergencies, her muscle memory meant she could react to sudden events without thinking, something which had saved her life more than once. To avoid disaster, she knew she needed to use the *Way of the Heart*, which, although her mastery of it was not yet complete, should be enough to control a simple horse.

The rider grabbed Shao Jun's waist to keep her on, and Shao Jun focused her internal energy to compress the two massive arteries that led to the animal's brain, causing it to kick even more fiercely before eventually calming. As she felt the danger pass, she gradually relaxed the pressure to avoid killing the creature, then sat up with a deep sigh of relief.

That had been close!

The rider soon relaxed her grip, suddenly ashamed to be clinging so tightly to this person she believed to be a man.

Shao Jun jumped to the ground, then used her belt to create a pair of makeshift reins. The horse, now gentle as a lamb, docilely lowered its head. It seemed safe to assume it wouldn't cause any more trouble for the time being.

A-Qian came running towards them.

"Big… big brother Shao!" she cried. "Are you alright?"

Before she could respond, the young Mongol woman, who had also just dismounted, spoke.

"You saved me! I don't know how to thank you, Mr… Shao?"

"Wang Shaoyang."

"Ah! Mr Wang, then. My name is Meng Gen. *Meng* means *silver* in my language."

Now they were out of danger, the young woman seemed to have become bubbly and talkative. Her mischievous eyes and the tiny imperfections in her refined Mandarin – perhaps even better than A-Qian's – made her quite charming. In addition, her sumptuous clothes clearly indicated that she held a very noble position.

"You owe me nothing, Miss Meng," Shao Jun responded simply, not wanting to linger.

But as she moved off, Meng Gen seized her by the wrist, something which would never be allowed for a young Chinese woman.

"Mr Wang," she insisted, "it wouldn't be right if I didn't express my gratitude somehow."

Just them, Prince Altan arrived at a gallop. He was closely followed by Ma Fang, who slid down from his saddle with remarkable grace to stand next to his lord before offering his shoulder to help him dismount. The Mongol heir's handsome face was creased with anger and concern. As soon as he hit the ground, he whipped his servant severely, tearing his clothes and opening bloody wounds on his shoulders.

"Ma Fang," he yelled, "how could you let the princess ride such a wild creature?!"

"Altan, stop," the young rider interrupted. "I insisted!"

The prince complied, but his anger did not cool in the slightest.

"You could have died, Meng Gen! You know that only Ma Feng can ride this beast."

"I'm sorry, I thought I could control it… but fortunately, Mr Wang came to my rescue. Please, help me thank him as he deserves!"

Altan noticed Shao Jun and A-Qian for the first time. Learning that he owed them his sister's life, he bowed to them, his obvious contempt warring with his sense of honor. He even tried to address them in Mandarin.

"Mr Wang," he began, "I haven't had the pleasure of meeting you before, but you have my gratitude. I am Altan, prince of Mongolia. Welcome to our lands! Allow me to offer you a hundred sheepskins and ten horses to thank you for your actions."

"That's not necessary, prince," Shao Jun responded. "I didn't do it for any reward. And now, if you would excuse me, I must leave your company."

Meng Gen's eyes went round. Would this selfless altruism pleasantly surprise her brother, or would he be offended by the refusal? She quickly turned towards her brother's servitor to avoid having to see his reaction.

"Ma Fang, accompany Mr Wang. I'll join you shortly."

As she moved off, Shao Jun heard the young woman speak to her brother in Mongol reproachfully. No doubt she had wanted him to be more welcoming… After all the commotion, the former imperial concubine wanted to be alone for a moment.

"You can leave us," she said to Ma Feng.

"No, Mr Wang, I cannot. The princess gave me a direct order."

"Brother Ma," exclaimed A-Qian, "you speak Mandarin without an accent!"

"It's because I'm Chinese. I come from Yuzhou."

"Your parents must miss you!"

"They died eight years ago… the year I entered the prince's service."

It wasn't difficult to guess the boy's story, who couldn't be any older than fifteen or sixteen at most. He must have been taken prisoner as a child in a bloody raid on his village, located in the area near Xuanfu Fortress, several hundred lis east of Datong. While he'd had the chance to live, he'd seen more than his share of horror and suffering in his short life. The villagers in the border regions were always the first victims of war.

When they reached the two yurts hired by the acolytes of the Society of the Mind, Shao Jun invited the young man to enter.

"Come and rest," she said gently.

"No, thank you. But may I ask when you plan to leave the market?"

"Today. And tell your master this quote from Confucius: 'None is wise who is not also brave.' I want him to understand that real bravery comes from making fair decisions. Innocent citizens on the border have suffered too much for the quarrels between our two peoples."

"I'll pass on your words," he responded, impressed by the wisdom of this unknown young man.

Forty years later, when Prince Altan became the Great Khan, he concluded a trade agreement with China that marked the beginning of seventy years of peace for the region.

CHAPTER 5

"So you haven't discovered who he came to meet here…" Shao Jun murmured.

"No, big sister. I'm sorry."

Tang Yingde still felt responsible even though he had done nothing wrong. When he'd seen Hu Ruzhen in the crowd, he'd briefly nurtured hope of being the hero of the day, but his prey had quickly escaped him in the busier areas of the market. The disciple of the Society of the Mind, already shaken by the ambush he'd walked into in his previous tracking attempt, preferred now to proceed with caution. He had rejoined Zhuo Mingke, following spaced apart so they could both keep an eye on the captain from a good distance, then let him go when he returned to Zhuma Fortress to cross the border. If he was returning to China, it was because he had already completed his mission.

"Don't blame yourself, brother Tang," the young woman reassured him. "We simply arrived too late."

"Do you think Captain Hu is trafficking with the Mongols, big sister?" Zhuo Mingke asked.

His question, which had haunted them all for the last few days but which none had dared voice, resulted in a heavy silence. Jaw tense, Shao Jun lifted the canvas at the entrance of her yurt to glance outside. The season was almost at an end, and the market was in its last hours. Soon, the plain would return to its desert quiet and become a simple transit zone rather than a destination in its own right. The last rays of the setting sun shone on a crowd that was less dense but still active, buyers and sellers relentlessly bargaining as long as the light remained. The discussions taking place here benefited all, and, with rare exceptions, everyone here had the feeling they were leaving better off than when they arrived. The sight of Chinese and Mongols, rich traders and poor farmers, improving their lives by working together was pleasant to see. Here and there, the inhabitants of the steppe had lit celebratory fires around which they danced and sang animatedly.

While he was close to Zhang Yong, Hu Shangren was a man of sufficient integrity to have earned Wang Yangming's respect. He had avoided taking part in the atrocities carried out by the Eight Tigers, and as the model of a Confucianist official who loved his country, had never made a deal with Mongolia. His son's character remained to be confirmed for sure, but could the apple really have fallen so far from the tree? What's more, despite his methods and the hatred that filled him, Zhang Yong had not yet acted traitorously. While Wang Yangming and he had differed on how to make the empire prosper, they had been working towards the same goal.

So then, why had Hu Ruzhen's trail led them here?

A strident whistle rang out.

"Mr Wang!" called a familiar voice. "Mr Wang Shaoyang!"

It was Ma Fang, who had arrived on horseback. When he arrived in front of the yurt, he jumped to the ground and bowed respectfully before announcing:

"Mr Wang, by order of the prince, I bring you twenty horses and two hundred sheepskins. You can count them!"

Shao Jun had to stop herself from sputtering in surprise. That was double what he had initially offered... and what she had refused. But just as she was about to protest again Meng Gen also appeared. Mounted on a snow-white horse and dressed in trousers and a green satin *deel* jacket, she was a sight to behold.

"Mr Wang," she said, "Mongol custom requires that a borrowed horse be returned the same day. Please, don't think me ungrateful."

Despite her gentleness, she had spoken firmly and loudly, attracting the attention of all the occupants of the surrounding yurts. Trapped, and concerned about becoming the center of attention yet again, Shao Jun acquiesced.

"Thank you, Princess Meng Gen. Your generosity does you honor."

"Perfect! Then I'll also have the pleasure of seeing you tomorrow at the banquet being thrown by my big brother."

With these words, she drew an elegant invitation card from her sleeve. Feeling even more uncomfortable, the former imperial concubine disguised as a man took it calmly.

"I wouldn't miss it for the world," she replied courteously.

Excited by the prospect, Meng Gen broke into delighted

laughter, revealing two rows of teeth whose dazzling whiteness contrasted against the red of her delicate lips. Her reaction was refreshing, because in the Ming empire, the rules of modesty and decorum officially required women to avoid showing their teeth.

"That makes me so happy!" she exclaimed. "Ask for me when you arrive, and I'll come to meet you personally."

As she moved away, Ma Fang clasped his hands together and bowed in the traditional Chinese fashion before remounting and accompanying the princess.

They then had to find somewhere to store the two hundred animal skins, which were fortunately washed and treated with nitrate – without which the smell would have been unbearable – and find an enclosure for the twenty horses, which in this land were the equivalent of a small fortune.

"All of that is going to slow us down," A-Qian commented with an amused smile.

"I'll gift it to Governor Yang Yiqing on our return. The army always needs horses and winter clothes."

Shao Jun turned her attention to the invitation thrust on her by Meng Gen. The Mongols were not normally in the habit of making them, so they took the style of those that were in use in the empire instead. Decorated with beautiful colors, it comprised a poem written in exquisite Chinese characters speaking of magpies sitting on the branches of a plum tree. The text, a subtle piece, could not have been composed by Prince Altan or his sister, whose level of skill in the language would not have enabled them to attain such a level of literary elegance.

"Well then!" exclaimed Zhuo Mingke as he examined it.

"It's referring to the stele of Cao Quan, erected in the Han dynasty! Who would have thought the Mongols capable of such scholarship? And these brush strokes are incredibly graceful!"

Like all students preparing for the imperial examinations, the young man had spent many hours learning this famous poem, although he had never understood its deeper meaning. His remark drew the curiosity of Tang Yingde, who bent over to scrutinize the invitation in turn.

"Big sister," he soon said, "I think this is He Jiuliang's script."

"What makes you say that?" the young woman asked.

"The style of the *zhi* 之, which he is known for never writing in the same way twice. In the poem *Scaled brocade*, which he wrote for Emperor Zhengde, he managed to write it thirty-six different ways."

It was this artist's signature style which made him stand out from his peers with the virtuosity of his way of writing this tiny character, so simple, common, and difficult to stylize. Most calligraphers, less bold and paradoxically more demonstrative, preferred to flaunt their dexterity with more complex characters.

"Brother Tang," asked Zhuo Mingke with embarrassment, "who is this He Jiuliang? I've never heard of him…"

But it was Shao Jun who answered.

"He Jiuliang was a eunuch at the imperial palace… where he was Zhang Yong's apprentice." She paused. "He was sometimes known as the ninth Tiger."

"A eunuch? At the side of a Mongol prince?"

So, Shao Jun thought, now they had the opportunity to

check their suspicions, because if a person so close to Zhang Yong really was part of the entourage of the most important family in Mongolia, the collusion there would be indisputable. It was incredibly fortunate that Tang Yingde had identified his style, because given that he had already met the famous calligrapher at the palace, and even spoken with him, he risked being recognized if he attended the celebration organized by Meng Gen's brother. Shao Jun on the other hand had seen this ninth Tiger more than once in the Leopard Residence, but always from behind a screen.

"Brother Tang," she decided, "you'll deliver the horses and skins to Governor Yang in Datong tomorrow. We can't risk you being recognized by He Jiuliang."

"Of course, big sister."

"Big brother Tang," A-Qian said, "it's dangerous to travel alone… Be careful!"

"You too, sister Qian," he answered without conviction.

Early the next morning, Ma Fang reappeared to guide "Mr Wang" and his friends to Gün Bilig's encampment, lying halfway between the market and a vast body of green water where several herds still grazed despite the low temperatures. It was Lake Dai, the largest north of Datong, which the Mongols sometimes called a sea due to its salty water. At other times, the rich, verdant grass surrounding it had also led to it being known as the lake of paradise. In warmer periods, it was an essential pasture for the region's herders. The camp owed its moist and salty air to the lake, despite being situated around ten lis away.

Gün Bilig's yurt, gilded and three times larger than the others, was unmissable. Just before Ma Fang disappeared inside, Meng Gen appeared, twirling like a graceful butterfly, wearing a fitted pink satin dress in a decidedly un-Mongol style.

"Mr Wang," she exclaimed, "how wonderful to see you! Come in, come in, and don't let yourselves be intimidated by my brother: he's good at heart, despite his rough edges. I've had a tent prepared for your friends, and I'll have them brought something to eat and drink."

"Thank you very much, princess."

These thanks were very necessary: Meng Gen must have had to use her influence to ensure that in this highly hierarchical group, A-Qian and Zhuo Mingke would not be treated as simple servants condemned to jostle near the stables for nothing more than a cup of water.

Shao Jun hadn't expected to be separated from her companions, but thinking about it, she would likely attract less attention alone. What's more, while Gün Bilig was making the effort to tolerate several rich Chinese traders during these events for the sake of the good trading relationship between his people and the Ming empire, it was better not to test the limits of his good will. This grandson of Dayan Khan had often been tempted to ally with Bodi Alag to bring the Yuan empire back to life, and his younger brother, Altan, knew how to speak to him to stop him giving in to hatred. Simply holding this banquet was itself a powerful message of peace, a victory for peaceful trade over violence.

From his elevated seat, which was not quite a throne, Gün Bilig appeared even more out of reach than ever. He scrupulously avoided meeting Shao Jun's eyes when she was presented to him, whereas in contrast his gaze was full of tenderness when he looked at Meng Gen and Altan, whom he seemed to sincerely adore. Seeing them standing side-by-side in formal clothes, it became even more obvious that the two were twins, whose names were very fitting, meaning "silver" and "gold" respectively. The young princess then presented her dear "Mr Wang" to the rest of the gathering, which included many nobles of the Jinong ethnicity. Someone by the name of Buhe – a relative of Baoyin, if Dou Decai hadn't lied – spoke several polite words to her in Mongol, but most present made no effort to hide their hostility behind cordial greetings. The Chinese traders, happy to be in the presence of a compatriot, were much more welcoming, although clearly distracted and trying to make the most of the banquet. While the young woman felt very out of place with her much more modest clothing, she noticed that Meng Gen drew nothing but admiration and respect from those around her.

The princess finished going around the table by pointing at a small man slightly apart from the rest.

"And this is Uncle Liang. He's Chinese too."

"Pleased to meet you, yes," he responded distractedly.

Shao Jun almost fainted. Her worst fears had just been confirmed: it really was He Jiuliang, the ninth Tiger. So, Zhang Yong was allied with the Mongol princes... The young woman's heart clenched at the idea that her master, who had believed in his old friend's integrity right to the very end, could have been so wrong. Wang Yangming had died convinced that, despite their differences, and even despite the Great Rites Controversy, the members of the Society of the Mind and the Zouwu were cut from the same cloth. But Zhang Yong's treason had gone too far this time. Was his plan to trigger and influence an invasion of the Ming empire by Mongolia? Nothing seemed impossible now... But that question would have to wait. For now, the young woman had to continue making a good impression at the banquet to avoid raising suspicion. Sitting alongside her big brother, Meng Gen kept casting her discreet glances.

Deciding that now was the time to broach the subject, Gün Bilig picked up a golden cup and officially opened the banquet with a traditional address in the Jinong dialect.

"Thank you for honoring us with your presence," Altan translated in summary. "Long life to you all!"

Usually, festive Mongol feasts included beef and mutton, but this more refined celebration saw a string of lamb dishes with rich and varied flavors. On the other hand, the alcohol was an extraordinarily strong drink made from fermented mare's milk, typical of the steppes where it was served warm to combat the harsh climate. Sitting down next to her savior once more, the princess drank a glass of it in one gulp, sending her cheeks delightfully rosy. Gün Bilig's mood began to lift after a few glasses too. Three rounds later, his obvious drunkenness cheered even the most reticent of the Jinong nobles, who began to dance and sing with the rest of the guests. By dusk, the khan would prove himself worthy of the illustrious emperors of the Yuan dynasty, known for their bawdy and debauched banquets.

By the time the festivities had really got into full swing, He Jiuliang was alone in a corner of the tent able to drink without excess, far from the sometimes-intrusive offerings of other overly drunken attendees. As the sun began to set over the plain, he suddenly set his glass down and quietly left.

His departure didn't escape Altan's notice. He quickly stood, ready to follow him.

"Altan!" Gün Bilig called out to him. "Come drink with me!"

"With pleasure, brother, but first I need to get some air for a moment."

Focusing all her inner energy, Shao Jun made herself redden and feigned a grimace of discomfort to appear as if overcome by alcohol.

"Please excuse me," she whispered to Meng Gen, "but I need to go outside for a minute."

"Oh! Mr Wang, our jade wine is too strong for you! I'm so sorry! Please, let me accompany you to your tent."

Used to the princess's insistent nature by this point, the young woman didn't even try to protest. Of course, she would have preferred to disappear alone to discreetly spy on the discussion between the calligrapher and the prince, but perhaps she could at least regain her freedom once she was away from the celebration.

Her two followers, visibly unhappy at having had to spend so much time alone together, waited in her yurt in front of several plates of food.

"Brother Shao!" exclaimed A-Qian on seeing her elder's red face. "What happened?"

"Mr Wang drank two rounds of jade wine," Meng Gen explained. "Pour some water over his face, lay him down for a while, and he should feel better soon. But still, make sure he doesn't vomit in here…"

"Do you need to go and change your clothes, Mr Wang?" Zhuo Mingke asked in turn.

It was a means of asking if she wanted to go somewhere quiet where solitude could be expected. The disciple of the School of Mind had understood the subterfuge after Shao Jun sent him a quick wink, and it was an effective way to lose their new and overly attentive Mongolian friend.

"I'll leave right now," the princess quickly decided. "Mr Wang, it would be wise for you to remain here. You'll be invited to drink more if you go back to the main tent."

After being thanked with a wave of the hand, she finally disappeared.

"Big sister," A-Qian began, "the princess is falling for you!"

"Come on, stop joking around!" Shao Jun retorted in amusement before rinsing her mouth and adding, much more seriously: "He Jiuliang really is here. He's meeting with Altan at this very moment."

"What?" Zhuo Mingke almost shouted. "Zhang Yong has fallen in with the Mongols?!"

"Unfortunately, I don't see any other possible explanation…"

If two such influential figures were on the point of concluding an agreement or speaking of anything already agreed, it was essential to find out more. But there were numerous guards patrolling Gün Bilig's permanent camp, clearly preventing any unauthorized movement at ground level, particularly by the Chinese. The large Mongol yurts, on the other hand, held up by four central pillars and with a complex roof of beams, were topped with a lightwell. Shao Jun sent her rope dart wrapping around the top of one of these tamarisk wood structures, then tugged on it to check it was firm. Satisfied, she jumped agilely, as light and silent as a feather, landing without causing the slightest tremble in the tent canvas.

What incredible control! thought A-Qian. *Would I be as skilled if I had been Wang Yangming's student?*

From her perch, the former imperial concubine could now see dozens of yurts just like her own, some with a thin trail of smoke emerging from the top. To find the one she was looking for, she was going to have to use *Way of the heart*, a technique which would allow her to access the full vision of Buddha. While it hadn't helped her master spot the yuxiao hidden under the water in his confrontation with Zhang Yong, it didn't seem likely that He Jiuliang and Prince Altan would be speaking at the bottom of Lake Dai...

The universe is my mind, and my mind is the universe. Shao Jun repeated this mantra to herself as she concentrated on deepening her breathing. Her sight gradually blurred, then her eyes began to see differently, directly drinking in sensory information from all around up to sixty-five feet, beyond which the details became vague and confused. With training, it was possible to sense even further, but the training was long and demanding. Unfortunately, it was in this fog at the edge of her perception that she could make out two silhouettes, one large and one smaller, which had to be Prince Altan and He Jiuliang, behind a yurt.

Already exhausted by the effort required for *Way of the heart*, Shao Jun knew she had to try harder. It was too important for her to fail. Ignoring the crushing weight of the responsibilities which threatened to overwhelm her, she forced herself to push her mind further out. It was clumsy and wavering at first, but suddenly, she breathed deeply and felt like she could see her two targets as clearly as if they stood in front of her. Better still, she could hear them too.

"It's not difficult," Altan was whispering, "the two prisoners are ready. But each new transfer increases the risk of discovery. You know what we're facing."

"Don't worry, prince," He Jiuliang immediately responded. "The captain general will testify that the captives are in the pay of the Koreans. Creating an army of yujing requires a lot of raw materials after all… There's no need to be concerned about our deal either, we have Elesi…"

The mention of the terrifying superhuman creatures once created on Dai Yu Island shook the young woman to her core. Unable to continue, her vision began to blur, and she fell backwards, unable to catch the rope. Fortunately, A-Qian ran forwards in time to catch her inside the yurt, saving her from a potentially fatal fall. White as a sheet, sides heaving, Shao Jun seemed exhausted, and it was only with great effort that she was able to stand and stagger a few paces. Such was the price of the *Way of the heart*.

"Big sister, what happened to you?" her younger friend asked.

"It's nothing serious, I'll be fine after some rest."

"You can feign drunkenness even more easily now than when you left the banquet!"

Given his knowledge of the young woman's incredible abilities, Zhuo Mingke was all the more shocked at her condition. She must have had to put in an unusual amount of effort to be so affected. He handed her a cup of suutei tsai, a fortifying Mongol tea which helped the drinker cope with the huge variations in temperature between day and night.

"Drink this, big sister," he said to her. "It'll do you good."

Grateful for the offer, she gulped a mouthful before speaking quietly: "Mingke, do you know where Elesi is?"

"No, that name means nothing to me, why?"

"These monsters... I'm worried it's going to start all over again... at Elesi..."

"The monsters from Dai Yu Island?" choked A-Qian. She had seen the horror of their existence two years before.

Shao Jun nodded. While brief, the exchange she had overheard left no room for doubt: Prince Altan was sending prisoners to Zhang Yong through He Jiuliang to help create an army of yujing. The Zouwus' plans for conquest had not ended with the destruction of Dai Yu Island, and it was vital that they were stopped, particularly now there was the opportunity to act... That was the mission the disciples of the School of Mind had inherited from Master Yangming.

"Big sister, do you want me to follow He Jiuliang?" Zhuo Mingke asked.

"No, because you might end up facing Zhang Yong alone... We'll try to discover his destination together when he leaves the banquet."

Without departing from her haggard but authentic air, Shao Jun returned to the main tent to keep an eye on the conspirators who then stayed until the end of the festivities. For her part, she was the subject of all Meng Gen's attentions – the princess swore to stop "Mr Wang" from drinking and loudly insisted that he should spend the night in the Mongol camp. Confronted with a firm refusal, the princess then took it upon herself to accompany the Chinese travelers to the market itself when the banquet ended in the middle of the night. Fortunately, she finally left them when they reached their own yurt, just as Shao Jun was wondering if she risked compromising their plans... because, as A-Qian had pointed out, it was becoming obvious that the Mongol princess had fallen in love with her savior. She would never see her again: like many youthful passions, Shao Jun would vanish forever, leaving behind a romantic memory that the young woman would idealize over time. Better that she not learn the truth.

On the steppe, the only remains of the market were the rubbish on the ground and a sense of emptiness that hung in the air where the largest gatherings had been. Merchants and passersby had been replaced by a handful of indifferent shepherds. From there, travelers could head towards the military location of Zhuma Fortress, towards the luxuriant Lake Dai, or, to the east, towards the arid and inhospitable lands where treacherous quicksand preceded the desert. It was in this direction that Zhang Yong must have established his lair to be able to carry out his experiments without being disturbed, Shao Jun concluded. She lowered her eyes to the map Master Yangming had given her. While the empire had been carefully documented, it contained no useful information on the places beyond its borders. To flush out their enemy, they would have to throw themselves into the unknown – but instead of feeling fear, the idea of finally confronting Zhang Yong made her thrum with impatience. She no longer had Tang Yingde at her side, but the last of the Eight Tigers didn't have Hu Ruzhen's help either, since he had now returned to China, and He Jiuliang was no martial artist. And with the advantage of surprise, the young woman felt capable of winning the battle.

Looking towards the horizon, she simply said: "Let's go!"

CHAPTER 6

While Xu Pengju had agreed to watch over Bai Gui to please Shao Jun, he also prided himself on being able to adopt the flattering position of master in the face of this eager child. The prince of Wei's scholarship was inferior to his martial skills, as he had soon realized when tackling the teachings of *The Great Learning*, a Confucian classic that his current pupil clearly knew better than him. He felt shame and anger, because his relative ignorance was the result of the lazy habits which had characterized his privileged childhood. He had learned a lot from Master Yiqing, but he still had a long way to go before he could claim to be accomplished, and so every failure smarted, particularly when inflicted by a youth.

"Young man," he sighed after being embarrassed one time too many, "I'm supposed to be teaching you, but it is you who is teaching me!"

All acolytes of the School of Mind had long dedicated themselves to the study of the famous foundational text of

Master Yangming's school of thought. Shao Jun hadn't yet come to understand all its subtleties, but Zhuo Mingke and Tang Yingde had mastered it fully. The latter had also recently taken it upon himself to help the younger man explore this essential text, particularly the governing precepts of kings long past: *Things being investigated, knowledge became complete. Their knowledge being complete, their thoughts were sincere. Their thoughts being sincere, their hearts were then rectified. Their hearts being rectified, their persons were cultivated. Their persons being cultivated, their families were regulated. Their families being regulated, their states were rightly governed*[9].

To forget this embarrassment, Xu Pengju had to find ground on which he would be more at ease.

"Let's leave this," he announced. "An accomplished Confucian must not only master the Four Books and the Five Classics, but also the Six Arts[10]! Let's go out before it gets too late, I'm going to teach you how to ride a horse."

"Alright! I've never ridden a horse."

They walked towards the courtyard of the military school, currently full of shouting and strident trumpeting: Yang Yiqing was overseeing the distribution of the winter clothing that Xu Pengju had just delivered.

Before the governor had been assigned to lead the border army, the troops had suffered from obvious carelessness which had greatly harmed their mission. While they should

---

[9] Translation taken from http://classics.mit.edu/Confucius/learning.html

[10] The Four Books (*The Great Learning, The Doctrine of the Mean (Zhongyong), The Analects of Confucius, Mencius*) and the Five Classics (*The Classic of Poetry, The Classic of History, The Classic of Changes* or the *Yi King, The Book of Rites, The Spring and Autumn Annals*) are the body of philosophical reference texts, and the Six Arts are rituals, music, archery, horse riding, calligraphy, and mathematics.

have received new uniforms every year, some soldiers were wearing rags at least six years old due to the corruption of senior officers who embezzled the funds allocated by the government for their men. A dangerous aberration for a military force that was supposed to be the first line of defense for an empire facing the world's greatest cavalry... When he took up his position, Yang Yiqing had taken the situation in hand very publicly: he had imposed training for battle formations, doubled the number of daily training sessions, and mercilessly punished any who had dishonored their post. It was thus under his attentive eye that the leaders of each unit, after announcing the number of their unit and the number of men within it, circulated the piles of clothes along their columns of men. Each soldier was assigned two uniforms, one for summer and one for winter, to ensure they could serve the empire under optimal conditions.

"The governor is truly a talented man," the prince of Wei whispered as he admired the operation. "Thanks to him, the border is well guarded."

The soldiers then paraded for half an hour to show the public their discipline before leaving the school's courtyard to the sound of the bugle. Xu Pengju mounted the platform where his master stood to greet him. Now friendly and smiling, his master enquired after the health of Bai Gui, who had still been recovering from his travel sickness at their last meeting. He was happy to hear that the child was much better and that he was going to receive riding lessons.

"What a wonderful idea!" he exclaimed. "And since the young prince will also be learning to ride today, you will have two pupils, my dear Pengju!"

"Which young prince?" the young man asked.

"Zhu Tiangxian, son of the prince of Dai of course! He must be the same age as Bai Gui, I'm sure they'll get along well with each other."

Beardless, unmarried, and childless, the old scholar was sometimes mistaken for a eunuch. But while the absence of any of his own family may have been what allowed him to dedicate his life to serving his country, it didn't mean he didn't enjoy the company of children: in their presence, the great military chief was once more an old man of eighty years. The child he was expecting was the older son of Zhu Chongyao, one of the most important people in Datong, who had received the cartographer Luo Hongxian the day after he had arrived in the city accompanied by the acolytes of the School of Mind.

Zhu Tiangxian didn't seem pleased by being introduced to a child of lower rank but refrained from protesting out of respect for Xu Pengju. The latter, having been passably impressed by Bai Gui's talents moments before, viewed the young prince's ostensible contempt very unfavorably. As the proverb said, "the children of the rich enjoy easy success". Preferring to avoid making a fuss, he helped his two protégées mount their gentle-natured ponies and led them at a walk around the yard. Little by little, he taught them how to hold their reins and direct their mounts themselves, but boredom soon set in; in addition, the dust raised by their mounts' hooves stuck to their sweat, which ended up making the lesson a less than pleasant experience. Then he saw Yang Yiqing greeting the driver of a cart loaded with goods just entering the yard.

Wanting to find out more, Xu Pengju called out to a soldier to watch the two boys for him and ran over. Seen up close, it was obvious that the young man who had just arrived was not a trader, but a scholar. Yang Yiqing quickly introduced him.

"Pengju, may I introduce Tang Yingde. He studied with my brother in arms, the monk He Daoren, making you fellow students."

When the prince had requested Master He's advice at Chaotian Temple, the venerable martial artist had mentioned Tang Yingde as his top student. Continually stuck in Nanjing due to his hereditary post, but despite wanting to, the young man had never had the chance to seek him out and compare himself against him. What luck they had met here, within the empire! Amazed and delighted, Xu Pengju bowed respectfully.

"It's wonderful to meet you, big brother Tang! Master He had nothing but good to speak of you."

"It's a pleasure to meet you. I also know your name, of course, both as prince of Wei and as the heir of Master Yang Yiqing... I am your senior, but may I suggest that we exchange a few blows?"

This duel went far beyond a challenge between two young men. He Daoren, a brilliant man who was one in a million, surpassed Yang Yiqing in all areas except the use of a spear. Now the two scholars were too old and respectable for unnecessary combat, it fell to their students to represent them, and it was in hope of one day seeing them beat his old rival's protegees that the monk at Chaotian Temple had trained Zhuo Mingke and Tang Yingde with such determination.

This symbolic meaning was not lost on the Datong soldiers

gathered in the yard, jostling impatiently to avoid missing this historic moment. Furthermore, it would probably be their first chance to see the *Three Revelations of the baton*, a technique made famous by the governor but which they had never had the opportunity to see with their own eyes.

Standing on his platform, Yang Yiqing followed the preparations for dueling with a small smile. The two combatants, mounted on horses, wore black tunics and were armed with spears whose tips had been replaced with a piece of white chalk so they could fight without risk of injury. Undoubtedly the governor hoped to see his student triumph, because deep down, he admired the way the well-born young man had managed to avoid the arrogance typical of his rank, and had striven to perfect his art, never giving in despite the demanding training. He was however realistic: because of his duties, his protege had almost never had the chance to use his technique in real life, unlike Tang Yingde, who was as finely honed as a butcher's knife.

The reality of a mounted duel is vastly different from how they are described in literature. Reading the more romantic authors, you might believe that dozens of blows are exchanged as the horses constantly whirl around in a wild ballet which offers the combatants numerous opportunities for attack. Nothing could be farther from the truth, because in a real mounted duel, the riders gallop towards one another and have only one chance to strike: at the exact moment they pass each other. If no decisive blow is achieved, another charge takes place, but it is exceedingly rare for it to be over in anything less than three charges.

Even the two children learning to ride interrupted their

exercises so they wouldn't miss the spectacle. Despite his arrogance, Zhu Tiangxian couldn't help speaking first.

"Who do you think will win?" he asked.

"It's hard to say... They seem equal."

"Nonsense! Lord Xu is of royal blood; he wouldn't lose to a mere commoner!"

Bai Gui rolled his eyes. Clearly his companion had no idea that Tang Yingde was no mere commoner but was in fact a court official. But then, he also hadn't witnessed him slay a horde of bandits out on the steppe... Feeling mischievous, the young boy seized upon the opportunity.

"In that case, dear prince, what would you say to a small wager on this duel?" he offered. "If Lord Xu wins, I'll play horse for you."

The structure of this proposal had the benefit of exempting him from doing this in the event of a draw, but Zhu Tiangxian, unused to handling the subtleties of language, failed to realize.

"Very well!" he exclaimed scornfully. "And if he loses, you can ride on my back."

"Oh no, no! I'm just a common boy, it would be too demeaning... Here's what I suggest: if you lose the bet, you must accept me as your teacher and give me the respect due a master from their student. What do you say?"

"Agreed!"

Just as the children shook hands, the two riders began to charge.

Despite the oncoming dusk, Shao Jun could see a single solitary vulture soaring in circles over the steppe. Far ahead,

He Jiuliang had just stopped, perhaps to eat or drink some water. His cart was almost certainly full of the prisoners he had mentioned the night before when talking to Prince Altan, and he had traveled at a moderate pace throughout the day without seeming to be aware he was being followed.

A gloomy tower loomed on the horizon to the northeast, eroded by sand and wind, the last remnants of an abandoned stretch of the Great Wall that was said to be haunted. His rest stop over, this was the direction taken by He Jiuliang. This could be a problem, Shao Jun thought: until now, she and her acolytes had been able to hide in the crowd, in the cracks and vegetation of the landscape to avoid being spotted, but the ninth Tiger was now heading into the desert… He would soon notice a small group following him.

"\What are we going to do, big sister?" A-Qian asked.

"I'm going to continue alone and on foot. You'll both stay here, ready to intervene if needed."

"Big sister, no!" Zhuo Mingke argued. "This desert is even vaster than the steppe, you'll never be able to survive alone and without a horse. In the market, I heard more than one soldier mention all those who had ventured there and never returned… In addition, without landmarks, you'll only be able to use the sun and stars to guide you, and if the weather is cloudy, you'll soon lose your way. Look, I can already see clouds on the horizon! I know you can beat Zhang Yong, but no one can win against the elements."

Usually little inclined to argue against his elder's decisions, the young man's agitation made Shao Jun smile.

"Don't worry, you'll serve as my landmark. And besides, to flush out the tiger, we first need to enter its lair."

She jumped to the ground and drew the cloak given to her by Ezio Auditore from underneath the saddle. Instead of mastering the Eastern martial arts, members of the European Brotherhood used this key accessory to protect themselves against bladed weapons, moving more smoothly, and making huge leaps. However, the young woman rarely had the opportunity to wear it, because it was clearly of foreign design and was anything but discreet in the middle of a Chinese crowd. In the desert, on the other hand, the cloak was an asset.

The second object Ezio Auditore had given Shao Jun was the Precursor box, which had since fallen into Zhang Yong's hands... Would she get it back one day? She had to, but for now, she had to concentrate on her preparations. She also equipped herself with the flares used by sailors to communicate in bad weather, which she packed with a nervous sigh. While it was never pleasant to imagine the worst, she had to consider the fate of her companions.

"Watch the sky," she said to them. "If you see one of these fireworks, forget about me and get back to Zhuma Fortress immediately."

"Big sister..." A-Qian murmured, terrified at the thought of never seeing her again.

While more stoic, Zhuo Mingke was also worried. But the woman opposite him was strong and dignified, her cloak fluttering like a banner in the wind. Even if she was but a pawn on the chessboard of fate, she looked ready to face anything that destiny threw her way.

"Brother Zhuo," she said without turning, "take care of A-Qian."

Even if she failed, she thought, the Society of the Mind would live on. With Zhuo Mingke and Tang Yingde, Bai Gui would be well cared for, and Zhang Yong had gone too far for his misdeeds to go unnoticed. Strangely reassured by this idea, she waved at her companions one last time, adjusted her cloak, then strode forward in the same direction as He Jiuliang, who was now just a speck on the horizon.

Fortunately for her, it was difficult to drive a cart in the desert. The sand made it difficult for the wheels to turn, and she was certainly moving much more quickly than the calligrapher she pursued. Furthermore, even when she lost sight of him due to the darkness, she could continue to follow him thanks to the deep tracks left in his wake. After a few hours, however, they were less deep as the ground began to grow firmer, and the young woman noticed that the gusts that sometimes whipped across her face were moist and salty. But the only stretch of salt water for lis around was Lake Dai! It could only mean one thing: to confuse any pursuers, after heading to the east, He Jiuliang had traveled in a wide arc towards the west to return to his point of departure.

Shao Jun took advantage of the wind to advance even more boldly. She felt she was close to the end and almost invisible thanks to her cloak. Her eyes were accustomed to the ambient darkness, and she could soon see the lake, a huge black mirror that reflected the pale moon. The ninth Tiger's cart was stopped on the bank, and the calligrapher himself stood a few steps away imitating the cry of a falcon and drawing circles in the air with a candle. It had to be a signal … The young woman hid behind a small dune twenty feet away and grasped the handle of her dagger – she had chosen to leave her longsword behind. If Zhang Yong was about to appear, she had to give her all to make the most of this unique opportunity to kill him.

Then, another light shone in the darkness… on the lake. A boat without rowers traveled across the water at high speed, a single solitary silhouette at its prow.

Zhang Yong!

It was him; she was sure. His oppressive aura was like no other…

"Captain," He Jiuliang greeted him soberly.

His boat remaining almost supernaturally still, the last of the Eight Tigers seemed to walk across the water for several steps before reaching the shore. He slowly lifted his lantern to shine on the cart.

"Did you bring everything we need?" he asked.

"The prince kept his side of the bargain."

"Do you know why I asked you to make a detour, little Tiger?"

"I'd never dare to question Your Excellency's orders."

"Ha ha! Your diplomacy is admirable. But I think you might be surprised at what comes next…"

A cruel gleam lit his eyes, then, after taking a deep breath, he shouted as loudly as he could.

"Imperial slut! Come out!"

"What?" said the calligrapher, amazed. "Captain, who are you talking to?"

"Emperor Zhengde's concubine, of course!"

Hearing only the silent night, he became angry and shouted again.

"Refusing to show yourself, slut? Fine, have it your way… Feilian! Elai!"

He had just called out the names of the mythical bodyguards of the Shang and Zhou dynasties. According to legend, the first had been able to run sixteen hundred li in a day, and the second had superhuman strength. But the protectors that came forth were two large, black dogs that jumped off the boat to sit either side of their master, still as statues. Another word from him, and they ran straight into the night, and the faster of the two quickly flushed Shao Jun out from behind her dune.

How had the situation got away from her, and so fast? Her stealth movements technique was perfect, she knew it was, so how had Zhang Yong known she was there? Could she beat the last of the Eight Tigers without the element of surprise? These questions jostled in the young woman's mind as she reflexively plunged her dagger smoothly into the nose of the mastiff that had just thrown itself at her. However, instead of fleeing like any other dog, the beast redoubled its effort, moving its jaws from side to side, lacerating its face in the process. It was so strong that Shao Jun, despite firmly gripping the handle of her knife, was able to make use of the momentum to float in the air with her cloak spread around her like the canvas of a kite. And so, when the second dog attacked, its teeth found nothing but empty air.

The young woman could see the truth in the pale green eyes of the hellish creatures: they had the same look as the yuxiao! And for good reason. Zhang Yong had spent the last two years working on his unholy experiments using the knowledge bestowed by the Precursor box. Animals were easier to procure than human prisoners, so of course he had naturally focused part of his research on developing these bestial demons... and he was not displeased with the results. While he could not see what was happening in the darkness, he was surprised not to see the dogs returning with the body of the former imperial concubine. "The slut is a worthy successor to Wang Yangming," he cursed silently, half in admiration, half in irritation. Resolved to end things as quickly as possible, he turned back to the boat and shouted.

"Shentu! Yulei!"

Two more large black dogs, these named after the legendary guardians of the Peach Garden and demon hunters of the Jade Emperor, quickly surged from the waves. Unlike Feilian and Elai, which had been the Tiger's first two viable subjects, these two could move underwater and spend a long time beneath the surface. It was they who had propelled the boat across the lake. As soon as they were in the open air, these monsters launched into the night to attack Shao Jun. Overwhelmed by the number of canine adversaries but still safe thanks to her cloak, the young woman had to concede that she couldn't win this fight: she had to retreat. She sent her rope dart flying towards an anchor point on He Jiuliang's cart then, as soon as she felt resistance, tugged on it to send herself flying into the air and land on the back of one of the horses drawing the cart. Completely disorientated by their prey's sudden disappearance, the four mastiffs circled piteously around their master's feet.

"Gongong! Zhu Rong!" the Tiger called out, counting on his last two beasts to finish her off.

But by the time the final two, named after the gods of water and fire in ancient legend, burst from the water's surface,

Shao Jun had already sliced the harness of her mount, which reared with a furious neigh.

Having decided to take matters into his own hands, Zhang Yong had just appeared in front of her, blocking her way forward.

CHAPTER 7

While Zhang Yong was not fond of Tang poetry, he was well acquainted with Du Fu's famous verse: "Aim for the horse to reach the man; to kill the leader is to kill his troops." Rather than trying to injure Shao Jun when he could only reach her legs, and without the certainty of dealing a fatal blow, he aimed for her horse's neck: with its artery cut open, the beast wouldn't get more than five steps before collapsing. But his sword was blocked by her knife with a clang, repelling the Tiger with such force that he lost his balance and was thrown back as the rider disappeared into the night.

The former captain of the imperial guard was stunned. Unhappy with being thwarted when the former imperial concubine had escaped his demonic canines, he had severely underestimated her reflexes and strength. Of course, she'd taken advantage of her mount's frantic movement to add power to her move, but he would be remiss if he failed to recognize the virtues of her cool-headedness and fighting skills. This brief encounter had been completely beyond He Jiuliang's skillset, and he had been wise enough not to interfere. Aware of his deficiencies as a fighter, he had chosen not to get in his master's way.

Shao Jun's heart beat like a drum. She blamed herself for once more failing to deal with Zhang Yong, but the discoveries she had made this night were a victory in themselves. Once his treason was exposed, the former captain of the imperial guard would lose all influence at court and, most importantly, Yang Yiqing's support. Thus isolated, his defeat would be only a matter of time. But to reach that point, first she had to get back to Zhuma Fortress alive... She glanced behind her: the two traitors weren't even trying to pursue her, instead leaving that task up to their hellhounds. But the canines were much too slow to catch her, and she gained a little more distance with each second that passed. She allowed herself a deep sigh of relief. All hope wasn't lost yet.

It was then that a dark shadow struck her mount's head with a high-pitched cry. Its eyes blinded, her horse reared before collapsing to the ground, leaving Shao Jun only a fraction of a second to jump down to avoid being crushed. She rolled on landing, then quickly unsheathed her dagger to face this new, unknown threat. Since her eyes were already accustomed to the darkness, she could make out the massive silhouette of a great eagle of the Mongol plains, a powerful bird of prey able to lift lambs and, according to legend, even the children of unwary nomads from the ground. Seated on the head of the agonized horse, it watched the young woman with glittering green eyes. That supernatural gleam left no room for doubt:

the bird was one of Zhang Yong's monsters, just like the dogs that were threatening to catch up with the young woman at any moment.

So that was how he'd known He Jiuliang was being followed!

Shao Jun was filled with anguish. Once again, she had underestimated her opponent and fallen straight into his trap. Worse still: this cursed bird might have revealed Zhuo Mingke and A-Qian's position to its master, putting them in great danger... Without a second's hesitation, she slid the flare she'd taken care to bring with her from her sleeve. When she removed the cap, the flints inside it rubbed against those at the base of the projectile, generating sparks which lit its short fuse. The flare flew into the sky almost immediately, lighting the night with a long trail of fire for several seconds. Both the eagle and the dogs, who were only a few steps away, were momentarily dazzled, giving Shao Jun a brief window to deploy her cloak and glide a dozen feet. Unfortunately, as she knew all too well, it was nowhere near enough. As soon as she touched down, she bent her legs slightly to lower her center of gravity and held her dagger out in front of her, ready to defend herself.

The first hound jumped at her, an enormous four-foot-long beast that Zhang Yong had named Yulei, only to be met by a devastating blow to its shoulder from her dagger. Despite their power, these animals lacked intelligence, so it had been easy for the young woman to dodge at the last minute, blade held in front of her, letting the monster's own weight and momentum inflict a wound that would have been fatal to any other creature. To Shao Jun, it felt like her dagger had hit a rock. Seeing the dog land on all fours and prepare to attack again as if nothing was wrong, she realized that, like the yuxiao she had faced two years before, she had to destroy each animal's vital organs to kill them. All six dogs had now encircled her while the eagle wheeled in menacing circles overhead. They seemed to be waiting for something… or someone. Strangely, in the deathly silence, she was reminded of Wang Yangming's words.

> *The mind itself is neither good nor evil. Good and evil are born of intention. Discerning good and evil is an essential knowledge. Studying the ten thousand things enables one to work for good and eliminate evil.*

It seemed like an eternity since the day she had first read those four wise sentences in the hall of High Virtue at Jishan University. The meaning of the first sentence had always eluded her, and her master had been intentionally vague in his explanations to ensure his disciple would have to solve the mystery herself. The venerable sage had founded his philosophy on Confucianism and Taoism, but also included aspects of Zen Buddhism, which emphasized learning through personal experience. As soon as she'd had the opportunity, Shao Jun had asked for clarifications from two of the master's best students, Wang Ji and Qian Dehong. The first had told her that as the mandate of heaven is pure goodness and that the mind, knowledge, and the ten thousand things all come from the heart, that both good and evil are superficial to the point of non-existence. The other had said that the outer world pollutes the heart, which is neutral by nature, inspiring good or bad intentions within it, and that you must examine yourself three times a day in order to discern them.

Their interpretations differed so much that Shao Jun was just as confused as she had been at the start.

But now, imminent death imbued her with a new-found lucidity, and she understood that good and evil only existed in relation to each other. In a world without predetermination, where both the best and the worst were permitted, the heart is neither pure nor impure: it is empty. And so, to Zhang Yong, the former imperial concubine was a detestable being who constantly thwarted his plans, while anyone who abhorred violence saw him as evil. In his infinite wisdom, Wang Yangming had simply accepted that their paths had diverged, without trying to pass judgment on their respective choices. Wang Ji had understood this to mean avoiding allowing oneself to be compromised by worldly opinions, and Qian Dehong believed that everyone aspired to act in accordance with the arbitrary laws of the world, but neither had achieved such a state. Astounded by her own revelation and stunned by its trivial essence, Shao Jun felt like laughing.

At least, she said to herself, *the Society of the Mind will survive!* Now the new generation was ready to take up the mantle, her fate was a mere distraction.

Zhang Yong finally made his appearance. He had arrived calmly and silently to stand behind his monsters and contemplate his enemy. The scene had a special significance for him: his beasts represented his future victory, and he gained a certain pleasure from seeing them surround the one person able to disrupt his plans. While he had long despised the former imperial concubine, he now couldn't help but feel a deep respect for her. She reminded him of Wang Yangming in many ways. It was ironic that, after annihilating so many of his opponents through subterfuge or assassination, the leader of the Eight Tigers had been forced to kill his oldest friend with his own hands... The death of his disciple, which he would soon witness, would be a somber echo of that bitter victory.

"Concubine, know that this old eunuch has much respect for you," he said solemnly.

In his mouth he carried a small, high-pitched whistle, an essential tool for animal trainers on the steppes, and blew it. The six dogs, who had been well trained before their transformation, leapt onto their prey in a single bound. These animals had been carefully selected for their obedience and physical strength. If one of them caught a sheep by the head and another by the tail, they could tear it apart in a single movement. Suffice to say that if a fragile young woman fell between their jaws, she would have no chance of escape.

In the almost total darkness of the dry and biting desert cold, Shao Jun could only follow the movements of the dogs by the gleam of their eyes. But when they fell upon her like lightning, their teeth closing on thin air, she was able to avoid them all.

Zhang Yong would have applauded if he hadn't wanted so badly for it to end. The young woman's grace and agility were truly incredible. Seeing her in action on more than one occasion, he could appreciate just how superior she was to Wei Bin, who had been the most skilled by far of the Eight Tigers. But unlike the monsters she currently faced, she was not tireless: they could keep attacking forever, but she would quickly become too tired to continue avoiding all their attacks. The former captain of the imperial guard blew his whistle once more.

One of the dogs managed to close its jaws on Shao Jun's arm, but it was fortunately protected by her cloak. In revenge, she stabbed her dagger into the animal's head. It was the same creature which had been the first to taste steel back at the lake, but this time she succeeded in splitting its skull. However, its jaws gripped tighter rather than loosening. Another, smaller dog set its teeth into the young woman's unprotected calf. She felt a wave of pain so intense that her heart almost stopped. Her leg gave way and she fell to the ground, at the mercy of the pack.

It was all over this time, she was sure of it. Eyes fixed on the sky above, she silently apologized to Master Yangming. Despite all her efforts, she hadn't managed to put a stop to Zhang Yong's machinations. Other than this nagging regret, she was ready to leave this world.

But just as a beast was about to close its jaws around her neck, a spear flew through the air and planted itself between its green eyes. The dog was thrown backwards and nailed to the ground. Shao Jun's first thought was that only Yang Yiqing himself was capable of such a throw in almost total darkness, but of course, the governor of Datong would never venture out into these lands alone...

The figure that collected the weapon was none other than Zhuo Mingke.

Nether he nor A-Qian had been able to force themselves to follow Shao Jun's instructions, so they had run towards her when they saw her distress signal. And the young man's lightning-fast attack, amplified by the speed of his galloping horse, had come at just the right time. As he tore his weapon from the body of the creature he thought dead, he was surprised to see it snort then shake itself, ready to pounce again. His unexpected arrival seemed to have made him the pack's new target and they circled him, growling. He immediately realized these were no ordinary animals, and that his skill with the spear wouldn't be enough to get him out of this sticky situation. It was likely he would have to use *Blocking the six meridians*, the ultimate teaching bequeathed to him by Master He. It was an attack of last resort because the martial artist using it risked suffering irreversible internal injuries. The technique required him to block six of the twelve meridians in his body to double his strength for a brief time: if he diverted his internal energy from half of its normal paths, those remaining open would logically benefit from an increased flow, which translated into superhuman agility, speed, and strength. It was an unnatural state of being, so no one could sustain such an effort for long... But what other choice did Zhuo Mingke have?

"Help big sister Shao escape while I keep them busy!" he panted to A-Qian.

She quickly made her way to Shao Jun, cut off a piece of her tunic and expertly wound it around the other woman's ankle. The latter was now able to stand and grab the saddle of the horse her saviors had brought for her, but as she was putting her weight on her uninjured leg to jump onto her mount's back, a draft of icy air ruffled her hair. Instead of mounting, she drew her longsword from the sheath on the horse's side and turned just in time to parry a thrust which would have struck her in the heart.

Zhang Yong!

The old Tiger had to admit his surprise. Despite what Shao Jun had feared, he hadn't expected his enemy to have company. But the problem would be quickly dealt with. As the young woman reeled from the blow she had just blocked, he thrust his blade into her horse's neck before swiftly moving towards the next horse. Clear-minded even in the heat of battle, he had decided that his priority was to deprive the three members of the Society of the Mind of any means of escape, because they didn't stand a chance against an eagle and six demonic canines.

Immediately realizing the danger, Shao Jun tried to rush to stop him, but as soon as she put weight on her injured leg, a shooting pain lanced through her like a knife. She fell to the ground, powerless, as Zhang Yong felled Zhuo Mingke's horse. He was momentarily distracted by his redoubtable enemy's vulnerability, contemplating the possibility of giving in to temptation and finishing her, but then resolved to continue with his initial plan and turned towards the last of the horses... to find A-Qian standing in front of it, armed with her twin blades.

Her mixed, unpredictable style belonged to all schools and none all at once, because she had learnt to fight among pirates from all walks of life, borrowing from a range of styles and executing them expertly regardless of their origin. After taking her under her wing, Shao Jun had helped her consolidate her strengths and rid herself of bad habits, but she was still far from the mastery of a martial artist who had benefitted from training worthy of the name. But what she lacked in training she made up for in courage and ferocity as she twirled her two swords like butterflies trying to force Zhang Yong to retreat. The latter, far from being impressed, easily blocked her clumsy blows, and pricked her with his sword in numerous places. Then, he pierced her shoulder with a quick thrust, but not enough to end the combat. Teeth clenched, she forced herself not to scream.

"Jump into the saddle, big sister!" she shouted.

Behind her, Shao Jun struggled with watching her take part in a duel that she had no chance of winning, but her young disciple was right: with her injured leg, she would be more mobile on horseback. Driven by the energy of despair, the former imperial concubine hoisted herself onto the back of the last living mount and spurred it to rescue A-Qian, whose tunic was soaked with blood. How many wounds were there on her skin? Twenty? Thirty? She lost count. But as Shao Jun drew up alongside her, she hit the horse's flank with the flat of her blade to force it into a gallop, despite its rider's protests.

Zhang Yong's eyes grew wide: so, this incompetent girl and the spearman who would soon fall to his beasts were ready to sacrifice themselves so the imperial slut could live? He couldn't allow it! And yet, his enemy was once more disappearing into the night…

Strangely, A-Qian and he were both thinking of the same person: Wang Yangming. The former master of the Eight Tigers thought of their past friendship, the deep and sincere friendship that had given way to hatred in his heart, and wondered which was more valid. He had hoped to be able to dispose of Shao Jun this night, to rid himself of his rival's most formidable disciple, but she had been saved by two young people who were clearly ready to give their lives for hers, a selfless gesture which he was certain no one would ever do for him. Such a spontaneous act could not be commanded: it had to be deserved. Throughout his long life, the founder of the School of Mind had put teaching at the heart of his relationships with others, and the seeds he had sown were bearing fruit far beyond his death. A-Qian had been astonished by her meeting with the old scholar several years before, when he had contacted her brother to persuade him to join his cause. He had pleaded for an end to the raiding, generously handed out several pearls of wisdom, and forever changed the life of a young girl who would later renounce all piracy to travel the empire at Shao Jun's side. Bai Gui had joined them, then Zhuo Mingke and Tang Yingde... It was the beginning of a movement that would only continue to expand.

Zhang Yong thought he could still use *Fire lotus* to catch Shao Jun, but he still couldn't afford to let her get too far ahead of him. The young girl with the undisciplined style before him had already delayed him too much, and he began to find it insulting that she refused to give up even after being so injured. It was time to end it. He still carried his high-pitched whistle in his mouth; one side commanded his dogs, the other his eagle. As soon as he blew it, the dark shadow of the eagle swept through the air to rake its sharp, powerful claws across A-Qian's head. Overwhelmed with pain, she had still had enough presence of mind to avoid attacking the bird, because to do so would have given Zhang Yong a fatal opening. Instead, she crossed her two blades then parted them in time with her steps forward, a formidable technique known as the *Sakura cut*, which she had learned from a Japanese pirate.

"Doesn't she fear death?" the old eunuch wondered as he avoided her swords. He was impressed that his young opponent had withstood the terrible attacks from the jewel of his demonic menagerie. Because while it was easy to find obedient dogs to experiment on, even with the risk of losing most of the subjects, trained birds were much rarer; in the end he had only been able to procure three. And so, he was furious when a spear flew into the animal's body.

It had been thrown by Zhuo Mingke. After successfully dealing a fatal blow to the worst of the six dogs and given he was secretly in love with her, he hadn't been able to bear hearing A-Qian's suffering only a few steps away any longer. Fearing she would soon succumb to either the eagle's talons or Zhang Yong's sword, he had chosen to intervene to give the young woman a chance to escape, aware this gesture would probably cost him his own life. Ready to defend her to the end, he leapt to his weapon to collect it but suddenly felt a sharp pain in his right calf. A dog had just bitten it, tearing off a large chunk of flesh. The young man shouted in pain and fell to the ground as the raptor, still alive despite its wound, pumped its wings to return to the air.

As the pack of dogs rushed towards him to tear him to pieces, Zhuo Mingke whispered the name of his beloved one last time. At least, he consoled himself, he had given her the chance to escape…

But when he turned his head towards her, he was horrified to see A-Qian throw herself at Zhang Yong once more, aiming at his legs with wide, disordered sweeps of her blades. It was no longer kung-fu, but the frantic, desperate moves of someone who had given up on victory and their own safety. She had decided to buy Shao Jun as much time as she could, because it was on her that the survival of Master Yangming's teachings depended, and nothing in the world mattered more. Her efforts had paid off, because the former imperial concubine was now too far away for him to reach her.

Fully aware of his failure, Zhang Yong was overcome with murderous rage. With a powerful roundhouse kick, he sent his young adversary's twin blades flying, as she clung tightly to his ankles to prevent him from moving away. He thrust his rapier into her back with a rough, imprecise movement, sadly missing the heart of his poor victim. He had to repeat this two or three times before the young woman finally let go, but when she rolled onto her back to take her last breath, there was a smile on her lips.

CHAPTER 8

Crack! Regulars at the military school were used to the sound: the sound of a spear breaking.

Like a wave, the crowd rose as one to applaud the duelists. Having jumped up from his seat, Yang Yiqing also held his breath. It would be terrible if one of the two brightest representatives of the next generation of Chinese martial artists were seriously injured during a simple exercise... but the two rivals remained in the saddle, their broken weapons in hand, then galloped around the yard before approaching the governor's dais at a walk. Relieved to see them unhurt, he waded through the crowd to greet them. When they dismounted, he studied the traces of chalk on their tunics: Tang Yingde's was marked on the shoulder, and Xu Pengju's on the arm. Neither had lost their proud, arrogant bearing, but they had both been secretly surprised that their opponent was their equal. They conceived a form of mutual respect which assuaged their respective frustration at not having triumphed.

Yang Yiqing had felt his rivalry with He Daoren revived through this duel. And for good reason: Tang Yingde had just used *The sound of the crane taking to the skies* which he had inherited from his master. Xu Pengju had been able to pivot in time only to be caught on the arm; he would have been knocked to the floor if it had hit him in the chest. The old governor himself had once paid the price for this powerful technique which he had never mastered, and seeing a young man succeed where he had failed made him a little nostalgic. While his own disciple had hit first, he had to recognize that his brother's had been superior. But only a little. So little in fact, that he was able to pronounce the outcome of the match with complete honesty: a draw.

"I'm grateful to you for not humiliating me in front of my master, brother Tang Yingde," declared Xu Pengju with hypocritical politeness.

"You're too kind, Lord Xu... The truth is that I wasn't able to win despite my best efforts."

The two children in the prince's care then arrived, leading their horses by the bridle. As always, Yang Yiqing was both amused and moved by the young Zhu Tiangxian's solemnity as he asked which of the two fighters had won. Though born and raised in luxury, the child had grown up far from the big cities and had therefore not absorbed the manners of those places, instead adopting an affected chivalry undoubtedly influenced by his reading. It was the source of that interest in riding and fighting that had won him the old governor's affection.

"Lord Zhu," he replied, "Lord Xu and brother Tang are equal."

The young noble quickly reddened in irritation, realizing that he had lost his bet. Fortunately, Bai Gui chose to be diplomatic.

"Dear prince," he offered, "let us simply say that neither of us won."

"Yes, brother Bai Gui, Lord Xu and brother Tang are both highly skilled fighters. But this equality of skill between them should have won you your bet, should it not?"

"That is a fair question, prince..."

While Yang Yiqing wondered if He Daoren would come out of his retirement after learning the outcome of this duel, the two young martial artists changed, then walked together to the private residence. Taking the opportunity to exchange a few words, they were pleasantly surprised to discover that their fighting styles originated from the same source; despite themselves, they had to admit to themselves that they would be good friends if circumstances ever gave them time to develop their relationship. When they reached their destination, Xu Pengju turned towards Tang Yingde to ask him the question which he had been burning to ask.

"Tell me, brother Tang, do you know when Miss Shao will be back?"

"Big sister plans to come back here after Gün Bilig's banquet, so by tomorrow at the latest."

"Very well, thank you for telling me."

The young prince couldn't help but smile in satisfaction as he noted that Shao Jun was "big sister" to his companion while she was "Miss" for him. On this front at least, his victory was unchallenged! He left with a lighter heart, relieved to finally be free of the embarrassing Bai Gui to whom he clearly had nothing to teach…

That evening, the child practiced his calligraphy and the writing of official documents in the company of Tang Yingde, who knew the subject like the back of his hand. When they finished, it was clear that their companions were not returning that evening, and so they stopped waiting and went to sleep in the large central room.

At the same time, far off on the steppe, Meng Gen meditated in the glow of a Chinese candle. She always bought them when she found them in the market, despite their price, because they were odorless and gave off less smoke than the unpleasant-smelling tallow candles made by the Mongols. Staring at the flickering flame, she longed for the elegant "Mr Wang." Would they see each other next year? Could they get to know each other better? But he might be married… Crushed by the weight of these considerations, she felt as gloomy and desolate as the plain would be in a few days, when the last traders had left and the encampment would be gone. The coming silence was already oppressive.

As she blew out her candle to go to sleep, she heard someone calling her from outside her tent. It was Ma Fang, the small Chinese man that Gün Bilig valued for his incredible riding skills. But while her brother didn't hesitate to beat him whenever he was in a bad mood and needed to take it out on someone, Meg Gen had always been friendly to him, as she was with all the servants. Nonetheless, it must be urgent for him to dare disturb her at such a late hour.

"What is it, Ma Fang?"

"Are you alone? You have a visitor…"

"At this hour? Fine… let them in."

The servant pulled back the entrance flap and stepped forward into the light, supporting an exhausted and bloodstained Shao Jun. Meng Gen immediately recognized the Wang Shaoyang who had left just several hours before. Filled with a whirlwind of emotion that included confusion, fear, and joy, she felt tears coming to her eyes.

"But what happened to him?" she asked Ma Fang.

"I don't know. I simply saw him fall from his horse when I was out for a walk. I didn't even recognize him at first…"

"Have you told anyone else?"

"No, but he came galloping from the north. I got the sense he was being pursued."

"From the north?"

Meng Gen frowned. What would a Chinese man be doing in the north? The closest border was Zhuma Fortress, to the southeast.

"Princess," Ma Fang murmured, "we must help him."

"Go back to where you found him and erase any tracks left by his horse, then make some new ones leading in a different direction."

Ma Fang wasn't stupid: he knew that if a Chinese was fleeing to the south on the steppe, it could only be because he was being pursued by Mongols. He was a native of the Ming empire himself and had been touched by the simple kindness shown to him by this Wang Shaoyang when they briefly encountered each other in the market. He had taken a risk by asking his mistress for help, but he knew her kindness to those in need, regardless of their nationality. Deeply moved, he kneeled before her and laid his forehead on the ground as he thanked her profusely.

"Thank you, Princess Meng Gen," he choked out. "Thank you!"

It's said that at the time of death, those leaving this world drink the soup of forgetfulness before crossing the River Nai and entering the kingdom of the dead. The old woman Tao had told Shao Jun about this legend shortly after her arrival in the imperial palace, as she watched the eunuchs dispose of the body of a concubine who had just passed away. Young as she was then, she had been overwhelmed by the sight and its implications, becoming scared and hiding to cry her heart out. Back then she had been lost and alone, isolated in a world with no place to call her own. She finally found that place when the elderly Tao took her under her wing, though she too had crossed the River Nai in the end…

Lying comfortably, Shao Jun felt a warm liquid flow into her mouth. Had her time come? Should she drink the soup of forgetfulness?

The memory struck her like a knife. She relived Zhuo Mingke's sacrifice, and then that of gentle A-Qian, who she had come to think of as a true sister over the last two years. Imagining the suffering she must have endured was unbearable, especially now that her mind, slowly emerging from unconsciousness, reconnected with the pain in her body. She hadn't been so seriously injured since her fight in the Xiaoling Tomb, when she had been on the trail of the Eight Tigers. Once again, she felt like she had cheated death... but the price of her survival had been far too great.

When she tried to get up, her entire being felt bruised. She tried to cry out, but a hand clapped itself across her mouth to keep her quiet.

"Are you awake?" a voice whispered in her ear.

With a shudder of dread, she recognized Meng Gen's voice. So, she hadn't made it back to Zhuma Fortress... Even worse, she must be in the heart of the Mongol camp, a stone's throw from Zhang Yong's allies! She forced her eyes open, and slowly, painfully, pulled herself into a sitting position. She was wearing a traditional Mongol dress, alone in a tent with the princess, who looked at her with confusion, but without anger or fear.

Seeing that her guest was relatively calm, Meng Gen offered her a small bowl filled with a warm concoction.

"Save your strength and drink this," she said gently. "Everything will be fine."

"Meng Gen, where am I?"

"In my yurt."

Nevertheless, the princess still needed to ask the most obvious question, which she did with a hint of disappointment in her voice.

"Miss, as it's quite obvious that your name isn't Mr Wang... Who are you really?"

"There's no point avoiding the truth, not now. My name is Shao Jun."

"That's just what I feared... Altan and Uncle Liang are looking for you. To hear them tell it, you're the devil himself."

"I doubt I can convince you otherwise. I won't blame you

if you decide to hand me over to Zhang Yong. It will simply be fulfilling my fate."

Such fatalistic and calm resignation surprised Meng Gen, who remained silent for a moment. But as she was about to continue, she heard the sound of hooves echoing outside her tent and went out to see what was going on. She recognized a senior Mongol official known for being Gün Bilig's confidante. As princess however, she still had sufficient authority to compel him to answer her questions.

"Buhe," she asked, "where are you going?"

"We're following Altan's order to pursue an outlaw who is trying to reach the Ming empire, princess."

"Have you caught him?"

"Unfortunately not. He escaped us after we chased him for most of the night… His trail doesn't seem to lead anywhere."

Unable to speak Mongol, Shao Jun didn't understand the conversation, but she heard Buhe's name and guessed he was talking about pursuing her. She didn't know what to think when Meng Gen returned to the tent and sat down next to the bed. Why hadn't she given her up? Had she decided to protect her? As the silence between the two women dragged on, Ma Fang asked for permission to enter the tent, which was granted by the princess. His face lit up when he saw that Shao Jun had found the strength to sit.

"You seem better, Mr Wang!" he said enthusiastically.

"Come, Ma Fang," Meng Gen interrupted, "you can clearly see she isn't a man! You must call her Miss Shao from now on."

"I'm so sorry, Miss Shao, please excuse my rudeness."

The servitor knelt before his mistress.

"Princess," he declared, "I'm sure Miss Shao isn't a bad person. I beg you, please protect her! If Prince Altan is after her, it must be some sort of misunderstanding…"

Although she said nothing, Meng Gen was roiling on the inside. Like her servant, she had instinctively wanted to help Shao Jun, who had shown courage and kindness under the identity of "Mr Wang", but it was impossible to ignore the gravity of the situation. One thing was certain, however: the fugitive would die if she was handed over to Altan and Gün Bilig. What's more, the princess had to decide quickly, because dawn was coming and men were beginning to dismantle the Mongol camp.

Far off, she heard Altan reprimanding Buhe for his failure. As far as he was concerned, their prey must have already reached the border…

As he mechanically told Bai Gui the history of Datong as a morning lesson, Tang Yingde worried for Shao Jun, Zhuo Mingke and A-Qian. They should have been back the day before after returning to Zhuma Fortress the day before that, but there'd been no news of them since their departure for the Mongol banquet. What could have happened?

He was snapped out of his thoughts by the arrival of a messenger come to invite them both, him and his student, for a meal given by the prince of Dai. The man liked to surround himself with people of quality and was already hosting the cartographer Luo Hongxian. He was delighted at the thought of bringing together Yang Yiqing's skilled nephew, Tang Yingde, and Prince Xu Pengju, having heard of his presence in town, together under one roof. Aged around thirty and a self-proclaimed scholar, he was part of the new generation that would build the China of the future, so he was interested in meeting others he might work with to make the empire prosper. And to top it off, it would also be a rare opportunity for his son to spend time with a child his own age.

The Ming dynasty had granted the title of prince to eighty-seven families, of whom sixty-five still had an heir in office, each assigned to a specific prefecture. Eternally indebted to the empire and those who had gone before them, they enjoyed as many privileges as they had duties. The current prince of Dai, Zhu Chongyao, was the fifth generation of his family to reign over this remote but prosperous city which had made its own fortune, where life was good since the region had been pacified by governor Yang Yiqing. General Xu Dayin had built Datong long ago, during the fifth year of the reign of Hongwu. Covering an area of thirty lis, it was protected by a wall forty feet high and five feet wide, making it the most fortified city in the northwest of the empire. The prince's residence was located in the northeast of the city, covering an area of twelve acres. It was even more luxurious than Xu Pengju's own residence in Nanjing, something he immediately noticed on his arrival.

Although the soil of Datong wasn't fertile and the city was several days' journey from the nearest coast, the banquet featured some of the empire's most delicious dishes. The meal was sumptuous and accompanied by enthusiastic discussion, with Zhu Chongyao constantly asking his guests' opinions on every subject that came to mind or that he cared about, constantly feeding the flow of conversation.

While Tang Yingde was too preoccupied by the fate of his friends to make the most of the occasion, Xu Pengju and Luo Hongxian talked and made more than enough noise to occupy intellectual space. Eventually, just as the debates turned political, the young Zhu Tiangxian grew tired of it all and allowed Bai Gui to leave the table to explore the palace. Driven by some instinct specific to children born of the nobility, he also took the opportunity to show off his wealth to remind his companion – who was clearly much more educated and skilled in martial arts than he – of his place.

The demonstration had the desired effect: having grown up in a modest military home, the series of luxurious and ostentatious rooms, the passageways and wide corridors, the gates and doors which went to make up the residence of the prince of Dai made Bai Gui's head spin. Even though his grandfather had taken him to visit the residence of the prince of Liao, which he guarded, several times, it was still far smaller than this.

The two children's wanderings took them outside the palace and onto the main path which crossed its grounds. Walking past altars to the wind, mountain, storms, and rivers, they reached the Temple of the Earth and Sky but only stayed briefly, since Zhu Tiangxian was ashamed of his inability to read the philosophical inscriptions. Deeper in the gardens, they arrived at the Pavilion of Virtue, a place of retreat where the princes sometimes went to relax or ask the emperors for advice. Normally the building was quiet and still, but today it seemed buzzing with servants. Noticing the two children, one of the eunuchs charged with guarding and maintaining the building approached.

"Hello, young prince," he said. "What brings you to the Pavilion of Virtue today?"

"What is all this activity?"

"Your father has decided he is going to come and stay here for a while, so we are cleaning the pavilion from top to bottom to prepare for his arrival."

It was a strange contrast: even as Prince Zhu Chongyao gave a banquet that was representative of his normal thirst for social and intellectual pleasures, he was preparing for a ten-day retreat far from the tumult of his life as a social and cultural figure. His staff took their work seriously, carefully dusting and rearranging the pavilion to make it clean and comfortable once more.

The huge building was designed by the monk Lei, a disciple of Anigo, the illustrious architect from the beginning of the Yuan dynasty. For the Pavilion of Virtue, he had created a garden worthy of a royal manor, depicting an entire country in miniature, with rivers and mountains, laid out in such orderly disorder that could have been chosen by Mother Nature herself. Somewhat neglected in recent years, the luxuriant vegetation had taken on the look of a jungle, but the prince's gardeners had worked hard to try to restore it to its former glory. Even Zhu Tiangxian, who lived there but rarely visited this part of the grounds, was amazed by the sight.

While he had never really ventured into the pavilion beyond its terrace, his role as guide emboldened him, and he led his friend along the path to enter the main room, surrounded by a small connecting courtyard which the servants were busy sweeping. He suggested they visit the Swallow Palace, the section of the pavilion which housed the prince's own quarters, which made Bai Gui uneasy: the place was too intimate for him to feel comfortable getting close. It could mean trouble, particularly for him, who wasn't a member of the ruling family.

The children then noticed two old eunuchs carrying a heavy copper chest out of the palace with much huffing and straining. One of the handles on their burden suddenly gave way, sending the chest crashing to the floor. Already weakened by the passage of time, the impact broke the lock.

"You two!" Zhu Tiangxian called authoritatively. "What are you doing with that chest?"

"We're taking it out of the Swallow Palace, Your Highness. It was just sitting there rotting."

Moving closer, Bai Gui recognized the seal of General Guo Deng, Count of Dingxiang, whose exploits he had heard that very morning from Tang Yingde. The skilled soldier, a key local figure, had defended Datong against the attacks of Khan Yesen after the latter had captured Emperor Yingzong during the battle for Tumu Fortress. These exploits earned him his post in the city, which he filled with thousands of riders and made the most impregnable bastion in the northwest. Even today, the inhabitants of the region still maintain that it is his fierce soul watching over them that prevents the Mongols from marching on the border, and that Yang Yiqing is the reincarnation of this legendary warrior.

"Young prince!" exclaimed Bai Gui. "This chest belonged to General Guo Deng!"

Zhu Tiangxian, who had never heard of him, naively asked, "Was he powerful? How was he compared to… say Yang Yiqing?"

Though the governor of Datong was for the children of many notable locals the main reference for prestige and authority, the question was really very unfair. In addition, Guo Deng enjoyed the incomparable legendary aura that is often granted posthumously to great figures; and so, historians had acclaimed the general as "wise and just, able to unerringly predict any enemy attack", which seemed too eulogistic to be completely true. Indeed, rather than losing himself in a lesson on the merits of this historic figure, Bai Gui would have preferred to open the chest as quickly as possible to discover what it contained.

"It would be unfair to compare great men who did not live in the same era," he answered diplomatically. "I wonder what might be in the chest..."

His curiosity piqued, Zhu Tiangxian turned to one of the eunuchs.

"You," he called out, "open this chest!"

Stating that the original lock hadn't been replaced by the reigning prince and that he would therefore not be committing any infraction, the servant opened the chest. The lid opened to release the strong odor of camphor and revealed three small coffers. Disappointed not to have laid eyes on some shinier or more glitzy treasure, the prince still picked one of them up to examine its contents: a delicately bound book with snow-white pages, quite different to the brown rice pages more commonly used through the empire. Zhu Tiangxian could only read the last character written on the cover.

"Big brother Bai," he asked, holding the book out to his friend, "what does it say here?"

"*Volume One of the Diagram of the Device of the Gods.*"
Bai Gui opened it to the first page, where he recognized the
first four verses of the *Field of Battle*, a poem by Guo Deng
which he had already written out in the company of Tang
Yingde. For a soldier with limited literary scholarship, the
famous general had a certain way with words.

> *One night, the wind swept away the Ming banner, and the*
> *battalion scattered like a cloud of falling stars,*
> *The minister is alone with the cold of winter, the general*
> *endures the anger of the country,*
> *Those brave fallen on the Central Plain, what do the gods*
> *of our temples say about them?*
> *Sunset, the river becomes white as bone, and the grass is*
> *red as blood.*

The words laid bare the emotions of the general crossing
the battlefield after the battle, and his questioning the
compassion of heaven for the soldiers who died in vain. It
was rare for a soldier with such a reputation to display his
humanity so openly.

The following page, entitled *Diagram of the Elite Dragons*,
featured an extremely detailed diagram of a soldier's uniform.
It must be equipment designed by the general for his own
men! Bai Gui's heart raced. It was a major discovery, one
that Governor Yang Yiqing might be able to take advantage
of. Feverishly, he seized the second book, which was, as he'd
hoped, the second volume of the *Diagram of the Device of the
Gods*.

"Prince," he said solemnly, "these works are much too

important to be ignored. Could you ask your father to have them taken to Governor Yang?"

"But what are they?"

"The life's work of General Guo Deng! He must have left them here so that the fruit of his military research could benefit future generations... Prince, if you help pass this knowledge on, you might even become a hero too!"

Zhu Tiangxian's eyes lit up. He didn't need to be convinced further.

"Come on, quick, let's show them to my father!"

In the banquet hall, the pitchers of wine had circulated around the table more than once, and only Zhu Chongyao was still hanging on the words of Luo Hongxian, who had lost himself in telling stories of his many travels. Despite the impression he cultivated, the prince had studied little, and was fascinated by the wealth of experience recounted by the great travelers whose company he sought. As the cartographer spoke of a ten-foot fish he encountered on the southeastern coast, Zhu Tiangxian stormed into the great hall, in defiance of all the social conventions expected of his rank.

"Father!" he cried. "Father! Look what I found!"

"You little brat!" the prince admonished him, unable to allow himself to lose face in front of his guests. "What happened to your manners?"

Used to only being reprimanded in private, the child hadn't expected his father's tone to be so harsh. He froze as if petrified, shaking and seconds away from tears. Fortunately, after spending several days in the residence, Luo Hongxian had developed a certain charitable sympathy for him.

"Prince," he interceded gently, "let's look at what your son has brought."

"Very well."

Stepping forward with a fearful expression on his face, Zhu Tiangxian held the three chests out to his father, who opened them and immediately recognized the writings of Guo Deng. The general had been a friend of the prince at that time, Zhu Shiwei, and had often stayed in the residence, so it wasn't surprising that he had left personal belongings behind. Zhu Chongyao was relieved that his son had been serious. If his son had disrupted the banquet for something trivial, he would have learned to fear his wrath even more than that of the heavens.

"Gentlemen," he announced to his guests, "this is the *Diagram of the Device of the Gods*, left here by the Count of Dingxiang."

Xu Pengju, Luo Hongxian and Tang Yingde jumped to their feet. They had all heard of the military models created by the legendary hero of Datong, but none of them had dreamed that such documents would one day become available. Pleased by his guests' clear fascination, the prince held out the first volume to Xu Pengju, the holder of the highest rank among them, the second to Luo Hongxian, and the third to Tang Yingde. Each immediately plunged into the books, all aware that they might be experiencing a historic moment.

"Prince," declared Xu Pengju, "General Guo Deng dedicated his life to this research, and now here it is, resurrected once more! It's a unique opportunity!"

"Exactly, my prince!" Luo Hongxian added. "And your

son had the wit to recognize the importance of these books, which truly proves the quality of his education."

"Let's not exaggerate, gentlemen," the prince cautioned. "I'm sure that he had no idea of the real value of his find!"

Only Tang Yingde had still said nothing. While he had treated Yang Yiqing coolly in the name of the rivalry between his own master and the governor, he knew that these works would be in safe hands with him.

Out of curiosity, he leafed through to the last page in the book, and what he saw there left him speechless.

"Prince," he finally said, "is there a Kui Xing pagoda in the city?"

"Yes, northwest of the residence, facing the north gate... Why?"

"According to this book, it has a hidden underground chamber which holds a big secret."

CHAPTER 9

"There's Zhuma Fortress, Mr Wang," Meng Gen sighed.

While she now knew the truth, she continued to call Shao Jun by her assumed name. As soon as the injured woman had been able to get up and climb into the saddle, the two women had discreetly crept out of the Mongol camp to head towards China. Once in sight of the border fortress, they had made a small detour onto a less frequented path to avoid the main road which was full of carts. The time to say their goodbyes had come.

"I don't know how to thank you, Meng Gen," Shao Jun said. "You've risked so much to help me..."

Even after the young woman had told her about Zhang Yong's terrible plans, it still hadn't been easy for the Mongol princess to betray her brother, but once she had made her decision, she hadn't considered going back on it for even a moment. Nonetheless, her concern was written all over her face.

"Mr Wang," she murmured, "will the Mongols and the Chinese ever get along?"

She knew the question was too big to have any real answer, but her anguish couldn't have been any better expressed. It was even more relevant given that Zhang Yong's dark designs were once again casting the shadow of war over the region... Deep down, Shao Jun was convinced that the responsibility for any conflict lay less upon the people than on the powerful who manipulated their passions.

"Princess," she said after a moment of silence, "a wise man once told me to follow my heart when I felt lost."

"Your heart?"

"Yes. You need to follow the path that makes you happiest!"

"When I was a child, Khan Bars Bolud, my dead father, fulfilled my every wish. But now, I can't have the one thing which would make me happy... and I have no one to open up to."

"Princess, there is a Chinese poem that says that 'only three or four of the eight or nine worries that plague us can be shared'. The solitude of our secret gardens is our lot."

Zhu Jiuyuan, Shao Jun's first mentor, constantly overwhelmed by the collapse of the Society of the Mind and the weight of his exile, had often cited these lines by Fang Yue of the Song dynasty. Meng Gen's level of Chinese didn't usually allow her to read poetry, but this sentence was simple enough for her to understand its meaning. She repeated it to herself several times to memorize it, then turned her big black eyes to Shao Jun and spoke, her voice cracking with emotion, "Leave, Mr Wang, and never return!"

"Very well, princess, I will never return. I wish you happiness and a peaceful life."

"I wish you nothing but good, Mr Wang, for you and your family."

With this awkward formula, whose origin she couldn't remember, the Mongol princess spurred her horse and leapt into a gallop across the steppe.

Alone with her thoughts and her guilt, Shao Jun bitterly regretted having lied to her about her identity. She hoped the big-hearted young woman could quickly forget her "Mr Wang" and everything he had meant to her… As she traveled toward Zhuma Fortress, she was alarmed to hear the thunder of hooves.

"Mr Wang, wait!" someone called out.

Turning around, she recognized Ma Fang, whose mount seemed to fly across the plain. There was no doubt about it, he really was the best rider on the Mongol steppes. He stopped his horse and dismounted with remarkable grace, holding a bag out to the young woman. This time, no longer worried about being overheard, he used her real name.

"Miss Shao, as the princess told me you were leaving on an empty stomach, I've brought you some cheese. It can be eaten fresh, but the Mongols usually dry it to transport it more easily."

"Thank you, Ma Fang. Please thank the princess for me and tell her again that I'll do everything I can to stop Zhang Yong's evil plot, just as I promised."

While she had no details of the arrangement between the two men, Shao Jun suspected that the former captain of the imperial guard had promised Altan a generous sum of money in exchange for his services and land to conduct his experiments. He was probably never planning to pay him, but once Zhang Yong had an army of almost immortal monsters at his command, that would be the least of the Mongol prince's worries... Even Meng Gen, who didn't usually involve herself in politics, could see the threat hanging over Mongolia and the Ming empire.

"One last thing, Miss Shao..." Ma Fang added. "Earlier, in the camp, I learned that Mr He Jiuliang, who was one of the men sent out to search for you, is also returning to China today. I wouldn't be surprised if he waits at the border, hoping to catch you. The princess wanted me to warn you."

"Thank you very much, Ma Fang... But in this case, perhaps I'll be the one to catch him!"

"Oh... I suppose he is an important witness."

The young Chinese man understood where Shao Jun was coming from: the celebrated calligrapher's prestige would lend invaluable weight to his confession. If he spoke in front of the emperor, or even in front of Yang Yiqing, Zhang Yong would be permanently compromised, deprived of all the official protections he currently benefited from. If she couldn't defeat him with martial arts, the young woman could take him down with politics instead.... Yes, he'd made a big mistake when he sent He Jiuliang after her!

"Look after yourself, Ma Fang," she said. "And the princess."

"If you need my help in future, Miss Shao, leave a stone at the edge of this path. It's rarely used, but I come through here every morning to train the prince's horses. I'll understand the message and find you as soon as possible."

"You're a good man, Ma Fang. Thank you for everything."

Deep down, the young rider was Chinese before he was anything else. But as Shao Jun returned to her country, he headed back into Mongolia and towards Meng Gen.

When he and the princess arrived in the camp, the frenzied activity there having disguised their absence, they learned that He Jiuliang had already left. While he was a calligrapher and Zhang Yong's disciple first, the old man had no personal desire to become a master or an accomplished scholar. His real, very prosaic, passion was money: he was leaving Mongolia with a cart full of beautiful animal skins, high-quality merchandise which he would undoubtedly sell for a fortune in China. His heavily loaded cart was unable to move quickly, but he had no reason to rush. As far as he was concerned, the former imperial concubine who he was supposed to watch out for had escaped them long ago, and he hadn't the slightest chance of finding her... The afternoon was thus mostly over by the time he reached Zhuma Fortress, where he took his place in the line of carts waiting to be examined by the local soldiers. The inspections took place under the watchful eye of General Tao, the commander of the border post, whom he had seen at the top of a guard tower. When his turn finally came, he presented himself to the men at arms under the pseudonym of Liang.

"Mr Liang," the inspector repeated mechanically, "what goods do you have to declare? I must remind you that, like all travelers, importing weapons to the empire is strictly prohibited."

"I'm only carrying skins."

A soldier and two assistants lifted the canvas to examine He Jiuliang's load, as he passed the time distractedly admiring the fort and its operations, which had been flawless since Yang Yiqing's arrival in the region. He knew that the inspection of his load was a mere formality: who would dare present themselves at the border post with illegal goods?

"Arrest this man!" shouted the soldier inspecting his cart, pointing at him.

Two guards rushed him and threw him to the ground. Despite his protests, he was completely powerless to prevent them taking him prisoner.

"What are you doing?" he said indignantly.

"You have tried to cross the border carrying Mongol weapons!"

Gesturing as he spoke, the soldier brandished a knife apparently pulled from underneath his animal skins. The calligrapher cursed. How ironic! He who had spent so much time toying with others at the palace, now fallen victim to a vulgar setup. All the attention of the soldiers and travelers around was fixed on him.

"Someone who wishes me ill must have hidden these weapons in my cart without my knowledge! Commander, please, be reasonable!"

The officer in charge of the search completely ignored his vain pleading and pathetic attempts to prove his innocence by emptying his pockets in front of everyone. He ordered his men to drag the old eunuch a little further away and move his cart out of the way of the line of vehicles it was blocking. Men at arms quickly stuffed a rag soaked with pork fat into their prisoner's mouth to stop him from shouting, then blindfolded him and threw him into their cart, which quickly began to move. Shaking in fear and frustration, He Jiuliang wondered was going to happen to him. Would he be stabbed to death and abandoned in the desert? Unlikely, because under Yang Yiqing's governance, the border guards had iron discipline, and that wasn't procedure... But on the other hand, if the governor hadn't reestablished order within the fortress, it would have been easy for him to bribe the soldiers to guarantee his passage. He wouldn't even have had to disguise himself as a trader to travel between the two countries. Honest men were cursed! Anguished and tossed about in the back of the cart, he eventually managed to get to sleep.

He was woken by the cart coming to a stop.

"These orders from General Tao are in order... You may pass," he heard outside the cart.

Clearly, a guard had just allowed the driver and his cart to enter a city full of hubbub, noise and animated discussion. It could only be Datong.

A short time later, the vehicle stopped again. He was taken out and the blindfold and the rag stuffed in his mouth were removed. It took him a moment to become accustomed to the blinding light, but as his sight adjusted, he made out the silhouette of an old, white-haired man wearing a long robe.

"Governor Yang Yiqing!" he cried.

"You're right, Shao Jun," the governor said to the person standing next to him.

He Jiuliang trembled. Now his sight had fully recovered, he saw with horror that the former imperial concubine was looking him up and down with a severe expression. What was he going to do? The situation was desperate: if he refused to cooperate, he would be in terrible trouble, but if he betrayed Zhang Yong, it would be even worse!

Completely indifferent to his torment, the governor of Datong addressed the soldier who had brought him his prisoner.

"Take him, and make sure his presence remains unnoticed."

Shao Jun had gone to find General Tao as soon as she arrived in Zhuma Fortress to ask him to trap He Jiuliang. The officer had been reluctant at first, but a few days earlier Yang Yiqing had asked him to ensure that the young woman and her companions were able to travel between Mongol territory and the empire without issue, and he couldn't refuse a person who was clearly so close to the governor. His men had therefore lent themselves with some amusement to the age-old tradition of planting fabricated evidence.

Shao Jun let out a sigh of relief. Though Zhuo Mingke and A-Qian were dead, Zhang Yong might yet be defeated with such a prisoner. After the eunuch had disappeared, she turned towards the esteemed master at her side.

"This scoundrel's confession should be more than enough to incriminate his master, but do you know who to send it to once we have it?"

"To Xie Qian, of course…"

Now aged over eighty, the old official had borne a deep hatred for the Eight Tigers since Liu Jin had dismissed him from his duties. Emperor Jiajing had since restored him to his position, but there was little doubt that he would be the ideal man to turn to defeat the Zouwu. The greatest obstacle to gaining his ear would be his fierce mistrust of Yang Yiqing, as he took a dim view of his closeness to Zhang Yong. For similar reasons, he had also systematically refused all invitations to lecture at Jishan University once sent by Wang Yangming.

And yet, he hadn't been able to restrain his tears when he learned of the death of the founder of the School of Mind. Either way, he could not afford to refuse a confession of such importance, regardless of its origin.

"You're right," Shao Jun admitted, "Xie Qian would be a good contact. But first of all, do you think our prisoner will talk?"

"If he doesn't answer our questions of his own accord, he'll have a taste of the techniques reserved for traitors to the nation, and he won't last a day after that before he confesses everything he knows."

"I hope it's quick. As soon as we have his confession, I'll take it to Xie Qian myself. You can't leave your posts, and Tang Yingde and Xu Pengju are too young… It has to be me."

"How are your injuries?"

"Better, thank you. The wounds aren't infected, and my shoulder isn't as damaged as I feared. The bite on my foot might be serious, but that doesn't stop me riding a horse. Can I ask you to watch over Yingde and Bai Gui?"

"Tang Yingde doesn't need to be chaperoned, and your young student lacks neither wisdom nor wit. He spent the last two days exploring the treasures and secrets of the pagoda!"

"Excuse me? Sorry, I'm afraid I don't know what you're talking about…"

"We've just discovered that General Guo Deng buried real treasures at the time he controlled Datong… You need to see them with your own eyes!"

He summoned a soldier named He to accompany his guest to the Kui Xing pagoda, an old temple dedicated to the Taoist god of exams and literature which was built in year 38 of the reign of Emperor Wanli. Its doors had been boarded up for many years and, abandoned due to a lack of funds to maintain it, it had gradually fallen into ruin, until Bai Gui and Zhu Tiangxian's recent discovery had persuaded the prince to reopen it. Shao Jun found it protected by soldiers who contained the crowd eager to find out what was going on inside. Seeing her accompanied by one of their own, the guards allowed her to enter: inside, she looked down at a gaping crater in the tiled floor of the great chamber on the ground floor. The hole revealed an even larger lower level, the excavation of which had required many tools and significant works. There, she saw several men bustling around stacks of wooden crates avidly opened by the researchers dispatched to the building. Among them she recognized Luo Hongxian, who was unrolling a calligraphy written on a roll of silk.

"This diagram shows where the handle should be located," he said aloud.

At his side, Shao Jun saw Tang Yingde, Xu Pengju and Bai Gui, who noticed her and greeted her joyously. The cartographer was surprised to see a young woman who bore a strange resemblance to the man who had escorted him on the road to Datong standing there. Nevertheless, he was impressed to hear Tang Yingde refer to her as "big sister", which implied that she was his better in martial arts.

"It is a great honor to meet a master of your level," he said. "I was myself a student of Master Nie, so we both belong to the same martial family."

He spoke the truth: his master was the current prefect of Suzhou, known as "the most honest man in the empire". This honorable figure had been deeply affected by the fundamentals of the Way of the Mind and had clearly fully embraced it after meeting Wang Yangming on two occasions. Later, he had even asked Wang Ji and Qian Dehong, two of his direct students, to teach him. He had then passed on these valued teachings to Luo Hongxian, seventeen years his junior, who had taken on this martial tradition despite not being a member of the Society of the Mind. Shao Jun was happy to see her master's school of thought living on through the generations, but his absence had never felt more painful.

"Brother Luo," she said, "Master Yang Yiqing told me about the treasures hidden here by General Guo Deng…"

"Yes! It was a find by the young prince and Bai Gui which led us here. It's a major discovery… There might be enough here to reconstruct or complete the experimental weapons and uniforms he designed to protect the city despite the deficiencies of his garrison."

The young man then launched into the discourse of an enthusiastic historian: after the disastrous battle of Tumu Fortress, Guo Deng had closed the gates of Datong, which still contained only several hundred soldiers. He then began to develop new weapons to face the Mongol cavalry, which was said to be the best in the world, and repelled the attacks of Khan Yesen for another nine years. Then, when he was removed from office at the end of his life, he hid all his research underneath the Kui Xing pagoda. His great friend Prince Zhu Shiwei knew, but the secret was lost over generations of incompetents submerged in alcohol and vain intrigue.

Although the story was fascinating, Tang Yingde burned

with impatience to speak alone with Shao Jun. Her paleness worried him as did the absence of Zhuo Mingke and A-Qian from her side. He took it upon himself to cut off his comrade.

"Brother Luo, I think big sister Shao must be tired from her journey, we need to let her rest."

"Oh yes, of course!" the cartographer responded, embarrassed by his rudeness. "I'm sorry to have bothered you, big sister."

"No harm done, brother Luo," the young woman reassured him gently.

She then turned to Xu Pengju.

"Thank you for taking care of Bai Gui for the last few days, Lord Xu. When do you leave?"

"In a few days."

"We'll make sure to visit when we pass through Nanjing, lord. Please excuse me for now, I need to speak with Tang Yingde."

"Of course, go ahead."

The prince was disappointed to be thus dismissed, but he wasn't a member of Master Wang's school. Yet, despite the affairs which waited for him in his own prefecture, he had delayed his departure as long as possible, both so that he might have the chance to speak with Shao Jun, and to explore Guo Deng's treasures.

Bai Gui was extremely disappointed at having to leave, but his mother's mood was so serious that he didn't dare protest. He also found it strange that A-Qian, who was normally always at her side, wasn't accompanying her. Despite his youth, he distinctly felt that something serious must have happened, and so gave no protest as he returned to the private residence with Tang Yingde and Shao Jun. They were met at the door by Shen Zhiwei, the steward.

"Miss Shao, Mr Tang and Mr Bai, welcome back. Are Miss Qian and Mr Zhuo not with you?"

"No…" Shao Jun said as neutrally as possible. "They were held up."

She then sent her student to work on his calligraphy in his room. But the child, far too curious to remain there, prepared his ink and gathered his equipment with excessive slowness in a nearby room so he could listen to what the adults were talking about in the courtyard. The broken voice of Tang Yingde, forcing himself to keep it together despite the tears that threatened to spill from his eyes, reached him first.

"Don't worry, brother Zhuo is a resourceful man. He always finds a way out of the worst situations."

"Brother Tang," Shao Jun responded, "I need to leave for Beijing to deliver He Jiuliang's confession to Xie Qian. The evidence against Zhang Yong is damning, but I fear he'll try to kill his minion here in Datong before he can talk. While they're close, I'm sure he wouldn't hesitate for a moment to put his own interests above his friend's life… And even if Yang Yiqing is now on our side, we don't stand a chance of convincing the emperor without this witness."

"Don't worry, big sister. As long as I'm in Datong, that demonic Zhang Yong won't even get close… But you need to let your wounds heal. Go rest."

With this, he turned and walked quickly out of the courtyard so he could let his tears fall freely. Zhuo Mingke and he had been as close as brothers; the thought of never seeing him again was unbearable… As for A-Qian, he'd always tried to ignore his feelings because, as Huo Biyao wrote: "Why build a home when you still have enemies to threaten it?".

Seeing her acolyte's back shaking with sobs broke Shao Jun's heart.

Zhang Yong, she thought, *I swear I'll spend the rest of my life doing everything I can to kill you!*

When she returned to her room, she found Bai Gui working on the calligraphy of *Yecheon Palace Inscription,* which he reproduced with hard, angular characters where they should have been rounded and smooth. His expression was colder and more murderous than she had ever seen it…

"Mother… Aunt Qian and big brother Zhuo aren't coming back, are they?" he asked without turning around.

"No," she choked out. "No, they won't be coming back."

The child didn't say anything more, but his paper disintegrated under the hard, angry strokes of his brush.

CHAPTER 10

Moving at speed, you could travel from Datong to Beijing in three days. That was Shao Jun's goal, as she planned to make as few stops as possible despite her injuries. He Jiuliang had written and signed his confession quicker than she had expected; clearly, the eunuch couldn't take much pain and wasn't sufficiently at peace with himself to welcome death with serenity. The young woman had set off as soon as she had the precious document in hand. The day after her departure, she had reached the district of Lingqiu, then angled east where she entered the capital region through the Zijing pass.

After the debacle at Tumu Fortress, the Oirats had reached inner passes – Juyong, Zijing and Daoma – where the Minister of War, Yu Qian, had pushed them back by making use of the narrow, twisted, and abrupt mountain paths. At altitude, the snow made the rocky soil slippery and treacherous, which together gave this unavoidable route towards Beijing a natural defense against large armies.

And now, it was Shao Jun who suffered from their effects. Despite her haste, she was forced to accept that she had to stop before her route became too dangerous, if only for her mount's sake. Ears trembling and covered in sweat, the poor beast seemed ready to collapse, so she slipped to the ground and led it by the reins as she searched for somewhere to eat and rest.

As the sun set, at the end of a path the young woman finally saw a small, rudimentary building built from rough wooden logs with chinks of light shining out between them. The only room in this refuge for hunters and travelers was full of draughts, but any shelter at all was preferable to the rigors of the night and wind. Through the cracks in one of these wooden walls, she could make out the back of a single man sitting at a table inside.

But as Shao Jun prepared to knock on the door, an icy shiver went down her back, as if the air around her was filled with murderous intent. It was an ambush!

Her forehead began to drip with sweat despite the chill of the oncoming dusk. How had her enemies followed her here? She had been extremely careful as she left Datong… She steepled her fingers as she considered her options. Jumping into the saddle and galloping to the next stop would be risky, firstly because her mount was so exhausted, and because the darkness could hide a multitude of enemies. To confirm her suspicions, she used *Mind sight,* the range of which she had been able to extend to six hundred and fifty feet after pushing her limits in the Mongol camp. Yes, there were at least thirty men hidden nearby. Even knowing where they were hidden, there were too many for her to stand the smallest chance of fighting all at once or escaping. In that case, should she enter and fight from inside the small structure? Strategically speaking, the idea seemed more reasonable, but the man inside must be a skilled martial artist to offer himself up as bait for the trap, someone who would certainly be able to survive until reinforcements arrived. If she was able to subjugate him however, she might be able to take him hostage. She would then have to find out what his life was worth to the people with him...

Just then, her thoughts were interrupted by the mysterious man calling out to her from inside the cabin.

"Who goes there? Come on, don't stay out in the cold, come on in!"

Shao Jun's blood ran cold as she recognized Hu Ruzhen's clear, distinct voice. How ironic! The young woman had followed his trail to Datong, and now here he was, having tracked her in turn. She had underestimated both his talents and Zhang Yong's responsiveness, but if the captain was here, it was undoubtedly to kill her.

Lacking any other options, she tied her horse's reins to a tree and pushed the door open.

Hu Ruzhen was sitting in the center of the small room, dressed elegantly but surprisingly lightly for the season. *Fire Lotus*, the powerful technique passed on to him by Zhang Yong, must protect him against the cold.

"Please sit, big sister," he said in a neutral tone, "and please accept my apologies for not having any tea or wine to offer you! I wasn't expecting any visitors, so I was passing the time by working on my calligraphy."

"It's a pleasure to see you again, young master Hu!" Shao Jun responded as she sat cross-legged on a mattress folded against a wall.

The rickety table on which the captain was writing, made from four poles and a roughly cut plank, was purely functional, designed only to accommodate the quick meals of hunters passing through before continuing their journey. Seemingly unbothered by its instability, the Huizhou guard captain wrote his characters in a light, precise hand on a piece of paper in the clerical script, characterized by its easy readability. Hu Ruzhen broke the silence as he diligently scribed a concave line to the right.

"When I was young, my father sometimes told me that no one was free to follow their heart. It was only after meeting Master Zhang Yong that I realized the bitterness of this statement."

Shao Jun perceived an infinite sadness behind his words. This well-educated and lettered young man, a skilled martial artist and fine amateur poet, would be suffocated in a rigid military career in which he would be constantly required to obey orders which he did not necessarily agree with.

"Young master, your words remind me of a phrase by the great poet Tao Yuanming which my master often cited. I've always liked it, but I fear I've never quite understood its full meaning. Could I tell it to you?"

"Of course, I'm listening."

"It's an extract from the *Song of Return*: 'The path of my misguidance has not yet led me too far; I realize that I am true now while I was false in the past.'"

This text was of particular significance to the young woman, as it was the first which Wang Yangming had her study on her return to China to begin to make up for her lack of education. Just as he did with his students at the university, he had encouraged her to focus on each individual line, one after the other, and meditate on their meaning. These especially seemed a perfect illustration of the respected master's state of mind when he chose to resign from his post as an official to move away from the spheres where he no longer felt he had a place. Shao Jun hoped to appeal to Hu Ruzhen's own inner struggle, because she was still convinced that a man of such integrity, who held Wang Yangming in such esteem, couldn't feel at home among the Zouwu. Perhaps it was time for him to join the Society of the Mind.

The captain smiled as he recognized the text, one which he appreciated.

"Big sister," he responded, "I suspect you understand these lines perfectly. But rather than continue this charade, what do you think of this?"

He pushed his brush through the sheet of paper and, with a precise throw, launched it so that it flew to embed itself in the cabin wall, displaying his calligraphy for all to see. What skill! Now she could read his poem, written with clean, rich, and rounded lines.

Hanging in the celestial vault, the stars lower their heads. Wings outspread; I fly for thousands of lis. I was vigorous when the red dust rose from the ground. Fall reclaimed its dues; the dream became a lie. Blood and tears ran. My young heart rebelled and refused to live under anyone else's yoke. It took off and flew into the sky, hot as the sun, bright as the full moon in the black night.

Shao Jun found the long, rebellious text incredibly

intelligent, but didn't recognize it as belonging to any poet she knew.

"Young master," she asked, "who is the author of this text?"

"Me... It's a work from my youth entitled *Entering adult life*. I wrote it as I was reading the *A New Account of Tales of the World* by Liu Yiqing, and there was one sentence that particularly threw me: 'It cannot be passed on to future generations, the filth cannot be destroyed.' My father mocked me when I read this text to him. I decided then that if I couldn't live according to my ideals, I would have to resign myself to being part of the filth of the world."

What awful thoughts for such a young man...

When they met at sea, Shao Jun had told him that her master had said he was one in a million, but had carefully avoided mentioning that according to Wang Yangming, any promising young man whose development is interrupted is doomed to forever wander in the limbo of moral ambiguity. While she had hoped that this omission would push him to pull free of Zhang Yong's evil yoke, she understood now that his troubles were much older and deeper than she had imagined. Hu Ruzhen wasn't bound to become the servant of the old captain of the imperial guard: he was destined to become exactly like him, or even surpass him! Like him, he seemed prepared to do anything necessary to achieve his aims. Like him, he was lying to himself and in the end would cause more harm than good. And finally, like him, he would find the Society of the Mind dogging his every step. This one-on-one with Shao Jun echoed the one that had once cost the life of Wang Yangming... which saddened the young woman, who still couldn't stop herself from seeing in her opponent what he could have been rather than what he really was. Her heart sank at the idea of having to fight him, perhaps even kill him. But it now seemed inevitable: she would have to take Hu Ruzhen hostage to have any hope of getting out of the Zijing Pass alive.

The young woman's body tensed, ready for combat. Her shoulder and ankle didn't hurt anymore, but she worried that they were still too fragile to take any sudden movement. She knew that her greatest advantage was her speed, which had allowed her to defeat men who were physically much stronger than her on more than one occasion. She was so swift that she could unsheathe her weapon and slice a candle in two faster than the eye could see. Could she get her knife against his throat before he had time to react? That would be the most favorable outcome by far.

Just as she was about to try her luck, Hu Ruzhen declared solemnly, "Big sister... During my visit to Jishan University, your master suggested that I apply myself to the essential knowledge, but I'll admit I don't really know what he was talking about. You were his student and heir; can you explain the meaning of these words?"

Shao Jun had learned enough from Zhu Jiuyuan and then from Master Wang Yangming to clearly understand this philosophical concept inspired by Mencius' notion of conscience. Her master had also taught, as one of his fundamental principles: *"The mind is neither good nor evil. Good and evil are born of intention."* Hu Ruzhen's questions proved that he wasn't yet wise enough to escape this essential dichotomy. He was undoubtedly at a turning point in his moral and intellectual journey, and while he might have unfortunately begun to follow the path taken by Zhang Yong, perhaps it wasn't too late for him to fully embrace the path trodden by Wang Yangming. Long ago, Shao Jun had been just as lost, but she had been lucky enough to meet the right people at the right time. Could she play the same role for him in turn?

"One day," she murmured, "Master Yangming told me that Uncle Zhang and he were both looking at the same paradise on the other side. But where my master would have built a bridge so everyone could reach it safely, Uncle Zhang was prepared to turn the sea red with blood to brave the storm on his ship and enjoy paradise alone."

"But sea quickly forgets the blood that once turned it red…"

"What is paradise worth, if you must cross an ocean of bodies to reach it?"

The young woman hadn't spoken loudly, but her words resonated in Hu Ruzhen's ears like a drum. Because this question, here amplified by a clear metaphor, was the same one he had asked himself repeatedly without ever finding an answer able to appease his tormented conscience. He saw himself again as a child, confronted with the four founding principles of the School of Mind displayed in the Hall of High Virtue at Jishan University: *The mind itself is neither good nor evil. Good and evil are born of intention. Discerning good and evil is an essential knowledge. Studying the ten thousand things enables one to work for good and eliminate evil.* At the time, his father hadn't been able to help him fully understand the depth and scope of these sentences, and his younger self had been convinced that he understood them perfectly. It was only later, once free of his juvenile impetuousness, that he had returned to them and begun to glimpse the infinite wisdom they concealed. And this discussion with Shao Jun had just shed more light on the importance of studying the ten thousand things.

The School of Mind placed enlightenment as envisaged by Zen Buddhism at the center of its teachings, the idea that it is possible to elevate one's own consciousness above material considerations by understanding the very essence of things. But young people with the potential required for this transcendent state were also the most emotionally unstable, which is why they needed guidance from wise, well-intentioned masters. It wouldn't have taken much for both Shao Jun and Hu Ruzhen to take the same path. Unfortunately, while Shao Jun had been able to learn from Zhu Jiuyuan then from Wang Yangming, his own admiration for the founder of the School of Mind had transferred to Zhang Yong when he became an adult. But he had recently begun to doubt his master's instructions, especially since he had intercepted the shipment of medicinal plants. Devoted to his country, the young captain could only view any collusion with Mongolia in a bad light. He'd had more doubts than ever when he received the order to stop Shao Jun, not only because he knew that the young woman was Wang Yangming's student, but also because he was thoroughly convinced of her good nature.

However, as usual, Hu Ruzhen had complied and carefully executed this ambush, which was now bearing fruit. An avid reader of books and the classics since he was very small, he had been transported by the *New Account of the Tales of the World* as well as the texts by Mencius, and had embraced the protection of the empire as his personal duty. As a good soldier, he had the conviction that noble ends sometimes justified forceful or violent acts, but did paradise really require that he sacrifice thousands of lives? And, in a much more prosaic way, was it possible that Zhang Yong wanted the former imperial concubine dead because, if the rumors were true, he had killed Wang Yangming with his own hands? The more the young man thought about these questions, the more inevitable it seemed to him to consider the possibility that Zhang Yong, who had never shared the detail of his plans with him, was only using him as a pawn. But pawn or not, he couldn't continue fighting a battle when he didn't know the stakes.

Without understanding the exact thoughts running through his mind, Shao Jun saw the confusion on Hu Ruzhen's face. Should she take advantage of it to attack? It would be easy to take such a distracted opponent by surprise … but that would go against the principle of discerning good and evil. And the young captain's hesitation was a good sign, because it resulted from a good education, and the beneficial influence of his father still acted as a safeguard against him becoming another Yu Dayong or Ma Yongcheng. His mind simply needed to separate what was right from what was wrong.

The moment seemed to last for an eternity, but it was broken by the tearing of paper. The rice paper nailed to the wall, gradually weakened by the moist air full of snow that entered through the cracks in the logs, had just ripped across the center. Only the first two phrases of the poem were still readable, but the ink had run, giving the characters a grotesque appearance.

"Thank you for your explanations, big sister," Hu Ruzhen said with a smile.

His eyes were bright, his voice calm and pleasant. He drew a small reed flute from his sleeve and played four sorrowful notes.

"I am a poor musician, but it's my way of bidding you goodnight... While I hope we'll see each other again someday, for now, your destiny awaits. The mountain paths may be treacherous, particularly after sundown, so please take care on the road."

With this, he turned away from Shao Jun, as if to demonstrate, without any ambiguity, his complete lack of hostility. Perplexed, the young woman decided to seize the opportunity.

"Take care of yourself, young lord," she murmured as she stood.

When she opened the door, the chilly air rushed into the refuge and set the lamp flickering. The shadows dancing across Hu Ruzhen's face lent him an even more tragic air. His eyes distant, he constantly repeated "discerning good from evil..." like a mantra he hoped to make his own.

After traveling around half a mile into the night, Shao Jun was reassured to note that none of the soldiers hidden nearby had attacked: the captain had indeed acted honestly. Personally, she was proud to have seen philosophy triumph over violence. The end of Zhang Yong's omnipotence seemed closer than ever.

Haunted by the memory of his lost companions, Tang Yingde couldn't sleep. Much more sensitive than his hot temper would suggest, the young man tossed and turned in his bed, unable to accept that he would never see them again. From now on, wherever he went and whatever he did, the shadows of A-Qian and Zhuo Mingke would hang over his heart and taint even his greatest joys with a bittersweet melancholy. But for now, he had to try to put his pain aside, or at least distract his tormented mind from it for a few minutes.

He stood, picked up his spear, and went out into the private residence's courtyard to perform training routines in the snow, hoping to find some solace in the martial practice. There was something in these movements he had repeated a thousand times, in the physical demands and transcendental space created by the perfect choreography, something simple, pure, and true that he desperately needed in that moment.

When he began to sweat, he stopped for a moment to refresh himself from a well in the courtyard. The air was so cold that the water seemed almost lukewarm, but when he poured some on his face, he felt an icy wind cruelly bite at his exposed cheeks. Strangely, this stinging pain echoed the pain in his soul, and he welcomed it with masochistic satisfaction. Eyes closed, he whispered several lines by Mencius which often helped him overcome challenges: "When heaven wants to test a man's reliability, it frustrates his intellect and his will, tires his muscles and his bones, causes him hunger and ruin, harasses and abuses him to stimulate his mind, harden his nature, and develop his skills."

However, on this night these wise words seemed hollow. Never mind the will of heaven, and never mind the responsibilities that awaited him, nothing could be worth the loss of his friends!

The snow was now falling in large, cotton-like flakes. He returned to his practice.

His exercises naturally led him to reminisce about his time at Chaotian Temple, and the figure of the man who had taught him how to use his favorite weapon quickly came to mind. Master He had been Yang Yiqing's brother in arms and had even surpassed his younger brother at arms during their first years of learning. Yet against all expectations, he remained unable to beat Yang Yiqing despite his obvious superiority, and his frustration had been one of his main drivers for entering Chaotian Temple, where he had chosen to dedicate himself to the development and teaching of his art. It was there that he had invented *Spear strikes the void* based on the famous *Three revelations of the baton*.

The first levels of his technique drew their name from the four stages of the universe in Taoist cosmogony: Taiyi, Taichu, Taichi, and Taisu. Then, an accomplished martial artist was supposed to reach taiji, the ultimate height of proficiency, but no one had ever reached that level, not even Master He. This level, the key to moving beyond ying and yang, opened only to hearts so pure that they had liberated themselves from the intrinsic duality of man, a state of manifest perfection that any other scholar would have despaired at reaching.

Master He had continued to train in the hope of one day touching this ideal. It was only after an entire decade of constant practice that, faced with the decline of his own physical aptitudes, he was forced to admit the hard reality that he would never achieve taiji. He thus transferred his hopes to his disciples, and specifically to the most brilliant, Tang Yingde, who welcomed this burden as an honor. Indeed, the young man had hoped to approach this supreme height several days earlier during his duel against Xu Pengju.

Now, with the weight of his loss weighing upon him and reminding him of the impermanence of all things, he found himself incapable of taking this quest to an ever more fleeting horizon seriously. *What a pointless crusade*, he thought disappointedly.

Nonetheless, abandoning himself to his spear work had been undeniably soothing. He passed his weapon from one hand to the other with wide, circular movements that were so fluid and fast that not a single snowflake landed on him. When he noticed, he stopped to tip his head backwards and allow the flakes to fall on him once more.

It was then that a large, dark figure swept a short distance overhead. He was intrigued, because it couldn't be a cloud, and it was much too large to be a bird … Then he remembered with horror the tale Shao Jun told him of her flight from Zhang Yong after their confrontation on Dai Yu Island: he had escaped aboard a giant balloon floating in the sky! The story, which had greatly excited the young Bai Gui, seemed straight out of a fairy tale, but after all, Yu Dayong of the Eight Tigers was known for his bold and innovative inventions. Yes, it was a safe bet that the former captain of the imperial guard still had the device at his disposal and that he wouldn't hesitate to use it to travel at night.

Was he preparing a surprise attack? He Jiuliang had betrayed him and had mountains of information, so knowing Zhang Yong, he intended to cut He Jiuliang's throat himself. After Shao Jun departed with his confessions, the prisoner had been confined in the secret underground chamber of the Kui Xing pagoda, which had been entirely emptied. Yang Yiqing had also increased the number of soldiers at the guard posts, and the number of patrols, taking care to communicate Zhang Yong's description to all his men. But of course, no one would expect him to come to the city by air...

Tang Yingde rushed into the house to knock on Bai Gui's door. While he had thought him long since asleep, the child was wide awake and fully dressed on his bed. His head was still full of the extraordinary discoveries made over the last few days in the company of the brilliant Luo Hongxian, with whom he had examined the marvels of General Guo Deng. The scholar, who had certainly merited his first place in the imperial examinations, had undertaken the construction of an auxiliary vehicle intended to be attached to the side of a chariot, and had put Bai Gui and Zhu Tiangxian to work. Both had been delighted to serve as his assistants in recreating the invention designed by Datong's famous hero.

But on hearing Tang Yingde knock on his door, the young boy had feared that his elder had come to tell him off for not being asleep. Feeling guilty, he had quickly slipped under the covers and pretended to sleep. The young man came into the room to wake him and whispered rapidly.

"Xiao Gui, get Yang Yiqing, quick! Zhang Yong is here!"

Then he disappeared.

Momentarily stunned, Bai Gui considered the importance of his mission. He jumped out of bed, put on his shoes, and ran outside. There, he suddenly stopped dead as he saw the darkness and snow. How would he find the governor of Datong, alone, in the middle of the night? The answer came instinctively: he would have to go to Xu Pengju, who was staying only two roads away and was certain to be able to gain the governor's attention.

He picked up an umbrella and left, his mind in turmoil. He burned to know how brother Tang could be so sure that their enemy was approaching, but that question would have to wait. This situation could have been a thrilling chapter in one of the adventure novels he devoured when he had time. Except of course that this time the danger was real, and that if any fighting happened, the iron spear tips wouldn't be replaced with harmless pieces of chalk. But he reassured himself to dispel the anguish that threatened to overcome him, the heroes always win.

CHAPTER 11

History records that the first human flight was by the Montgolfier brothers in November 1783. However, some two hundred years earlier, Zhang Yong flew over Datong in a balloon created by Yu Dayong, based on the floating lanterns used in popular Chinese festivals. In the middle of the day and with clear weather, such a device would have drawn the attention of the entire city, but the curfew imposed by the governor was less strict than in the capital, requiring residents to remain at home, so the roads were deserted. Not even thieves dared come out, because as one of their sayings said, "you can steal in the wind but not under the moon; you can steal in the rain but not in the snow". The cold was so biting that the guards stayed in the warm inside their tower and barracks, only occasionally stepping out to glance around outside.

His back straight and his expression severe, Zhang Yong

used *Fire lotus* to protect himself against the glacial wind that whipped across his face. Contemplating the deserted city below, he bitterly regretted the loss of Yu Dayong and his other Tigers, competent and influential collaborators upon whom he been able to rely for carrying out his dirty work. Several years earlier, he would never have taken it upon himself to personally assassinate a filthy traitor to stop them from talking. Involving He Jiuliang in his plans had been a terrible mistake. His calligraphy was beautiful, but that was really his only use.

The former captain of the imperial guard cursed. Since Wang Yangming's death, he had lost much of his aura of respectability, and Xie Qian's return to the cabinet had precipitated his downfall. If only he still had access to the incredible facilities on Dai Yu Island, he would have been able to continue his research under optimal conditions instead of being forced to flee to Mongol territory, but his old rival's student had caused the complete destruction of the mountain and its ancient knowledge. And now, to top it all, even Yang Yiqing was standing against him! He reflexively gripped the jade pendant at his neck, but it felt hot as an ember. Had he truly fallen so low?

Arriving at his destination, he grabbed a rope and jumped to the ground with supernatural ease. Any other man jumping from that height would have been dead or seriously injured, but he landed with the ethereal grace of a cloud. He then tied his balloon to a hitching post and strode towards the Kui Xing pagoda. It seemed to him a strange choice of jail, but it wasn't unusual for the army to store weapons there, and it was therefore usually well guarded. The old eunuch rested a hand on the solid wooden door, several inches thick and held closed by an enormous lock. Pressing on it lightly, he realized he couldn't force it. Even with a battering ram, it would take several charges.

He took two steps back to examine the pagoda's upper floors. There were three, with eaves that were narrower than most other buildings of this style, but their windows consisted only of a mesh as thin as a cicada's wing. No one had thought to reinforce these points of entry, because the first was a good ten feet from the ground. It would take more than that to stop Zhang Yong, who jumped into the air with enough power to reach the window on the first try. He felt an icy draught down his back.

"Take this!" someone shouted behind him.

He had used *Fire lotus* so often that it had become second nature. He had been able to react instinctively, even in midair: his entire body twisted in a fraction of a second, and the spear flying towards him brushed past and sank into the pagoda wall like a knife through butter. He certainly wouldn't have survived had the spear hit him. Seeing the iron tip sunk into the wood of the building, he nevertheless guessed that it wasn't Yang Yiqing trying to kill him, because the governor of Datong never threw his spears with excessive force. What's more, the voice that had shouted at him had been young and angry.

Whoever it was, this spearman had given him a great gift to aid his climb: he stood on the horizontal shaft and jumped onto the snow-covered ledge where his formidable agility ensured he didn't lose his footing. Once there, he sent the window crashing inward with a simple press from his palm.

But as he climbed through the window frame, he felt a new attack coming. He hadn't expected his assailant to be able to reach him so quickly. But who was this skilled young man?

He reflexively threw his left arm out behind him and intercepted a powerful punch. He hadn't been hit so hard since he faced Tiexin, but the fighter facing him now was far more skilled than a mere pirate. Even blocked, the blow thrummed down Zhang Yong's arm and threw him so off balance that he had to lean on the window frame, which immediately cracked under his weight. He fell onto the tiles then slid to the edge of the roof, his progress quickly followed by his attacker.

It was, of course, Tang Yingde!

As soon as he reached the ground, the young man collected his spear from the wall and adopted the *Qi begins to gather* pose, which belonged to the taichu level of *Spear strikes the void*. Despite his ferocious look, Zhang Yong's power had impressed him, parrying his punch with phenomenal strength. His arm still tremored with discomfort, and he realized that for a fighter as accomplished as Wang Yangming, *Fire lotus* was the only explanation. He drew on his rage to strengthen his resolve, because the man he was facing was undoubtedly Zhuo Mingke and A-Qian's murderer.

Zhang Yong was very curious to find out who he was dealing with. To his knowledge, the only young, high-level combatant currently in Datong was Xu Pengju, who he had met several years earlier when he visited Yang Yiqing. At the time, the prince was invited to face Wei Bin in a friendly duel; he had lost, but the old eunuch had still appreciated his talent and potential. Today, however, he was aware that he was facing someone else.

"What a daring young man!" he said mockingly. "But I don't think we've been introduced... Can I ask your name?"

Tang Yingde, filled with hatred and just wanting to fight, saw his apparent nonchalance as a clear insult. When he saw Zhang Yong climbing the Kui Xing pagoda, he had felt duty-bound to call out as he threw his spear, because it was dishonorable to attack an enemy who had no idea they were under attack, but these martial courtesies no longer applied. He hit the infamous old man with a powerful strike just as he reached the taichu level of *Spear strikes the void*, which began with *Qi begins to gather* and ended with *The form fades*.

While the move was sublime, Zhang Yong easily dodged it then drew a small whistle from his sleeve, blowing into it as hard as he could without producing the slightest sound.

A deep voice suddenly rose from within the Kui Xing pagoda.

"Who dared to break a window?"

It was Niu, a human colossus from Guangxi assigned to guard the building for the night and who had gone to sleep on the upper floor to escape the cold of the large chamber below. He had been dozing with his head under a blanket when he was woken, not by the fight between Tang Yingde and Zhang Yong, but by the gust of frigid air rushing through the broken window. When he looked out to see what was going on outside, he saw the two men ready to fight down below. But it was the enormous balloon floating a few feet above that drew his attention... and the two silhouettes rushing down from the basket to reach the pagoda's courtyard. Were they going to get involved in the fight? One carried a sword, the other a spear, but strangest of all was their indifference to the cold, even though they wore no shoes and were dressed in rags. When the soldier caught sight of their pale eyes, he saw that they were devoid of all humanity.

"G-ghosts…" he stammered, stumbling back in terror.

At first sight, Tang Yingde thought they were Zhang Yong's disciples or students, and he wasn't impressed. Certain of his abilities, he felt ready to take on three or four opponents if he had to. Admirably calm despite the intensity of combat, he spun his spear as he progressed from one stage of the technique to the next as he approached the "great extreme" with such speed that even his adversary was unable to follow his moves. Focused and serene, he ordered the chaos in accordance with the rules of Taoist cosmogony, lending great power to his *Three revelations of the baton*. Despite his agility, Zhang Yong was reduced to dodging the dragon-like fury of the attacks as best he could.

But just as the eunuch seemed about to lose, one of his companions lifted him from the ground as if he weighed nothing and placed themselves straight in the path of Tang Yingde's spear. Without any apparent hesitation, they grabbed the point in one hand and placed their other on the shaft. In the darkness, the young man concluded that this new assailant must be wearing gloves to still have all their fingers intact after coming into contact with his weapon's meteoric iron, which was able to draw blood with the slightest touch. He then began to saw his spear back and forth to try to slice through the fabric which had to be protecting his opponent's hands, but nothing happened: whoever it was, clearly impervious to pain, didn't let go. As he struggled, Tang Yingde became concerned about the strange turn of events... How could this man, who had appeared out of nowhere and dressed in the rags of a Mongol peasant, be so strong?

It was a yujing, the improved version of the yuxiao once created by Zhang Yong on Dai Yu Island. Unlike their predecessors, they had a limited ability to think, and were thus much more effective in combat because they didn't need to constantly be given orders. Each of these creatures, created in a less-than-ideal facility, had required months of work by the old eunuch. He had eventually managed to produce six and had brought two with him in his balloon in case he encountered trouble in Datong. He had been reluctant to use them because he wanted to keep their existence a secret as long as possible, but the current situation required a radical response. Each yujing alone was equal to several yuxiao, so he was sure that this young man who seemed determined to stand in his way wouldn't last long against them.

Tang Yingde's frenzied attacks seemed to have an effect, as the yujing suddenly let go of the weapon. It was enough for him to regain control of his spear and immediately attack. The creature was forced to shift to protect its head but was unable to prevent the meteoric iron tip from embedding into its left shoulder, breaking the bone instantly. Sensing that he had a solid anchor, the young man used it to propel himself towards the pagoda's lowest roof section where Zhang Yong had also just jumped as he tried to reach the building's upper floors.

While in the air, Tang Yingde attempted to strike an acupuncture point on the arch of the old man's foot that would have caused him to immediately lose consciousness, but just as his blow was about to connect, his own ankle was seized by the second yujing which had jumped after him. The spearman clung to the slippery tiles as best he could to prevent the monster's weight from dragging him down. Despite the intense physical effort, he focused just enough to use *One with the weapon*, a technique derived from the *Mind sight* that he had begun to teach Shao Jun. It allowed him to clearly see the yujing's position and strike the creature's hand with the end of his spear without even having to turn.

While blunt, this end of the weapon was pointed to cause severe injury, especially when used with enough force. It felt like he was trying to drive it into a tree, but Tang Yingde succeeded by repeating the move until he cut the tendons and the creature lost the mechanical ability to maintain its grip. By the time it tried to grab him with its other hand the young man had already stood back up, leaving it to tumble to the ground. Unfortunately, the fall wasn't enough to kill it.

As he was preparing to jump back up onto the roof, a shadow sprung out of the broken window to crash behind the two monsters with a muffled thump. It was Niu, who had gathered his courage to fulfil what he considered to be his duty as a soldier: stopping these malevolent ghosts. He had wrapped himself in his thick blanket to cushion his fall, then jumped out of the window; the snow had softened his landing even more, and he now faced the two yujing. He was a good soldier, and though he instinctively felt that he had no chance of beating them, he couldn't sit back and do nothing. While he'd also noticed Zhang Yong climbing the pagoda, he had decided that a small old man like that couldn't cause much trouble, so he had chosen to deal with what he viewed as the more dangerous threats.

Likewise, with his injured heel the yujing had concluded that Tang Yingde was no longer able to trouble their master. They thus turned to attack Niu. The first one tried to grab him, but it was left just holding his blanket, which seemed to confuse it. The soldier immediately took to his heels, closely followed by the two creatures. He had just unintentionally bought Tang Yingde a welcome respite.

With a heroic effort, the latter finally managed to reach the top floor of the pagoda, a task which would have taken no time at all if his leg hadn't been injured. When he cautiously leaned inside the room whose window Zhang Yong had broken, he immediately sensed that he was alone, and confidently climbed through the window frame. Reserved for storing gunpowder, lamps were forbidden on the upper floors and the rooms were in complete darkness. The former captain of the imperial guard must have quickly realized that the prisoner he sought wasn't there and gone down to search the rest of the building. He might even have reached the basement already.

Standing in front of the stairs, Tang Yingde sighed. The first time Shao Jun had told him about the monsters she had faced on Dai Yu Island, he'd thought she was exaggerating, no doubt blinded by his own ignorance. Now he regretted not believing her, because, he had to admit, he wasn't sure he could kill such creatures. And in this state, he had no chance of beating Zhang Yong without the help of governor Yang Yiqing. But he had no choice: if their enemy killed He Jiuliang, he would get the chance to save his name and his reputation, and thus continue with his terrible plans. A-Qian and Zhuo Mingke would have died for nothing.

He massaged his ankle to assess the damage. The yujing's grip had been like the jaws of some huge wild animal, and he could still feel the burn of those rough, powerful fingers which could have torn off his leg. At least the bone wasn't broken. He tore off a strip of fabric from his tunic and tied it tightly before descending the stairs.

In the streets of Datong, the breathless Niu still ran for his life. Competent but not exceptional, the veteran had hoped that guarding the Kui Xing pagoda would be an opportunity to end his career in peace, far from the more dangerous tasks, and the irony of the situation did not escape him. Too scared to turn around, he had no idea how close his pursuers were, and he had no idea what to think when he heard hooves, an unusual sound at this hour and time of year. By this point he was too exhausted even for terror to drive him any more, and realized that he was gradually running slower. The muscles in his legs refused to carry him further.

It was then that the icy hand of a yujing fell onto his shoulder.

He was immediately lifted off the ground, then surprisingly small fingers wrapped around his neck. His eyes bulging, lips turning blue, and legs dangling in midair, he felt the life begin to leave him but, strangely, his mind could only focus on one thing: how could such a small hand have such a grip? As an experienced soldier, Niu was used to combat, but he had never encountered such a thing. It defied imagining! As the last of his strength left him, he told himself that he would take this mystery to the grave. Everything around him turned white… then a dark shadow flashed in front of him, cleaving through the snow with sudden violence. The pressure on his neck abruptly ceased, and he fell to the ground like a rag doll.

Just as he was taking a deep, painful breath to reinflate his lungs, he saw a white horse with a majestic figure on its back: Xu Pengju! With fantastic precision, the young man had thrust his spear through the yujing's hand without even scratching Niu's neck.

Ever since the day he'd spent with Bai Gui, the prince of Wei had felt his lack of education more keenly than ever, blaming it on his own idleness amidst the comfort of his privileged life. Determined to take his life in hand, he had spent his time in Datong studying the literary and philosophical classics and practicing his fighting skills. Equally concerned with earning Shao Jun's esteem and respect, this evening he had decided to write several lyrical verses that he hoped would please her when she returned to the city. And so when Bai Gui had come to warn him of Zhang Yong's attack, he had found him fully clothed, sitting in the window as he searched for inspiration.

Xu Pengju had immediately armed himself and leapt onto his mount to rush to the Kui Xing pagoda, on his way encountering the barely clothed Niu running as if his life depended on it. He'd quickly recognized Zhang Yong's monsters from Shao Jun's description and had instantly leapt into action. For him, this was a chance to not only carry out his duty, but to prove his worth, because he saw his draw with Tang Yingde a few days earlier as a mark of failure. Several years earlier he had also lost a duel against Shao Jun in front of his own master, and he wanted to stop disappointing him.

Since then, he had made much progress in his pursuit of the *Three revelations of the baton*, as shown by the increased precision of his strikes. The yujing seemed impressed in their own way because they switched their attention from their initial prey to focus on this new opponent. Now that Niu could safely get away, Xu Pengju was free to fight or flee if he chose. But his father wouldn't have liked to see him flee a fight. He gripped his spear firmly and faced the two monsters five or six feet away. Everything else ceased to exist, and he felt a heavy weight settle on his shoulders. This burden, which he was now experiencing for the first time, was the same Shao Jun had borne since she had taken it upon herself to fight Zhang Yong, a responsibility he now took up in turn. Galvanized rather than paralyzed by the feeling, his heart beat like a drum.

When the first yujing rushed his horse, Xu Pengju thrust his spear into its hand before it could even touch the animal's muzzle. The spear plunged through the monster's fingers, tearing flesh and breaking bones, but the unexpected resistance unseated the young man, leaving him feeling like he'd dislocated his shoulder as he fell heavily onto the snowy ground. Despite the shock, he immediately stood to whistle for his mount, but unfortunately the yujing reached it before him, crashing violently into its side. Its ribs broken, the beast collapsed with a piercing scream of agony. Having traveled on its back all the way to Datong, the horrific sight broke Xu Pengju's heart.

But for now he had to worry about his own life. Was he going to die at the claws of these demons? Even the one with the mangled hand didn't seem affected. Unable to feel pain, it tried to attack as if it had never been injured. The young man brandished his spear, prepared to face his destiny. If this was to be his last fight, he wasn't going to make it easy.

Just then, a huge black horse surged out of the night and its rider drove a spear through the heart of the nearest yujing.

CHAPTER 12

It was Yang Yiqing.

He'd ordered his guard to mobilize as soon as Xu Pengju's messenger had told him about Zhang Yong's arrival, but his men needed time to prepare and reach the Kui Xing pagoda. Fearing for his student's life, he had immediately dressed and armed so he could quickly go ahead without them. Though he'd lived through many conflicts, he had rarely been so agitated, particularly after realizing that his old friend would stop at nothing, including the murder of a promising member of the empire's new generation of scholars and martial artists, to achieve his ends. And to think that during that night spent discussing their respective philosophies, the governor of Datong had passionately advocated the path of compromise… Recent events proved just how far gone those days were, and Yang Yiqing was ageing like ginger – aggressively.

When he saw a man attacking his student, his blood boiled

and he immediately attacked with all his fury. But to his great surprise, instead of falling to the ground, his victim turned towards him and seized the end of his spear.

Impossible!

He almost shouted in surprise. Just like the others, he had made the mistake of failing to take Shao Jun's stories seriously enough, and now he risked paying the price for his skepticism. For an accomplished spearman who had devoted his life to the study of his art, both its practice and its theory, this reversal was hard to take. However, his experience and absolute mastery of his weapon allowed him to swiftly react to get out of this predicament. With a series of movements as fast and precise as they were unpredictable, he was able to free his weapon to use once more.

Spear techniques use six basic movements: pulling, pushing, guarding, sweeping, stabbing, and thrusting downward. The last of these is probably the most devastating because it relies on a sudden downward motion, which increases the power of the move. While difficult to use, it almost always ensures victory. Yang Yiqing had of course integrated it into his *Three revelations of the baton*, which had been inspired by the ideas of *Verses on the Treasury of Abhidharma*, a fourth-century text which includes the line "in all realms of the universe, the flow is continuous and the breath without end." This explains why, for example, a person able to lift twenty pounds under normal circumstances can lift two hundred in an emergency: like water flowing through a fishing net, the strength of the human body always finds a way to circulate despite obstacles. Wisdom and discipline allow this flow to be channeled as desired, to make it a torrent to serve the needs of martial artists who have achieved complete harmony.

And so, Yang Yiqing thrust downwards at the yujing from atop his horse, breaking its ribs and piercing its heart with phenomenal power. He swept it up in the same movement to send it flying ten feet, then leapt to the ground to throw himself upon it. He executed *Boat of Samadhi*, a deadly series of moves that kicked up the powdery snow and shards of ice in a wide circle around him. He increased the number of blows with almost cathartic fury, letting out all his frustration and disappointment through sheer violence. His student had almost died, Wang Yangming was dead, Zhang Yong was a traitor to the empire, unnatural creatures had invaded Datong... The old man felt like he was seeing his lifelong accomplishments and ideals slowly winking out one by one, and the yujing, relatively light despite its great physical strength, was paying the price. Its body quickly became riddled with wounds that would have been enough to kill any human.

Witnessing the spectacle, Xu Pengju couldn't help but admire the perfection of his master's movements, seeing him in a real fight for the first time. Clearly blinded by his own youth, he had sometimes wondered if age or lack of practice might have diminished the respected governor's abilities, but seeing that was not true, he felt ashamed of ever having doubted.

He saw an unexpected movement out of the corner of his eye: the yujing which had crashed into his horse, and that he had believed irredeemably crushed under the animal's weight, was freeing itself from underneath the corpse. It extricated its arm from the dead beast's ribcage, then lifted the body and threw it straight at Yang Yiqing as if it weighed nothing.

Fortunately, the governor saw the threat in time and plunged his spear down into the monster he was facing before using the butt of the spear to counter the dead horse's body and send it flying back with even greater force. He noted that even the monster he had thought dead after relentlessly tearing it apart was still stirring. Worse, it struggled more and more, clearly determined to get up to continue attacking. Even for a great warrior like him, it was obvious that retreat, however temporary, was the only reasonable option.

He collected his spear and ran towards his own horse. Mounting quickly, he spurred it towards his student.

"Pengju, get on!" he shouted, holding out his spear.

The young man grabbed it as he passed and quickly swung himself into the saddle behind his master as they galloped through the snow. One of the demons barred their way, but the huge black horse jumped over its head with a powerful leap. As they finally escaped, Yang Yiqing hoped with all his heart that Zhang Yong didn't have an entire army of these creatures at his disposal, otherwise the entire empire was lost.

Disorientated, the two yujing could only watch as their prey sped away. It was after midnight and the snow quickly accumulated on their unmoving heads and shoulders, giving them the appearance of grotesque statues strangely erected in the middle of the street. While they were more intelligent than the yuxiao, this unexpected situation greatly exceeded their meager capacity for thought. But a familiar sound soon reached their ears.

Zhang Yong had just used his whistle. Panting, his eyes never left Tang Yingde, who had caused him no end of trouble this night. Both stood in the pagoda's hall, a vast room at the center of which stood a sculpture of Kui Xing, the ghostly guardian god of literature, a brush in his hand. His face and pointed teeth looked even more hideous than normal in the bluish gleam of the moon and snow. When the building was still a place of worship, a large ceremonial bronze bell had hung before the deity, but it was destroyed when the army took control of the pagoda, and only the wooden posts and chain which had once held its hammer bore witness to the fact that it ever existed.

"Young man," the old eunuch thundered, "tell me where He Jiuliang is hidden, and I'll let you live!"

The night certainly wasn't going as he'd planned. He hadn't expected the intervention of Niu, who had diverted his yujing, nor this conceited, unknown youngster who had been skilled enough to delay him. If he took too long, he risked Yang Yiqing joining the fray, complicating his task even further.

Wounded in the arm and ankle, Tang Yingde knew that he couldn't win this fight alone. He had never faced an opponent of this level and was painfully aware that he owed his survival to a simple technicality: his spear was longer than Zhang Yong's sword, which allowed him to keep him far away enough to avoid being cut to ribbons. But there was no question of him accepting his hated enemy's proposal. Wordlessly, he lifted his meteoric iron spear tip and defiantly pointed it at the old eunuch.

When Master He had taught him his art, he had taught him that a warrior's true strength wasn't found in his weapon, but in his heart. Yet it was about more than mere sight... When reaching the ultimate height of the technique, an accomplished spearman became able to perceive the heartbeat of everyone around them, and thus able to predict their movements. While the young man hadn't yet achieved this degree of mastery, he seemed to vaguely hear regular heartbeats mingled with his own. Was he on the right track?

"The universe is my mind, and my mind is the universe," he repeated to himself silently. Though he was a follower of the School of Mind, he had practiced the *Way of the heart* after joining the Society of the Mind. He was still far below Shao Jun's level, but he always came into his own in a crisis, and right then, he needed every technique at his disposal. Perhaps one that might help him make sense of these sensations...

"Jiuliang!" Zhang Yong called. "Make some noise, so I can come and free you!"

His voice, amplified by *Fire lotus*, reverberated through every wall in the building, even to the outside. After searching the entire pagoda, he was now certain his acolyte was imprisoned in a secret room somewhere. Just then, he heard two distinct thuds from the depths in response to his call. The sound was faint, but nothing escaped the old eunuch in his current state of awareness. The signal came from the base of one of the posts which had supported the old bell. Turning his attention to that area, he noticed that the stone slabs next to it were scratched and much newer than those on the rest of the floor. The dust was also lighter here. These two signs could only point to one thing: it had to be a trap door. Possessing a sometimes terrifyingly accurate instinct, Zhang Yong immediately realized that the chain from the bell's hammer had to be the key to activating the mechanism to access the secret chamber.

Distracted by his success, he was almost fatally surprised

by Tang Yingde, who had taken advantage of the opportunity to press his attack. The eunuch reacted just in time to move away and bring his sword down on the young man's weapon, causing him to stumble and slide.

Without wasting a moment, the old eunuch pulled on the chain, triggering the slabs to grind open. But then he sensed another spear flying towards him from an unexpected direction. He dodged at the last second and it drove itself into the red bricks of one of the pillars, shattering into splinters which drew a spray of blood. Without even turning, he knew exactly who had made that perfect throw.

Yang Yiqing!

It could be no one else. And it was the first time he'd attacked him … Yes, he thought sadly, the time of their friendship was truly gone. When he turned round, he discovered him at the top of the staircase leading to the first floor, accompanied by his student Xu Pengju, who seemed to have turned out well. Both cleared the entire flight of stairs in one leap to land gracefully between Zhang Yong and Tang Yingde.

"Brother Yang!" exclaimed the former captain of the imperial guard.

"I'm sorry that circumstances have led us to this, uncle Zhang," said the governor of Datong.

Never before had he called him "uncle", a title reserved for eunuchs in court circles. Until then, out of respect and despite the eleven years between them, Yang Yiqing had always called his old comrade "brother". From him, this change in register was worth a thousand words: nothing would ever be the same again.

"Do you plan to fight me to the death, big brother Yiqing?"

"Why ask a question to which you already know the answer, uncle Zhang?"

Despite his apparent coolness, Yang Yiqing was heartbroken. For this man of ideals, fighting such a close friend after discovering the horrific reality of his misdeeds was the end of a lifelong dream. But he didn't falter, in spite of the pain.

"In that case, brother Yiqing..." began Zhang Yong before he was interrupted by a terrible crash.

Someone was banging on the doors of the Kui Xing pagoda, which were as solid as those of the city of Datong and reinforced with thick beams attached with copper screws. Taking advantage of his enemies' distraction, the eunuch rushed toward the room entrance to lift the thick beam which held the sturdy doors shut. The two yujing then appeared in a cloud of dust, covered in snow that their cold bodies had been unable to melt.

Their master was about to order them to attack when a spear flew in his direction. It was Yang Yiqing, who, fast as lightning, had retrieved his weapon in an attempt to finish this increasingly uncertain battle as quickly as possible. But one of the monsters obediently interposed itself between the iron and its target with superhuman reflexes. Deep down, the governor of Datong was almost relieved. Despite what he now knew, and despite his keen sense of duty, it wasn't easy for him to sweep away whole years of sincere friendship in one fell swoop. While he was prepared to do anything to put an end to the former imperial guard captain's evil acts, he would prefer not to kill him with his own hands...

Zhang Yong's eyes widened. He would have been dead without the yujing, which was now keeping his opponent

Yan Leisheng

busy. But rather than waste time he didn't have thinking about his good fortune, he rushed towards the passage that had just opened up in the floor of the room. Unfortunately for him, this time he found his way blocked by the shaking but determined figure of Tang Yingde, his rage and desire for revenge the only things keeping him standing. To him, giving up now would be the greatest dishonor: if this traitorous dog wanted to get to the pagoda's basement, he would have to get through him first!

He still didn't know his name, but Zhang Yong was beginning to hate this young man more and more. Using his whistle once more, he ordered the monster not occupied with fighting Yang Yiqing to take care of the young man. In his state, he wouldn't be an obstacle for long. But this time it was the governor of Datong who surprised him: the old spearman thrust his weapon into the chest of the creature he faced, then lifted it and threw it forcefully to crash against one of the walls. Xu Pengju, who had rushed to his aid, was amazed to see that his master clearly needed no help. Meanwhile, Zhang Yong, who had hoped that his old friend might be diminished by age, was shocked.

Only Tang Yingde realized that he must have just used *Blocking the six meridians*, the dangerous technique taught by Master He. While the governor of Datong was in excellent physical condition for a man of his age, his body would nevertheless still be under extreme stress from the intense effort required for this measure of last resort. He undoubtedly risked his life and his health, even more than by facing some supernatural monster. The young man's eyes filled with tears at the nobility of this sacrifice. It was only the second time he had ever cried.

"Pengju, Yingde," cried Yang Yiqing as he leapt to face Yang Yiqing and his other yujing, "get He Jiuliang far away from here!"

The first of the two young men, used to obeying his master's orders without question, immediately acquiesced, and the second followed suit after muttering several words of apology. While he grasped the urgency of the situation, he was angry with himself for allowing his elder to fight in his place. It was neither the time nor the place, but he would have liked to demonstrate his respect. He finally understood why Master He had never managed to beat him...

"Brother Yang," Zhang Yong called, "you're surprisingly sprightly for your age... Be careful not to overdo it!"

"Do you know this verse by Wang Yue, uncle Zhang? 'To the sound of Mongol flutes, my hair whitened like snow; to the rhythm of the conflicts on the borders, my heart reddened like blood'... When you're already old enough to die, one day more or less makes little difference."

A minister in the reign of Emperor Hongzhi, Wang Yue had spent his life fighting the Mongols. The governor of Datong had immense respect for the elderly man who, like him, had led a brilliant career as a soldier and an official, and who, also like him, had good relations with Zhang Yong despite significant differences of opinion. This verse was taken from his *Song for myself*:

> *I deplore that generals prefer honors over Confucian values,*
> *because it is easy to speak to soldiers but difficult to make*
> *them act.*
> *For the soldier suffering in battle,*

the world is as cold as the wind that blows on the frontier.
Hair soon turns white as snow,
and the heart burns in the flames.
The courts render justice, but peace hangs by a thread.

His vision equally disturbed by *Blocking the six meridians* as by the constant flow of memories, Yang Yiqing was at peace with his potential impeding death. At over seventy years old, he was happy to hand over the burden of maintaining peace to a new generation of skilled young people. For now, at least, he had successfully forced his enemy away from the secret passage, which was a victory in itself. But his two adversaries gave him no respite, and the yujing he thought he'd knocked out was already trying to stand. With a forceful gesture, he pushed back the monster facing him to create more room to move. The blow hit the creature like an anvil thrown by a catapult… and yet only pushed it back several steps without incapacitating it.

It was then that Tang Yingde and Xu Pengju reappeared to slip one firmly bound and gagged He Jiuliang from his underground prison. The timing couldn't have been worse, because at that precise moment the governor of Datong was focused on the yujing he was trying to rid himself of. Anxious not to let this opportunity slip through his fingers, Zhang Yong darted his thin sword straight in front of him and threw himself on his old acolyte, ready to skewer him without mercy. The calligrapher felt as if his entire life flashed before his eyes, a life full of bad choices, the worst of which was undoubtedly his association with the former captain of the imperial guard. And to think that up until that moment, he had dared to believe that his master had come to save him, when in fact his only goal had been to stop him talking!

But the sword never reached him: it buried itself in Tang Yingde's shoulder as he courageously threw himself in its path. The young man then made the most of his enemy's surprise to immediately riposte and inflict a terrible wound which instantly rendered Zhang Yong's tunic red. He stifled a cry of pain, surprise, and indignation. It was the first time he had seen his own blood spilt.

"Get out of here with the prisoner!" Yang Yiqing shouted to his two companions.

"Master Yang," Xu Pengju protested, "you…"

"Don't argue! Go!"

There is no worse torture for a student than to abandon their master in the face of danger, and the prince of Wei was so intensely torn that it was almost physical. While he hadn't built such strong emotional bonds with the governor of Datong, Tang Yingde was a Confucianist, and respect for his elders was so deeply rooted within him that he also found it difficult to obey. Nevertheless, the two young men knew where their duty lay, and so rushed towards the pagoda's exit as Yang Yiqing vigorously held off the two yujing. Zhang Yong, however, managed to summon enough energy to follow them outside, and what he discovered out there made his blood run cold.

It was a moonless night filled with snow, but the torches of two hundred elite soldiers in shining armor lit the courtyard. It was the personal guard of the governor of Datong, a troop of men carefully trained who had finally just arrived after their master had alerted them in the middle of the night. Even Bai Gui, who no one had known what to do with and who had been more than happy to help with the soldiers' preparations, was there. Immediately grasping the gravity of the situation, the soldiers moved apart to allow Xu Pengju, Tang Yingde, and their prisoner through, before quickly closing their ranks to point their weapons at Zhang Yong.

Finally safe, the two young men cut He Jiuliang's gag.

"Uncle He," Tang Yingde began, "I hope you now understand that your master has every intention of ripping out your tongue. You know you're only alive because we need your testimony?"

"Yes, yes, Master Tang," the calligrapher moaned. "But... where is Master Zhang now?"

As he spoke, Zhang Yong had returned to take refuge in the pagoda, and closed the doors to keep anyone from entering.

"Master Yang!" cried Xu Pengju. "Master Yang is still inside!"

A huge explosion suddenly rang out, sending pieces of brick and flaming splinters raining in every direction. In seconds, the Kui Xing pagoda became a huge, incandescent torch. Fueled by the gunpowder stored on the upper floors, the fire was so devastating and ferocious that was impossible to approach more than a few dozen steps.

It couldn't be an accident: Yang Yiqing must have lit the first spark himself...

Overwhelmed with emotion, Xu Pengju fell to his knees and let his tears course freely down his face.

CHAPTER 13

"In memory of Yang Yiqing, master and governor." This sober epitaph was the only decoration on the plaque of the funerary altar in front of which Shao Jun was kneeling as she meditated.

After leaving Hu Ruzhen in the mountains, she had reached Beijing without issue, where Xie Qian had lent an attentive ear to all she had to say. The minister had then personally given He Jiuliang's confession to the emperor, who had immediately sent out a warrant for the capture of Zhang Yong. With the villain's treachery finally exposed, Shao Jun felt like a terrible weight had lifted. For the first time in years, she finally believed that her side might win... but when she returned to Datong, she was confronted with the tragic tale of the battle at the Kui Xing pagoda.

The explosion had been so violent that it had jolted half of the city awake. It had taken hours and dozens of soldiers to finally extinguish the fire, which had completely ravaged every floor of the building. However, after searching the debris, they had found nothing but ashes and three bodies: the governor and two huge, unknown corpses that could only be the yujing. There were faint footprints in the snow behind the pagoda, suggesting that Zhang Yong had escaped once again.

Shao Jun stood and turned towards Xu Pengju, who had welcomed her on her return to the city and told her about what had transpired. Yang Yiqing had no heirs, and so he had taken it upon himself to assume the role of son in the funerary rites, a task which he had been proud to perform. As a representative of the empire, it was also his duty to temporarily administer Datong, but the discipline which reigned there made him almost superfluous: the late governor's generals and subordinates were competent and trustworthy and were doing a fantastic job of managing the daily life of the city.

In one way, events had brought Shao Jun and the prince of Wei closer, as they had now both seen their respective masters die at the hands of the same man. Their hearts cried out for vengeance.

"Lord Xu," the young woman declared, "it's time for us to make Zhang Yong pay! His plans may have been revealed, but the empire is in danger as long as that traitor lives."

"Of course, sister Shao, but how can we hope to win where both our honored masters failed? Alone, that demon would make a powerful enemy, but by now he could have armies of supernatural creatures under his command…"

"We'll certainly need all the help we can get. Let's ask Tang Yingde for his thoughts."

Xu Pengju nodded. Since fighting together in the Kui Xing

pagoda, the two young men had given up on their initial rivalry and now considered themselves brothers in arms. The prince of Wei had immense respect for the tenacity, courage, and martial skill the disciple of the School of Mind had displayed that terrible night. His acts of bravery had resulted in serious wounds which he was still recovering from. They wouldn't have any long-term consequences, but Tang Yingde needed a lot of rest to fully recover.

But when Shao Jun and Xu Pengju rejoined him at the private residence, they found him performing his daily spear exercises, clearly determined to get fighting fit as soon as possible. All three of them discussed the situation until dusk began to fall, then the young woman went to her room to sleep. There, she was surprised to discover Bai Gui, who was supposed to be staying with the prince of Dai for the peace and quiet. The child was shaken by recent events and needed to focus on his studies.

On the night of the battle at the pagoda, before Zhang Yong had closed the doors, he had glimpsed what was going on inside, and one image would forever remain engraved in his memory: Yang Yiqing's powerlessness faced with the two yujing. He knew that the governor of Datong was one of the best spearmen in the country, and not even he had been able to stand up to those cursed creatures… And he had only faced two of them! Bai Gui couldn't stop trembling every time he thought about it. When his mother returned to the fight, she would meet these monsters again, probably in large numbers. How could she survive?

"Mother," he asked suddenly, "Lord Xu, brother Tang and you are going after uncle Zhang, aren't you?"

"Yes… But promise me that whatever happens, you'll find another master to continue teaching you martial arts. Don't give in to laziness!"

While young, the child understood the real meaning of these words all too clearly. Grief-stricken, he didn't want to even consider the possibility.

"Mother," he said, "I've identified the two main reasons Zhang Yong is hard to capture."

"And what are they?"

"Firstly, he's allied himself with the Mongol princes, in territory where the empire has little sway. He'll be untouchable as long as he has this support."

"Your maturity constantly surprises me, Xiao Gui. Yes, you're right. And the second reason?"

"Well… It's those demons that protect him. Do you know how many he has made, mother?"

"Many, I fear… But to tell the truth, I haven't yet seen them for myself: in the desert I only encountered his dogs and his eagle."

Bai Gui let out a deep sigh. This answer, while honest, wasn't at all reassuring. He decided to change to a lighter subject.

"Mother, Confucius teaches us that 'every good laborer must begin by sharpening his tools'. General Guo Deng left us many valuable resources… Why not use them?"

"You mean his treasure?"

Fortunately, the chests of prototypes and documents under the Kui Xing pagoda had already been transferred to the prince of Dai's residence when they imprisoned He Jiuliang, and so nothing had been lost in the fire. Luo Hongxian had been studying these finds night and day under Bai Gui and Zhu Tiangxian's fascinated gaze, and they hadn't missed a thing. Shao Jun's protegee now had an almost exhaustive knowledge of all General Guo Deng's legacy. He continued:

"The invention that would be most useful to us right now is the auxiliary vehicle that can be attached to the side of a battle chariot. It's a long iron box pierced with holes, equipped with a cannon and wheels; it's an invention the general assessed as 'viable' in his documents."

He then began to describe the details of the device and uses that Guo Deng had already tested. He had obtained satisfactory results in several battles on the border, but he had been restricted to only using his prototypes to push back offensives and had never used them to carry out his own, wanting to avoid any chance of them being captured by the enemy. On the battlefield, he always ensured that the device was protected by numerous swordsmen. In time, he had planned to build fully armored chariots equipped with guns, which would have been powerful weapons with an incomparable strategic advantage.

Two of the three volumes of *Diagram of the Device of the Gods* were dedicated to these inventions, and the chests underneath the Kui Xing pagoda already contained enough ready-made parts to make nine-tenths of a functioning model. This discovery couldn't have come at a better time, as the prince of Dai had the necessary resources and the desire to complete General Guo Deng's work, and Luo Hongxian was the ideal man to continue this noble task.

On her return to Datong, Shao Jun had paid little attention to the work underway at the princely residence, but Bai Gui's speech had piqued her interest. Her protegee was right: any incursion by the imperial army into Mongol territory would be taken as a declaration of war, but a handful of chariots could enter without causing suspicion, and if they were armored and equipped with cannons, they could be used to attack Zhang Yong's base with a good chance of success.

The young woman brightened for the first time in a long while.

"Xiao Gui, that's fantastic! Do you know where Luo Hongxian is?"

"He must still be working at the prince of Dai's residence. Do you want to pay him a visit?"

"Yes, take me there before it gets dark."

In the orange light of the setting sun, Shao Jun could again see a chance to avenge her master's death.

Several days later, on the steppe, Prince Altan came out of his tent to stretch while watching dawn creep across the horizon. The sun, huge and proud, seemed to be more determined than ever to conquer the sky, he thought. Under the reign of the great Genghis Khan, the Mongol people had also been like that: always ready to fight, driven by an insatiable thirst for victory. But what remained of that glorious era? Not much, unfortunately. The descendants of the warriors of old had grown fat and lazy, numbed by peace, happy simply trading with their neighbors rather than claiming their lands. Even the current emperor of China had been born a captive of the Mongol dynasty before it was shattered by internal conflict.

Altan despaired that each new generation would be even

less capable than the last to maintain an army that might at least reclaim the regions that had belonged to the Yuans. That was why he had been won over by Zhang Yong's projects and experience when they met two years before: each of his yujing were worth at least ten elite warriors, if not more. Everything he needed was an abundant primary resource. Since then, in the greatest secrecy, the prince had sent a constant stream of prisoners and brigands that he could make disappear without anyone noticing. Slowly but surely, he had supplied Zhang Yong with around a hundred men. When he had a thousand, he would finally be ready to march on the empire, to raise the banner of the Golden Horde in Beijing and engrave his name in history.

"Altan Khan…" he whispered to himself, savoring the sound of the title on his lips.

First, he needed to convince his brother, Gün Bilig, because no significant plans could be carried out without his support. What would his older brother think? Hard to say… He too wished with all his heart to restore honor to his country, but he would be wary of any alliance with foreigners, and particularly with someone as problematic as Zhang Yong.

Just then, he spotted an eagle gliding slowly towards the camp. The bird landed on top of the tent pole that secured the family's banner, then dropped a bamboo message tube from its beak before flying off again with several beats of its wings. Buhe, Altan's most trusted aide, collected it then brought it to his master, who opened it and unrolled the paper scroll contained inside. His face immediately lit up.

"Buhe," he whispered, "order our soldiers to prepare."

"So soon? And the other Jinongs?"

"Gather just our men. It's high time I had an important conversation with my brother."

Without another word, Buhe spurred his horse and left at a gallop towards the mobile barracks. Once alone, the prince reread Zhang Yong's message. It contained a single sentence: *It's tomorrow.*

Altan carefully tore the message into a thousand tiny pieces that he threw into the wind. Despite his excitement, he was confused: to his knowledge, in its current state, the army of yujing established by his Chinese ally was far from being powerful enough to take Datong, an essential precondition for a larger invasion. Thousands of the demons would undoubtedly ensure an easy victory, but what could be achieved with barely a hundred?

He would have liked to be able to brush aside these concerns. There was no going back now, and he wasn't someone to go back on his decisions anyway, but despite his pride, he knew he was still young and terribly inexperienced. He loved his country deeply and wouldn't ever be able to forgive himself if he was the one who precipitated its fall, even if it was in the process of trying to restore it to greatness. More importantly, if he failed, his cousin Bodi Alag wouldn't hesitate to take advantage to crush his branch of the dynasty once and for all. It would be the end of the line of Genghis Khan.

He was paralyzed with indecision. But it was much too late to hesitate: he couldn't show the slightest uncertainty if he wanted to persuade Gün Bilig of the soundness of his plans.

"Altan!"

He turned around. It was Meng Gen, his twin sister,

arriving at a gallop. Dressed in red and riding a white horse, she stood out against the steppe like an unexpected mirage.

"Did you ask Buhe to gather the men and horses?" she asked as she drew closer.

Clearly in the grip of intense emotion, her cheeks were pink, and her breath came in short gasps. The prince was surprised by her question, because he had always taken care to keep her away from official business. Besides, he had nothing to hide.

"Yes," he responded drily. "But it's got nothing to do with you!"

"You want to attack the Ming empire?"

"Yes!"

"Altan! Don't be fooled, this uncle Zhang is just using you for his own ends!"

"What do you know of uncle Zhang? And how dare you throw around these accusations! Where did you hear such foolish things?"

In tears, Meng Gen jumped to the ground to stand firmly in front of her brother.

"Altan, you mustn't trust this man! Now, listen carefully to what I have to say ..."

On the wall at Zhuma Fortress, General Tao Shen slowly walked towards his three visitors as they stared at the horizon. He already knew two of them: Shao Jun, who he had met when she crossed the border with a letter of recommendation from the governor, and Xu Pengju, who wore the customary uniform that designated him as Yang Yiqing's official successor. The soldier could refuse them nothing, but after hearing of the high official's death a few days before, and then the writ ordering the arrest of Zhang Yong, he feared that the shadow of war would continue to loom over the region even as he strived to maintain peace.

The criminal had gone to ground outside the borders of the empire, and his capture by the army could be used as a pretext for war by the Mongol authorities. And really, that was exactly what he planned: he was counting on manipulating Prince Altan so he would send his armies to attack Datong. While they pointlessly broke themselves against the walls like waves on a reef, the master of the Zouwu would take advantage of the confusion to take his one hundred yujing across the border, where they could then make their way to the capital.

As the war distracted the central authorities, he could easily seize power, and even Xie Qian would be able to do nothing about it. The plan was flawless... but it relied on Prince Altan's cooperation, and more generally, on the right wing of the Mongol rulers, who generally favored peace and trade more than Bodi Alag's left wing. What would the proud descendants of Genghis Khan decide? That was the question Shao Jun and her companions pondered as they observed the steppe.

While he didn't know the details of the terrible events that were brewing, Bai Gui also stared at the horizon. His adoptive mother would have preferred he remain safely at the prince of Dai's residence, but he had persuaded her to allow him to accompany her. He was also suffering from A-Qian and Zhuo Mingke's disappearance, and his knowledge of General Guo Deng's prototypes had been crucial. This fight was his now too.

"Mother!" he shouted suddenly. "Someone's coming!"

He was right: by squinting, the companions could make out a small cloud of dust on the plain. A man on horseback galloping at top speed soon came into view; he was almost at the fortress gates before they realized.

"What a rider!" Tao Shen exclaimed.

"General Tao," Shao Jun said, "that's the man I was expecting. Can you order your guards not to show any hostility towards him?"

But even before the officer was able to give the order, he let out a shocked cry as he saw the young woman jump into the open air. Pale as a ghost, he felt his heart stop until he realized she was attached to her rope dart, and therefore that the thirty-three-foot drop wouldn't kill her. Halfway down, she pushed the retractable blades in her boots into the wall and climbed down with disturbing ease. No sooner had she touched the ground than she hurried towards the rider and began to speak with him. Tao Shen felt a shiver run down his spine when he saw the man wore Mongol clothing.

"Can we trust this man?" he asked Tang Yingde. "Do I need to send your friend an escort?"

"That won't be necessary, general. She knows what she's doing."

The conversation was short, and the rider soon departed as he'd come, while Shao Jun returned to the top of the wall, this time using the gate and stairs.

"What news, sister Shao?" Xu Pengju immediately asked her.

"It's good news," she answered with obvious relief. "The eastern wind is with us."

As if summoned by her words, the fort's flag fluttered in a gust of wind, blowing towards the left.

"Long live the wind!" enthused the prince of Wei. "Heaven is with us!"

Several days earlier, Shao Jun had met Meng Gen in secret, and she had updated her on all Zhang Yong's plans and He Jiuliang's confession. The princess had promised to do everything she could to persuade her brother to end his collaboration with the traitor, and Ma Fang, his Chinese servant, had just come to announce that she had succeeded. Whether or not she realized the importance of her gesture, the young girl had just averted a bloody war which would have lasted for many years and whose consequences would have been terrible for both China and Mongolia. Now Zhang Yong no longer benefited from the protection of the lords of the steppe, all that remained was to attack his secret base.

"Let's go!" Shao Jun called resolutely.

General Tao had the greatest admiration for these three young people. And among them were both Yang Yiqing's successor and his nephew, a skilled martial artist. He assigned them nineteen elite soldiers each, specially selected for the occasion. The idea of a full-frontal attack had been discarded at first, because even a thousand men would struggle to vanquish an army of a hundred yujing, but General Guo Deng's chariots had changed the balance. Under the direction of Luo Hongxian, a dozen of the devices, perfected and improved by the input of modern technologies, had been fully constructed. The prince of Dai, deeply saddened by Yang Yiqing's death and keen to participate in anything that might avenge him, had disbursed his funds generously to ensure the craftsmen had the best materials. The completed chariots were drawn by horses for long distances, but once in view of the enemy they could be detached from the beasts and maneuvered using levers. Sheltering behind its armor, soldiers could attack through the openings without being vulnerable to external assaults. Like in any battle, the risk of death still loomed, but these inventions were a significant strategic advantage.

"Do your men know what they're facing?" Shao Jun asked.

"They all want to avenge Governor Yang."

The young woman nodded solemnly. She didn't need anything more than that.

"Mother, I want to come along," Bai Gui announced.

It wasn't the first time he had asked this, but his adoptive mother was firm on this point.

"You are the future of the Society of the Mind," she answered. "If something happens to us, it will be up to you to complete our mission."

While she had spoken softly, her tone was unambiguous: she had made her decision and that was final.

She took the fabric bag held out to her by General Tao and climbed into the basket of the balloon abandoned by Zhang Yong on the night of the battle at the Kui Xing pagoda. After being taught how it worked by Luo Hongxian, she had decided to use it to lead the assault on the secret lair. Its mechanism was quite simple, and clearly inspired by wishing lanterns; the real difference was one of scale, as in this case the hot air was generated by oil lamps and not simple candles.

When she examined it, Shao Jun couldn't help but be impressed by Yu Dayong's talent and skill. His work could have contributed to the advancement of the empire if he hadn't thrown in his lot with Zhang Yong. But now the balloon was just a balloon, and its nature remained the same whether it was used for good or ill. In the end, origins and allegiances were mere abstractions when faced with the reality of decisions and concrete actions. Hu Ruzhen, for example, was a member of the Zouwu, but he had chosen to follow his heart when the time had come to act.

Nothing is true, everything is permitted.

The balloon slowly rose into the air as the ropes tying it down were released. When the balloon reached several hundred feet above the ground, Shao Jun reduced the intensity of the oil lamps to stabilize its height and looked at the dozen armed chariots far below as they emerged from Zhuma Fortress onto the steppe. An easterly wind blew her towards Lake Dai.

In the Mongol camp, Meng Gen was not as reassured as might be expected. While she had nurtured the hope that she might persuade her brother to give up his plans in the name of peace, it was Zhang Yong's treason that had finally forced his hand. In reality, the prince had only encouraged trade over the last two years to help finance his ally's research and experiments, but now the fires of war had been lit in his mind, they would not extinguish any time soon.

Ma Fang had told the young woman that he'd passed on her message and that he had seen a large balloon and a dozen armored chariots leave the fort, but she had no interest in these political happenings. Learning Shao Jun's true identity hadn't stopped her from developing a real and deep friendship with her, and her heart sank at the thought that she might never see her friend again.

Because she had left out some vital information: if the Chinese failed to capture Zhang Yong, Altan would let his army loose on both parties to massacre everyone involved in this dark affair.

CHAPTER 14

Lake Dai took its name from the Mongol word meaning "sea". Thirty lis long from east to west and twenty lis wide from north to south, it was the largest body of water in the entire region. It had been renamed many times by previous dynasties before receiving its current name: it had been known as the Lake of Heaven under the Qins, the Fragrant Marsh under the Hans, the Salt Pond under the Weis, and the Sea Where the Waters End under the Liaos. Its southwestern shore was famous for being particularly treacherous due to its marshy ground, and many unwary travelers had perished in its quicksand.

It was there that Zhang Yong had established his base, built with stones recovered from the remains of the abandoned sections of the Great Wall. The work had been carried out by prisoners condemned to death by Prince Altan's tribe, poor wretches who believed they would earn their freedom through this forced labor but had later been transformed into yujing when the work was complete.

In two years, the traitor had created exactly one hundred of these demons, of which two had died in the disastrous battle at the Kui Xing pagoda. No matter: he still had more than enough to execute his plans. They were all there in front of him, standing perfectly still in neat rows. Due to their limited ability for thought, the yujing couldn't be left to their own devices for too long, so Zhang Yong sent them into a deep artificial sleep when he didn't need them. To do this, he used the Baihui acupuncture point located at the back of the skull, where he inserted a tapered needle with fast, practiced movements. The technique was so dangerous that the slightest error could be fatal, but the old eunuch's hand had never betrayed him.

After sending the monster he had just created to sleep, Zhang Yong sighed and contemplated his work with satisfaction. Two years before, he had feared that the destruction of Dai Yu Island would prevent him from ever producing his yujing, because while the Precursor Box contained the alchemical remedies, secret acupuncture, and moxibustion techniques required for the process, it also stipulated that it must be carried out in a specific place of power. But through his research, the eunuch had discovered that he could substitute a special blend of medicinal herbs to create the specific energy conditions present at the sites of the Precursors' civilization.

The heavens seemed to have chosen to assist him, but the winds had recently changed. Zhang Yong would have liked another six months to complete and train his army, a luxury he no longer had. The former captain of the twelve battalions of the imperial guard was disgraced. Only a show of unprecedented strength would allow him to appear once more as one of the empire's strongmen, even if it was to the detriment of the empire itself. Who better than he to steer China towards its destiny? Despite his age, his blood still ran hot as that of a young man.

Just then, he heard a loud rumbling in the distance.

Prince Altan alone knew the location of his base, but he only resupplied it once every five days – although half-dead, the yujing still needed to eat – and he wasn't expecting anyone today. The old man's sharp ears made out at least six chariots approaching, too heavily laden to be carrying anything but living cargo. More importantly, any undesirable visitor would first have to pass through the Mongol camp, an almost impossible feat. So, what could be happening?

Zhang Yong rushed to the door to glance outside. What he saw made his blood run cold: a convoy of armored vehicles was approaching at high speed!

Quick as lightning, he inserted his needle into the temple of a sleeping yujing near the doorway to reanimate it and ordered it to guard outside. The old eunuch wasn't someone to panic easily, and he believed the situation was still mostly under control. Even though he was concerned that his allies hadn't stopped these intruders from passing through, these newcomers weren't sufficient in number to present any real danger. His ninety-nine demonic soldiers were worth ten thousand ordinary men.

But he suddenly heard cannon fire, and his sentinel brutally exploded into a thousand pieces.

Zhang Yong's eyes widened. Heavy artillery? Mounted

on chariots? He cursed. It was unheard of! It could only be the doing of Shao Jun, who never ceased to surprise him and constantly thwarted his plans in unexpected ways. And to think that he'd thought he had a clear path after dealing with Wang Yangming... Back then, he had never expected his former friend's student to be equal to the master. But now wasn't the time for ruminating. He set to work waking as many of his sleeping monsters as possible before the enemy was at his door. If they wanted a fight, they would have it!

"Reload, and fast!" Tang Yingde cried.

The young man was responsible for that first shot. While he more often got the chance to shine in hand-to-hand combat, he was also an expert in artillery and firearms, and today he was delighted to put these skills to work in the name of vengeance. That dog Zhang Yong would pay dearly for the deaths of A-Qian and Zhuo Mingke!

Each team was composed of four men: the first two loaded, triggered, and cleaned the cannon, while the other two, armed with crossbows and spears, protected the chariot between shots. The maneuvers had to be carried out at great speed, because the yujing could only be felled by the heaviest balls. But in the confined and stifling space of an armored chariot, the heat quickly became unbearable. Tang Yingde and his three soldiers were already sweating profusely as one of them, wearing thick leather gloves, cleaned the smoking mouth of the cannon with a long brush to prevent the molten filings fusing to its walls. Luckily, the wintry wind that sometimes blew through the openings was just enough to prevent them from fainting.

"Master Tang, who are these men?" one crossbowman asked, worried to see even more enemies rushing towards the Chinese troops.

"They're demons," the disciple of the School of Mind responded without hesitation. "Today, we are demon hunters!"

As Tang Yingde prepared to reload the cannon, the chariot was shaken by a violent jolt.

"A dog!" one of the soldiers shouted.

Knowing that they would make the most difficult targets, Zhang Yong had released his entire pack of twenty demonic dogs. One of the two largest, the size of a small calf, had just rushed the chariot. Its powerful jaws could grip to pierce through the metal armor plates, but they broke the mouth of the cannon like the bones of a rabbit. As the men froze in horror, Tang Yingde loaded the powder and called out loudly.

"Fire!"

Suddenly shaken out of his stupor, the powderman obeyed; less than a second later, a furious cannonball pulverized the dog's head. And though unknown to anyone else, Zhuo Mingke was in some way avenged, because this beast, Shentu, was the one that had taken his life.

While the chariots gave the troops an advantage, the outcome of the battle remained uncertain due to their small number and the time required to clean and load the cannons. In addition, Zhang Yong was able to wake his monsters much more quickly than they could be killed, so they soon filled the plain, terrorizing the cannon teams facing them for the first time as they discovered with horror that their crossbow bolts were useless. As the saying goes, a mountain can only be destroyed one stone at a time, and so it was with this monstrous army... but this mountain hit back, blow for blow.

Tang Yingde's chariot was once again struck by a massive weight. *Boom!* Violently thrown against the metal wall, the young man was hit by a sudden worry: if several of them worked together, a handful of yujing could easily overturn a chariot, and thus ensure their victory. At that point, the chariots would stop being moving fortresses and quickly become tombs.

Determined not to let that happen, he ordered his soldiers to reload the cannon again then he opened the trap door above his head to climb onto the roof. Once in the open air, he enjoyed the cool breeze on his face and almost smiled as he saw that the four yujing surrounding them, rather than all standing on the same side, were on opposite sides of the chariot and therefore stood no chance of overturning it. He still needed to deal with them though, and so he cut off the hands of the ones on the left with a rapid slice of his spear, before repeating the operation on the right. Unfortunately, just then, one of the monsters grabbed the tip of his weapon before it lost its hands.

Tang Yingde didn't panic. After facing these creatures in Datong, he knew what to expect. Rather than trying to regain control by force, he followed his opponent's movements, pushing when it pulled and pulling when it pushed, to take control of its momentum and better turn it against it. When the time felt right, he suddenly tore his spear out of its hands and planted it in the monster's shoulder with enough power to make its arm unusable, before finally cutting off the hands of the last of his attackers.

Some distance away, however, three yujing on the same side of another chariot had just succeeded in tipping it over, crushing one of themselves in the process without even noticing. They then began to thump savagely on the metal walls to try to loosen the armor, drawing even more monsters to them. Gripped by panic, and with its walls threatening to give way, the chariot's occupants shouted in terror. Tang Yingde ordered his team to head towards them to help, but moving these chariots without horses was slow and clumsy. Would they arrive in time?

He didn't have to wonder, because Xu Pengju, who was much closer, emerged from his own chariot dressed in his white mourning robe to intervene. Inspired by Tang Yingde's courage, he left the relative safety of his perch to save their endangered comrades: thrusting his spear into the ground, he used it as a platform to launch himself into the air and try to skewer a yujing as he descended. His momentum wasn't enough to pierce the monster's thick muscles, but he immediately climbed up onto the overturned chariot to drive his weapon's tip into his attacker's armpit. By that point, the prince of Wei had reached the Samadhi stage of *Three revelations of the baton*, which allowed him to lift the monster to send it flying and crashing into the ground some distance away. Nonetheless, the effort required had been much more than he had expected, and he suddenly felt so dizzy that he almost dropped his spear.

This slight discomfort couldn't have come at a worse time, as another demonic creature was already approaching. But just as it was about to attack, a meteoric iron spear tip pierced through its chest.

It was Tang Yingde, who had just joined the fight. The overturned chariot in the middle of the battlefield was a considerable risk to the Qin forces, not only because they needed to be able to use all their cannons, but also because such a sight risked sapping their morale. In such an uncertain fight, psychology was key. As Confucius rightly said: "The three armies may change commander, but no one can change their ambition." In addition, despite the yujings' phenomenal brute strength, the Qin men had an undeniable advantage: they could help each other and coordinate their actions.

"Get out of there, all of you!" Tang Yingde ordered the team. "Lord Xu and I will hold these demons back while you right your chariot."

Galvanized by the presence of the two elite young spearmen, the soldiers calmed down and obeyed. The chariot still weighed some two tons, so they struggled to reach its tipping point. They wouldn't have succeeded if, taking advantage of a moment of respite, their protectors hadn't used their weapons as levers to give them the final push needed to complete their task. Despite this symbolic success, no one felt in the mood to shout with joy: with only twenty of their number dead, the yujing continued to flow out of Zhang Yong's base at regular intervals. It was easy to believe that they might keep coming forever.

"Chen Buhao directs the chariot to the far south," stated a reedy voice. "Chen Wenxiong commands the one to the far north, Cao Zhenying and Wang Lei are to the west, and the three chariots belonging to Lin Wen, Qiu Su and Qin Wendai are behind and to the east."

It was… Bai Gui! And from the sound, he was in Xu

Pengju's chariot, which he must have sneaked into right under the adults' noses.

After his initial surprise, Tang Yingde was actually quite impressed that the child – unlike himself – had remembered the names of all the commanders of the armored chariots and that he had chosen exactly the right moment to state their positions. Indeed, in addition to the obvious strategic benefit of such information, his intervention informed the surrounding soldiers that they were in the middle of all their comrades, and thus in the most well-protected part of the battlefield. They all cheered up immediately, and on resuming their posts they were once again ready to do battle.

Just then, a giant shadow fell over Xu Pengju as he returned to his own chariot. He looked up to see Shao Jun's balloon heading straight towards Zhang Yong's base.

The young woman had begun to lower the balloon as soon as Lake Dai was in view, but her descent had been much slower than expected. When she left the fort, General Tao had given her two bombs designed by General Guo Deng and with a payload doubled by Luo Hongxian. However, once their fuses were lit, she had to ensure she was no more than a hundred feet above the ground before throwing them, otherwise they would explode in midair without causing any damage. She had no room for mistakes, because as far as she could see, on the ground, victory was still far from assured for the Qin chariots.

Murmuring a prayer to the heavens, she dropped both her bombs at once.

In his base, Zhang Yong was still waking his yujing when he heard a sound like thunder rumbling through the building's foundations. Despite the heavy losses his army had suffered, he thought he had seen the battle turning in his favor. By now, he had woken half of his monsters, and according to his calculations, if he maintained this pace, they should eventually overcome their attackers. But the roof collapsed at the same time as his last hopes of glory, and he was only just able to save his own life by leaping through the open door as tons of stone wiped out the results of two years of demanding work.

He looked up to the sky and cursed. While he had expected his enemies to use the balloon he had been forced to abandon in Datong, he hadn't expected them to use it in this way. There could be no doubt, it had to be Shao Jun. She would pay dearly for this insult! He angrily drew the whistle from his sleeve and raised it to his lips.

In the sky, the young woman rejoiced to see that she had successfully accomplished her mission. With the flow of yujing interrupted, it was only a question of time before her side won the day. This was a setback that Zhang Yong wouldn't be able to recover from. But she couldn't afford to make assumptions: the old eunuch was a formidable martial artist, and so it was unlikely he had died alongside his monsters... And so, as she leant over the edge of her basket to examine the huge cloud of grey smoke below, she saw his silhouette escaping towards the remnants of the Great Wall, unseen by the rest of the forces on the ground.

Just as she was about to turn in his direction to avoid losing him from view, she heard a shrill cry sound from a little above her. Zhang Yong's three demonic eagles were tearing at the fabric of her balloon!

Shao Jun felt like her heart had stopped. But the terrifying birds of prey soon left without trying to attack her. The young woman wasn't out of the woods yet though; she'd lost control of her flight and was now falling towards the ground too quickly to survive the crash. It was pointless hoping to find salvation in the lake's waters: she was much too far away. No, her only chance was to jump out of her basket and use her cloak to glide to the dunes that the winds had formed against the remains of the Great Wall. The air currents would need to carry her for long enough and in the right direction, and she would need to control her speed to avoid crashing against either the wall or into the rocky plain beyond... But what other choice did she have?

She took a depth breath and threw herself into the air.

As she glided over the steppe, a fragile but graceful silhouette, she saw her entire life flash before her eyes. Her childhood in the heart of the Forbidden City, her introduction to the Society of the Mind, then the complete collapse of everything she had ever known and her flight to Europe, the teachings of her various masters, her return to China and tracking down of the Eight Tigers. She saw herself surrounded by the faces of Zhu Jiuyuan, Ezio Auditore, Wang Yangming, Zhuo Mingke and A-Qian... and that of Zhang Yong, her sworn enemy, against whom she yearned for revenge.

With a final swoop, she landed softly at the top of a dune.

EPILOGUE

Darkness had fallen over the steppe without warning, but Zhang Yong could clearly see Shao Jun's silhouette as she fell towards one of the highest dunes against the Great Wall. Even though reason said that no one could survive such a fall, he had come to realize that members of the Society of the Mind had an annoying tendency to achieve the impossible. At first, he'd thought her insignificant, but this young woman now dogged him at every step. And now, as the ultimate insult, she had just defeated his army of yujing! He would never again be able to field such a force.

Of course, he could still flee, change his name, wear more modest clothing, and spend quiet days in some remote province of the empire where no one knew him. But such an end would be... unworthy of him. No, he couldn't let it come to that. All he had left now was his honor, and the place could not have been better chosen, so evocative were the ruins of

Yan Leisheng

the Great Wall. Once, it had protected the empire. Once, men had stood here to fight for what they believed in. Once, it had seemed as if it would last forever. But time had done its work, the world had changed, and today it was nothing more than a crumbling wall in a place inhabited by no one.

"How have you been since our last encounter, uncle Zhang?" a female voice called from behind him.

When he turned, he saw the despised figure of the one he would recognize anywhere. Squinting until his eyes were no more than slits, he examined her carefully. She was completely uninjured. Now that was admirable. She confidently unsheathed the weapon she carried on her back to hold it above her head. Her blade gleamed eerily in the moonlight.

"Do you recognize this sword?" the young woman asked.

It was Green Lotus, Wang Yangming's famous sword. Those who had seen him as nothing more than a mere scholar would have seen only a simple, decorative object, but anyone who knew the martial skills of the founder of the Society of the Mind also knew this weapon was as sharp as a razor. The student carried her master's weapon to avenge his murder. The circle would be complete.

"Of course," Zhang Yong answered. "It's almost like seeing an old friend…"

With these words, he unsheathed his own thin rapier and threw himself at Shao Jun, who calmly parried with ease. Although this fight was probably the most important in her life, she was completely calm; she fought without hatred, filled only with distant respect for her adversary. While she still strongly rejected his beliefs, ideas, and methods, she had to admit that he had never deviated from the path he had chosen, just like she had never turned away from her own principles.

Quick as lightning, their blades swayed like dragons in the white light of the moon. The young woman and the old eunuch were both extremely agile and used fighting techniques inspired by both the East and West. Their skill was such that they fought in perfect silence, without leaving the slightest mark on the dune. Neither of them seemed able to gain the upper hand.

But just as they were about to clash once more, a violent gust of wind lifted a thick cloud of sand that momentarily blocked the moonlight, plunging them both into complete darkness. When it cleared, Shao Jun and Zhang Yong had switched places... and a crimson stain was spreading across the young woman's shoulder. With extraordinary skill, the old eunuch had managed to pull his adversary's protective cloak aside to expose her tunic and thrust his blade into her. Yet it was he who murmured in admiration.

"You wield a sword like no one else!"

Indeed, as he had lunged for that effective but far from fatal thrust, Wang Yangming's student had used *Mind sight* to put out both of his eyes, sending a flood of bloody tears rushing down his cheeks. He wouldn't die from it, but the duel was at an end. Was she going to take the opportunity to finish him? It would go against everything she believed in, and in this faithless world, her convictions were her only shield. She couldn't do it. It was no longer her sworn enemy that faced her, but an old, blind, and defenseless eunuch. What would be the point in cutting off the head of such a pathetic being?

"Uncle Zhang," she began. "Give me the Precursor Box and I'll let you live."

"You're so generous, concubine! Unfortunately, at the end of that night of debate with my friends Wang Yangming and Yang Yiqing, I made three wishes: the first was to bring glory to the Ming dynasty, the second to ensure the stability of my country..."

"You could have achieved those goals in another way!" Shao Jun couldn't help interrupting.

"Hahaha! So, it's not enough to ruin me, is it? You also feel the need to criticize what I have devoted my life to? Anyway... Would like to know what my third wish was?"

"I'm listening."

"I swore that I, Zhang Yong, would never kneel before anyone!"

With this, he used his whistle one last time to summon his demonic eagles, which surged out of the darkness to fall upon him.

Dignified and impassive, he didn't struggle or cry out as the sharp beaks and claws of the birds he himself had created ripped his flesh and broke his bones. Shao Jun recoiled in horror, but the unbearable carnage only lasted for a moment; the beasts quickly flew back into the sky, leaving behind a bloody carcass, a vague, nightmarish mass which was barely recognizable as human.

Uncle Zhang, Shao Jun thought, *while my path was different from yours, know that we pursued the same dreams. I hope you find eternal peace.*

In the distance, the young woman could hear a few final cannon shots. Now the battle was finally at an end, the chariots were methodically finishing off the last yujing still able to move. She took a deep breath and began to walk back towards the destroyed base, where she found Xu Pengju standing on his chariot, organizing the collection of the monstrous corpses scattered all around. He greeted her with relief as he saw her return on her own two legs.

"Dear Jun," he called, "did you kill Zhang Yong?"

"He's dead," she answered simply, without any joy.

To his great regret, Tang Yingde announced that they had thoroughly searched the ruins, but failed to find any trace of the Precursor Box. If the old eunuch hadn't been carrying it with him, and he hadn't hidden it in his lair, where could it be? They feared he had taken the secret to his grave.

"We've still got a long way to go…" Shao Jun sighed.

Although happy to see his mother unharmed, Bai Gui stood back a little, worried he would be reprimanded for sneaking into a chariot. The presence of a child on this devastated battlefield was so incongruous that he was impossible to ignore.

The young woman walked towards him and rested an affectionate hand on his shoulder.

"You've got a long way to go too, Bai Gui…"

Everyone then turned to the east to gratefully welcome the first orange rays of the morning sun. It had been a long time since the dawn had been so full of promise.

ACONYTE EXTRA!!

Explore the war between Assassins and Templars as it wreaks havoc in the Victorian era, with the first two chapters of a bold new thriller in the world of Assassin's Creed®

THE ENGINE OF HISTORY

The MAGUS CONSPIRACY

KATE HEARTFIELD

PROLOGUE

Simeon Price tried to shut out the sound of whispered prayer, and the groaning of the ship. He flopped one arm over his ear, but it was no good. He was, irritatingly, awake.

"Seasick again, Halford?" he mumbled.

The praying stopped. "Not tonight. Can't sleep, is all."

Simeon turned over with some difficulty in his rocking hammock. Private Sawyer Halford was a dark bulk against a line of similar dark bulks, lit up by a single lantern against the wall. The troop deck was stuffy this deep into the night, a stew of sweat and tobacco, iron and wood. Overhead somewhere, a rat scuttled.

"Thinking about what's waiting for us when we go ashore?" Simeon kept his voice low. He'd recently been given the appointment of lance corporal, which was hardly even a rank, but it did mean that he had responsibility over Halford and a few other privates of the 74th Highland Regiment of Foot. Anyway, Simeon liked Halford.

But going ashore was going to happen, and soon. They had sailed past Cape Town, the captain charting a course that hugged the southern coast of Africa to save time, speeding by steam and sail toward war.

"I suppose so," Halford said. "It was one thing being sent to Ireland. I knew what to expect, or I thought I did." There was a pause, during which they both thought about what they'd seen in Ireland: the houses burned, the children so thin. "But I'd never even heard of the Xhosa before we sailed."

"I doubt they've heard of you either, mate."

Halford might have chuckled or might have sighed; it was hard to tell which in the dark. "At least when my father went off to fight Napoleon, he'd seen a picture of the bastard." He paused, then said, even more quietly, "I've never killed anyone before."

Neither had Simeon, though he'd come close a couple of times in his father's public house back in Ealing. There had been one night in Tipperary when he had expected to be asked to kill women and old men. In the end, they had left the storehouse he was guarding without violence, gone back to their hungry beds, and Simeon had got very drunk. He had no words of wisdom for Halford tonight.

"I'm sorry I interrupted your prayer," Simeon said quietly.

"Prayer?" Halford chuckled. "Oh, no, Price. I wasn't praying. I always recite Shakespeare when I can't sleep."

"Which bit of Shakespeare?"

"It varies. Tonight, it's the sceptre'd isle speech. From *Richard II.*"

Simeon was surprised. "Ah, right. 'England, bound in with the triumphant sea, whose rocky shore beats back the envious siege of watery Neptune'... I can't remember the next part."

"'Is now bound in with shame, with inky blots and rotten parchment bonds. That England, that was wont to conquer others hath made a shameful conquest of itself.'" Halford paused. "Maybe not the best choice for tonight, but it was the sea that made me think of it."

Simeon opened his mouth to say he thought it was an excellent choice, when the ship lurched to a terrible stop, throwing him half out of his hammock.

There were shouts from above. Simeon disentangled his arm and stumbled to his feet. The hideous noise stretched on: a sickening crunch, the iron hull tearing open. The floor tilted from bow to stern. Simeon lurched through the jungle of hammocks and ropes, past the bewildered men just waking up. Out to the door and the stairs up to the deck, in his shirt and trousers.

It was a warm night, with cold stars above, the dark water below. The ship was now unnaturally still and lying at an odd angle. HMS *Birkenhead* was a Frankenstein's monster of iron and wood, converted from a frigate to a troop ship, steam coming from its great black funnel and sails furled on its masts, paddlewheels on its sides. There were men shouting up on the forecastle.

"She ran onto a fucking rock," said a passing sailor in uniform, seeing Simeon's face. "There was a light on shore that we thought was a lighthouse – but it must have been a fire. We're on the wrong course. The rock put a bloody great gash in the bow, and we're stuck fast."

"All right," said Simeon, as the sailor seemed to be looking for some kind of resolution, from someone. "Where are we needed? On the pumps?"

"Not yet. They're firing the engines to back us off the rock."

"But won't that bring more water in?"

The sailor shrugged. "Captain's orders. We have to get free, he says. Says the compartments will hold."

As if in answer, the ship came to life and heaved slowly backwards. Shouts from the front, and the bow dipped, throwing Simeon back the way he'd come. As he righted himself, he turned toward the stairs, and saw the water rising, covering the bottom of the stairwell. Those stairs led back down to the upper troop deck, where hundreds of men had been sleeping minutes before.

He slipped and slid down the stairs, into the water, wet up to his knees. The door had swung shut behind him, or he'd closed it – he couldn't recall now. Someone was pulling at it from the inside, and he shoved, and nearly fell onto Private Halford, soaked to the skin and panting.

"There are wounded," Halford said, and pointed back behind him, toward the bow.

Simeon and Halford waded, the ship tilting and throwing them onto each other as they tripped and slid. This deck, which had been built as a gunroom before the ship's conversion, was full of men, all in their nightshirts and frantically crowding to the door that led to freedom. The ship's engines were as silent as death now, and the water as cold. The fires must have gone out.

And all the while Simeon was thinking, There's another deck below this one. Where's the water coming in?

A man had hurt his leg – probably broken – and was trying

to keep his head above water as he staggered, the ship still shuddering beneath them and the water as full of waves as though there were wind inside the ship. Simeon and Halford put their arms around the man's shoulders and got him to the door.

Someone yelled, "Lance Corporal Price! You're needed!"

Simeon craned his neck back to see, up on the deck at the top of the steep stairs, a young lieutenant with a frantic expression. Lieutenant Grimes, that was his name.

"The horses," Grimes shouted down. "We cut them free but they're thrashing and kicking up here. We can't get anything done until we get them overboard. It's Bedlam. Look lively!"

Simeon pushed wet hair out of his eyes. "The horses are on deck, but the men—"

"The men, unlike the horses, will stay quiet," the lieutenant snapped.

Grimes was in the 74th Regiment, the same as Simeon. Where was Colonel Seton? Off doing something useful, presumably, which left men like Grimes free rein to issue orders.

Out of nowhere, someone slammed Lieutenant Grimes roughly down to the boards.

The figure wore a cloak, with a hood so close around his face that all Simeon could see was a square jaw, unshaven. Not a uniformed soldier, whoever he was, but he held an axe. He descended the stairs at speed.

"Come on," the figure growled, pushing past Simeon toward the lower deck and the rising water.

"Is he—" Simeon tried to see what had happened to the lieutenant.

"I haven't killed him yet … which might prove a mistake."

Simeon was stunned. Cloaked men didn't appear out of nowhere on Her Majesty's troop ships, and they certainly didn't knock officers down. But there was no time for questions. Whoever the stranger was, he was heading down, toward the muffled shouts and screams.

The water in the lower stairwell was blacker than the sky above. They had to pull themselves down, with the water over their heads. The door to the men's quarters wouldn't open. The stranger beat at the door with the axe, but the water slowed his movement. Eventually he resorted to a kind of scraping and slashing. When the wood of the door split, Simeon pushed his hands in and pulled the door apart, he and the stranger working at it until the door was splintered open and their hands were bloody and there was no air in their lungs. Then Simeon started to black out.

He lost his grip and floated to the middle of the stairwell, and hardly knew whether he was drowning or not. Somewhere, high overhead, yellow light from the ship's lanterns swam in his eyes. His head was free of the water as he grabbed for the steep stairs.

Then the cloaked man was at his side, pushing a coughing and spluttering soldier up into the air.

Simeon was shaking from cold and panic. He seemed to have to think about every breath. But the cloaked man was going back below, pulling himself down the thin stair rail. Who was this bloke, anyway? A stowaway? A paying passenger? A sailor out of uniform?

There would be time to think about that later. Now, every moment was a life lost or saved, and Simeon had enough air in his lungs to do his part.

Simeon took a deep breath and followed the stranger back down into darkness. They found one more man thrashing, trying to get through the broken doorway in a panic. The stranger battered at the door, and this time, it opened. They pulled him out and up.

Their third descent found a man floating limp, halfway between floor and ceiling, and they pulled him out too, pushing his nightshirt off his unconscious face. The stranger rolled him to one side and then the other, shaking him, shouting at him and pushing on his abdomen, but it was very clearly no good. As Simeon and the stranger lay on the stairs, retching and coughing, a dead man lying beside them, the cloaked man gasped, "Go on. You don't want to survive this just to be courtmartialed."

A memory leapt into Simeon's mind. It had only been weeks ago, but it felt like years. The hot sun beating down, as all of the six hundred troops on board the *Birkenhead* were paraded to watch a young stoker receive his fifty lashes, punishment for leaping overboard and swimming for the coast of Sierra Leone. Punishment for desertion.

"What about you?" Simeon croaked, his throat aching and tight from their trips under water.

"I don't answer to them," said the man, pushing back his hood. Simeon didn't recognize him: a middle-aged man with light brown skin, sharp cheekbones and a few days' worth of beard on his angular chin. He was panting, his hand to his chest. "But you took the Queen's shilling, didn't you? So go on. There's no one left to save down here."

The stranger stared sidelong at him, as if it were a dare. Beneath the battered cloak, he didn't look any more soldierly.

He must be a stowaway, although for what reason, Simeon couldn't dream. And why was he risking capture, not to mention his life, to save the men everyone else seemed to have given up for lost? What would happen to him if he went up on deck?

"I don't know who you are, and for the moment I don't care. I want to know you'll be safe," Simeon said. "Can you make it to the boats? Come on, we'll go together, and I'll make sure no one gets in your way."

The man's face contorted into a smile. "Maybe he was right about you," he muttered.

"Who was?"

"Listen, if you ever find you want to give the Queen back her shilling, make your way to Vienna. You'll find us there. A brotherhood that believes in taking orders from conscience alone. Nothing is true, everything is permitted. Will you remember that?"

Vienna! It seemed as unreal as Fairyland. They were on a sinking ship on the far side of Africa. He seemed unlikely to set foot on land ever again, and if he did, it would be a country where he'd never been before. Even if they survived the night, the 74th Regiment was meant to fight and die for British settlers in their attempt to subjugate the local people. A brotherhood that believed in … ? Fairyland indeed.

Simeon wasn't sure what to make of any of the stranger's instructions, except that it was too long a speech for a man to make if he was in danger of dying. He nodded, briefly, not sure what he was agreeing to. The whole encounter seemed unreal, but everything was unreal at the moment: the screams of the dying, the water gurgling and frothing through every crack in the ship, the stink of wet coal and vomit and tar. Lieutenant Grimes was still roaring commands above. He had work to do, and more people to help. The horses would be frantic. And Simeon was, still, a soldier.

Simeon shook the stranger's hand, in thanks and farewell, then scrambled up the steep wet stairs, suddenly dog-tired. The ship was rocking wildly, the mast swinging from one star to another.

There was Private Halford, looking as worn out as Simeon felt. Grimes was nowhere to be seen, for the moment. A few men were running from one part of the ship to another, without any apparent logic to their movements. Others, like Halford, seemed to be stunned, unsure what to do.

"The horses," Simeon said, weakly. "I've got orders to see to the horses."

"Already overboard, and swimming to shore. If the sharks don't get them, they'll be better off than any of us."

"What's next then? The boats?"

Halford shook his head, glumly. "They want us to pump. Fifty men at a go, until they tire, then the next fifty."

"But surely—"

"We got the women and children into the cutter and launched it. That's done, at least."

In the rush to save the drowning down below, Simeon hadn't thought about the officers' wives near the stern of the ship, and their children – there must have been a few dozen all told. A couple of the women had given birth on the journey.

Halford continued, "We tried to get the bigger boats down into the water. Rusted winches and rotten ropes – the boats are no good to us, that's the long and short of it. Can't get two of 'em off the ship with the winches busted, and the third was swamped when the rope broke."

"No good at all?" Simeon was shocked. Dozens of people, maybe hundreds, could have fitted into those boats.

"The rest of us, we're to stay on board and pump out the water." Halford paused. "Do you… do you think that's what we should do?"

Simeon tried to think. He was wet and cold, and couldn't seem to stop his shoulders from shaking.

The ship juddered backward and there was an all too familiar crunch and scream of iron against stone, a crack of wood breaking. The ship tipped backward this time, as water rushed into a fresh hole, this one in the stern.

Captain Salmond strode toward them, the way only a sea captain could stride on the watery deck of a swaying ship. His dark hair was wild, and so were his dark eyes.

"She's going down," he said. "Anyone who can swim for it, do so."

With an aye-aye or two, a few men scrambled to find a place to jump overboard. Halford and Simeon climbed up to the poop deck and clung to the railing. The unbalanced ship was rocking wildly; sometimes the sea was a few feet away, and sometimes it was a great deal further. The prospect of diving was terrifying, but the captain was right. If they stayed on board, the suction of the ship as it went down would pull them under, or they'd be caught in the rigging, and they'd have no chance of swimming to shore or surviving long enough to be rescued.

They climbed the railing as if it were a ladder, and Simeon considered stripping off his wet clothing. It would be a terrible sunburn, on the coast of the Cape, if he made it that far. Instead, he tucked his shirt well into his trousers, to keep the thing from billowing and dragging in the water.

"Beat to quarters!" came a scream from behind them. "Beat to quarters!"

They turned to see Lieutenant Grimes, and all the surviving men, half of them in uniform and half in their shirts, standing as steady as they could on the tilting deck.

You took the Queen's shilling, the stranger had said. Simeon had wanted to become anonymous, to make a quiet living, one man in a crowd. It was either north to Manchester and a factory or off to the army, and the army had seemed less likely to result in injury. He'd wanted to stop thinking, to stop making all the wrong decisions. To stop making any decisions at all.

But under the stars of the far side of the world, on a breaking ship full of the newly drowned, Simeon found himself saying, "The captain's orders were to swim for it."

"And I say beat to quarters, damn you!" The lieutenant took a few unsteady steps to them, and spoke quietly, almost intimately, as though showing the great patience he had for this insubordinate lance corporal. "If these men swim, they'll swim to the two lifeboats out there, which are full of women and children. They'll try to get into the boats, and they'll swamp them."

"Or," Simeon said through gritted teeth, "they won't do that, because they aren't monsters. If they swim, they have a chance."

The lieutenant whirled on his heel and yelled, "Beat to quarters! Stand firm, and stand for Her Majesty! Men, you can be proud of this moment. You have carried out your orders calmly. All has been done with the utmost regularity."

Halford slid down off the rail and followed the lieutenant toward the ranks of men, who were indeed standing in silence, dripping and staring.

"The utmost regularity," repeated the lieutenant, and then the ship broke in half.

It sounded like a cannon and felt like an earthquake. The great black funnel came crashing down, right on top of several men, including Private Halford. Simeon ran forward but as he reached for Halford, the private's body skidded down the rocking deck, coming to rest at the lieutenant's feet. Dead eyes stared up at the officer, blood poured from his lifeless head. Halford wouldn't have a chance to worry about killing a man.

All of the shouts and groaning had stopped. The only men left alive were holding on and staring at each other. The world was silent for a moment.

"Beat to quarters!" screamed the lieutenant again, as the two halves of the ship slipped and groaned, each in its own direction, down toward the sea. Men grabbed for the yardarm, for the masts, for anything. "Beat to quarters!"

CHAPTER ONE

All around the hippodrome, golden gaslights framed the indigo sky. Pierrette loved the early evenings, when humans and gods seemed to be competing for who could dazzle the night. Let them do their utmost; Pierrette was about to give them all a run for their money.

Tonight, she'd perform the troupe's most dangerous and astonishing act. She wasn't exactly *grateful* that the usual performer had broken his collarbone and declared he was done with circus life for good. Still, if this was her chance, she was ready to seize it.

Major Wallin was not convinced, though, even now when the band had started up, and the stands were filled. They were always filled. The new hippodrome in Kensington Gardens was only a few steps away from the imposing Crystal Palace housing the Great Exhibition, filled with wonders from all over the world. There had never been a better place or time to be a performer than London in the summer of 1851. There was so much demand that the hippodrome had several troupes performing. The long oval ring had only just been swept of ostrich dung and chariot wheel-ruts from the afternoon's Astonishing Antiquity performance when a fresh audience streamed in for the horse show.

But Major Wallin, the leader of the Aurora Equestrian Troupe, looked nervous. He stood under the performers' entrance in his crisp blue and gold jacket, a simulacrum of the Swedish cavalry officer's uniform he had worn in his former life. He regarded Pierrette with skepticism.

"You know that I can do it," she said, speaking in French as she always did with Major Wallin. "I've done it a dozen times in rehearsal."

"But everyone will be expecting a man!" Major Wallin scratched one of his graying muttonchops. "Mazeppa is always performed by a man. It only makes *sense* for a man, because the character in Byron's poem was lashed to the galloping horse as punishment for an affair with a countess. You cannot play that part."

"You don't think people will believe I could seduce a countess?" Pierrette put her hand on her hip. Her one-piece costume, which Nell had hastily constructed that day for the Mazeppa role, was the same pinkish hue as her skin.

She was teasing, and he blushed. The Swedish major and his late Italian wife (the Aurora who had given her name to the troupe) had taken Pierrette with them when they left France three years previously, in the wake of the bloody Paris uprising when her parents were killed. Major Wallin had been a second father to her, and she respected his judgment. He was the master of all the horses, and he made every call.

But Pierrette was nearly nineteen now, old enough to know her own mind, and she knew she could do this and make it the talk of the town. She *needed* to do this. Her destiny lay in the lights, in the air. There was no way the world could see her talents if she only did what every other equestrienne did: the somersaults, the standing on bareback, the vaults. All of it was dangerous and all of it took a great deal of skill, but people wanted more. They wanted drama. They wanted a story. They wanted baying wolves and growling thunder and a galloping horse, foaming and frenzied (or at least made to look like it was – dear old Attila would be fine). She needed an act that would tell make world take notice.

She smiled fondly at the major, and said, "Mazeppa hasn't really been about the poem for years. It's about tying someone to a horse and having that horse gallop into rocks and be chased by wolves and up the ramp. Imagine how our troupe's reputation will soar when people hear that a *woman* has performed Mazeppa! And with my hoop act at the end to fetch my trophy, it will be different to any Mazeppa ever performed."

The major grumbled. "There is something to be said for tradition. We are not mere spectacle. We are artists." But this was a speech he'd given enough times to bore even himself, and he was looking out at the crowd.

"The tradition is that someone performs Mazeppa at the end of the show. Everyone will expect it. And I am the only member of this troupe qualified to perform it tonight."

He'd lost, and he knew it. He sighed, and said, as one last

salvo, "I promised your parents I'd keep you safe. Mazeppa is the opposite of safe."

But Pierrette had a salvo ready of her own. She tucked one of her dark curls behind her ear and quoted two lines from Byron's poem, in English: "'No matter; I have bared my brow full in Death's face – before – and now.'"

The brass band's music went low, the horns quiet and the drums suspenseful. The evening's entertainment began. First up was "The African Hercules," who was really Hugh Robinson from Manchester, riding two horses around the ring, a foot on each saddle. Beside Pierrette, Hugh's wife watched from the wings, her arms folded over her neat blue bodice with its pearl buttons. Nell Robinson was the troupe's accountant and business manager. More than once, Major Wallin had asked her to perform, but she'd said she had seen too many Black women dressed in skimpy furs as "femmes sauvages" to consider it, and always refused to talk about it any more than that.

Then it was the rope dancer, the beautiful and lithe Ariel Fine, billed as "Neither Man Nor Woman But Sprite of the Air," performing intricate steps on a somewhat slack rope, with a balance bar in their hands.

The music took on a military air for Tillie Wallin, the Major's eight year-old daughter, on her pretty mare. She always charmed the audience with her blonde curls, and she could perform as well as any adult Pierrette had seen. The major was so proud of his daughter, and had trained her in the careful maneuvers and jumps of the *haute école* tradition.

Jovita Ferreira, a Brazilian woman who'd left her husband

and literally run away to the circus, performed Pierrette's usual act of somersaults, vaults and Amazonian feats.

Then it was Pierrette's turn. Mechanical covers rose up to dim the flames of the gaslights as she strode out into the ring. Major Wallin tied her to Attila's broad back, and there she was, staring up at the darkening sky. They hadn't told the audience there was a change in performer tonight, and whispers went up in the front row as the lights went bright again.

Pierrette Arnaud was about to show the world what she could do.

She was Mazeppa, the poetic hero, condemned to a terrible journey across Eastern Europe. First, Attila picked his way through a course of "rocks" made of plaster. Then out came the dogs to chase him, although they were good friends of Attila's now.

The brass band did its best imitations of wolves and wild horses as Attila raced three times around the ring. The poem, which she had read purely to find an argument for the major, whispered in her mind: *"The skies spun like a mighty wheel; I saw the trees like drunkards reel."*

But there were no trees inside the hippodrome, only a fair few actual drunkards. They were the greatest danger, because the Mazeppa act required the performer to ride quickly up a ramp that they'd put right over a section of the seating, sacrificing a few tickets to create a thrill. Being so close to the audience, there was always the danger of someone pulling at the ropes or grabbing the performer's leg.

It was, in fact, safest to go as quickly as the horse could go, and Attila knew his business. He carried Pierrette confidently on the final run across the dirt, toward the ramp.

But he was sweating, and so was Pierrette – even London was hot in July. She could feel herself slipping inside the ropes. If she got tangled in his gait, or he faltered and fell, she could be crushed. Performers had been dragged to their deaths before now.

Out of the corner of her eye, Pierrette scanned for any likely troublemakers in the stands. There was a woman holding an opera glass in her hands, and a man over her shoulder, looking at the woman. A pickpocket, probably, but too far off to cause Attila and Pierrette any concern.

Up, up, and she took her last look at the purpling sky in the center of the open hippodrome. She could not manage the horse at all, not in this position, sprawled on his back with her legs and arms pinioned. But the people were cheering. It was a roar in her ears.

And then Attila reared, Pierrette lurched backward, and the audience gasped.

It was all part of the show. A way for Attila to come to a stop and get his carrot. In the darkness just behind the curtain hanging from the roof that covered the stands, Tillie fed Attila his treat. Major Wallin sliced the ropes, and Pierrette emerged back into her adoring gaslight, stumbling because her character had been broken and was waking from a faint. And stumbling because she'd just been untied from the back of a leaping horse.

She had three breaths to recover her equilibrium so she could perform the last part of the act: receiving a trophy from a beautiful woman. The audience reacted first to Pierrette staggering, free and alive, and then across to the beautiful woman in question, who was Jovita in a new costume, lowered in a hoop that hung from a high crane that the apprentices had wheeled out into the center of the hippodrome. Jovita was high in the air, out of reach. But there was a series of hoops on cranes, and Pierrette would swing on each until, dangling from her knees on the last one, she would catch the trophy as Jovita threw it, in midair.

Another hoop descended from the roof over the stands, at the base of the ramp.

Her heart beat with joy as she staggered down the ramp. She loved this part.

Off to her right, the woman with the opera glass now had four men around her, and they were all turning to her. She was nearly obscured by their broad shoulders and bowler hats. Four men. That wasn't pickpockets.

Focus, Pierrette ordered herself, and ran down the ramp toward her hoop. At the last moment, she leaped up, caught it in her hands. Now she had to get the hoop moving. A series of climbs and twists, hanging from the hoop, as it started to swing. Then on to the next hoop, and the next. Finally, she dropped to her knees, keeping her eyes on Jovita and the trophy. The final moment was nearly here.

And the man behind the woman with the opera glass now had his gloved hand over her mouth, and she was wriggling, her eyes alarmed, her arms restrained, no sign of the opera glass now. They started moving her through the stands, but backward, and nobody around her seemed to be paying any attention – or they didn't care. *Help her!* Pierrette wanted to scream. The woman would be out of the audience altogether in a moment, taken by these men for who-knows-what purpose.

All eyes were on Pierrette. Except her own. If she was the only witness, well then, so be it. She was the only one who could help.

Instead of turning to catch the trophy, Pierrette leapt back to where she'd started, hoop by hoop, and then dangled from her knees over the audience, as they reached up to her, unable to touch her, shouting their praise. She was almost low enough. She could do this.

She swung the hoop sideways, again and again, back and forth, turning it into a pendulum. A little more, and she'd be nearly over the abducted woman.

Down to her ankles, looping her feet to hold herself steady, she reached down and grabbed the woman by her arms. It never would have worked if it weren't for the fact that the men around her were so startled by this phenomenon that they slackened their grip and ducked as though from an aggressive seagull.

Under her wide green skirt and yellow cape, the lady was a tiny, bony thing. Even so, the weight was too much, and she made it worse by kicking and squirming. Pierrette's ankles were screaming. Her body was contorting in all the wrong ways. A few more seconds was all she had. As the hoop swung backwards, its arc shortened now, she dropped the woman onto the ramp where she and Attila had galloped a few moments before. Pierrette dropped beside her, skinning her knee and jarring her wrists. But the lady was sprawled face first.

Pierrette glanced up at Jovita, still high in her hoop, frozen in a dramatic posture, the trophy forgotten in her hand. Her eyes were wide, and her other hand gripped the hoop so hard it was rotating.

Everyone in London, these days, knew that it was pointless

asking for help from the police. Most of them were in cahoots with various gangs and criminals, and there was no telling which ones were the good ones, at a glance. Anyway, there were no bobbies to be seen in the hippodrome that night, good or otherwise, but there were four men who seemed determined to get their hands on this woman.

So Pierrette took the woman's arm and whispered, "Run," and lifted her to her feet.

She didn't need to say it again. The scrawny lady ran like a frightened cat, gathering strength from who knows where, her skirts in her hands, and her heeled shoes slipping on the runway, down into the ring, across to the performers' entrance, and out of the hippodrome.

And whether out of some performer's instinct for a dramatic ending, or because she didn't seem very likely to get to safety on her own, Pierrette ran with her.

They tore past the rope barrier that kept people without tickets from getting close enough to see inside the hippodrome. People milled beyond those ropes, out for the evening in the shadow of the Great Exhibition. Men and women, some well-dressed, but most with worn shawls and patched coats, some with children on their shoulders, little dogs yipping on leashes.

The lady ran into the crowd, tripped, and collapsed in a heap of bottle-green poplin.

Pierrette snatched up the lady's bonnet just before a dachshund could, then helped her to her feet. The people around them were murmuring, gasping, smiling, confused – a mixture of reactions on every face.

Someone said, "Is it part of the trick?"

Pierrette turned and smiled at the man. "I'll get my trophy yet, by gum!"

At that, everyone around her laughed. She knew her English was a bit accented, and that was probably part of what they were laughing at, but that didn't matter. She was who she was, and she would use all of it, with every audience, until they shouted her name, stamped their feet, whistled and clapped.

Pierrette glanced behind. There was a man in a bowler walking toward them with purpose, but whether it was one of the abductors, she couldn't say. And there was a roar from the crowd back in the hippodrome, but in reaction to what? Maybe Jovita and the others had found some way to make it all look intentional. Maybe Pierrette's performance wouldn't be thought a total disaster. All the same, Pierrette wasn't looking forward to seeing the look on Major Wallin's face.

Cursing herself for not leaving well enough alone, Pierrette ducked down by the lady on the ground. "Come, just a little further."

She pulled her to her feet one more time, and they walked over mostly green rolling ground toward the Crystal Palace. In the evening it was lit like a fairy palace. Pierrette had been inside three times already, and had seen a lump of rock billing itself as the Koh-i-Noor, to which she had said, if *that* was a diamond, *she* could be anything she wanted. Tonight, she had no desire to pay the shilling admittance, or to walk through the crowds in her skimpy flesh-colored maillot.

But there was a line of hansom cabs on the road on the far side of the Crystal Palace.

She asked the lady, "Have you got money? For a hansom cab, I mean. As you can see, I have no pockets at the moment."

The lady grimaced, as though she was in pain. She had probably hurt herself in the scramble. She was older than Pierrette: in her thirties, at a guess, and very thin.

"There's no need," the lady said, her voice clear and determined. "I'll have no trouble reaching my house on foot – it's just on the other side of the park."

Pierrette frowned. Hyde Park could take a half an hour or more to walk through. She couldn't let the lady walk alone, but Major Wallin and the others would wonder what had happened to her.

As if in response to the frown, the lady said, breathlessly, "No, you've done enough. I'm quite used to walking on my own. Thank you for your help tonight. You will call on me, won't you? I'm the Countess of Lovelace. Ada, to my friends. I think it's right that you and I should be friends. That poem you performed tonight. Mazeppa. It was written by my father."

Pierrette had met people before who thought they were Napoleon, or Wellington, or both at once. But she believed Ada. There were the clothes, for one thing.

But also, there was the man in the bowler, again. Walking in a straight line toward this corner of the park, with his coat flaring, his eyes on them.

"I won't let you walk through the park alone, Lady Lovelace," she said. "The show is finished for tonight, anyway. We must hurry."

Pierrette imagined the map of Hyde Park in her head: a great green rectangle in the midst of London. The Crystal

Palace, home of the Great Exhibition, was in the middle along the southern edge. That was on their right now. Beyond it lay busy, bright streets, which might be safer. But if Lady Lovelace was trying to get to the northeast corner, it would be much faster to go diagonally through the park. That meant crossing the bridge over the Serpentine, the lake that cut the park in half.

She pulled Ada to the left, urgently, taking a gravel side-path. As they approached the Serpentine, Pierrette looked back. There was the shadowy man, and he'd been joined by another, loping along beside him like a hound.

"*Bande de salauds*," Pierrette grumbled. Then louder, to Lady Lovelace: "Who are these men and why are they so persistent?"

"Creditors," Ada said, out of breath. "I assume, anyway. I do have rather a few debts, you see. I have a wonderful plan – I can guess the horse races – but it hasn't quite worked out. Or I suppose it might be…" She broke off.

"What?"

"Or they might be someone else," Ada whispered.

At the near end of the bridge stood another two men in bowlers, just at the edge of a circle of light cast by the nearest gas lamp. In the hippodrome, the thugs had counted on the crowd's attention being on the performance. Here in the open, they'd be looking for darkness and isolation.

Pierrette took Ada's hand and hurried her toward the path that led to the bridge. They fell in behind a group of three school-aged children following an irritated governess. The children glanced at Pierrette, in her pink maillot, but the governess seemed too flustered to care. They were so terribly late and their poor mother would be so worried, her posture announced.

Past the men and over the bridge. One of the children ran toward the wooded shore, eager to make friends with a pair of swans. The governess groaned, lifted her skirt and ran after her charge, with the other two following.

They were alone and exposed again.

Pierrette glanced behind to see four men now, matching their brisk walking pace. They crossed a broad road, the earth packed hard. Pierrette considered taking it north, but there were only occasional carriages on it at the moment, and it was lined with trees that would cut them off from public view. Besides, on the road, they'd be easily bundled into a carriage.

They struck out on the footpath leading diagonally across the park. Here the land was open, but it was so dark now. The pursuers were still behind them, and she could see two more men approaching on the path ahead, little more than dark shapes.

She looked frantically around. Toward the south, on another path, a couple was strolling arm in arm. Would they help, if she called for it?

Pierrette pretended to stumble, crying out. Lady Lovelace stopped, but Pierrette waved her concern away. It was a test. The couple on the other path paused, but didn't change course or even turn their heads. The selfishness of some people! The men were closing in.

"This way," Pierrette whispered, and grabbed Lady Lovelace by the elbow. By the time the men were almost within grabbing distance, they were passing the couple. They settled in front of them, still close enough that the man's pipe smoke billowed around them, and slackened their pace.

Before long the odd procession – Pierrette and Lady Lovelace in front, the irritated couple behind, and four men trailing them – passed two more men in bowlers. They might have been the men who'd been approaching on the other path. For a moment, Pierrette wondered whether they might attack all four of them, including the oblivious couple. But the thugs simply touched their hat brims and sneered.

The end of the park at last. Ada was walking steadily, one hand on Pierrette's arm. Park Lane was bright and busy, and Pierrette didn't chase after the couple when they took the first opportunity to leave the path. Once there was no sign of the men in the bowler hats, Pierrette risked slowing down for a moment to rest. People walked all around and past them: a sea of silk, felt and beaver hats in all states of repair; shawls smelling of oysters, jackets smelling of beer.

"I used to ride out in the park," Ada said with a wistful glance behind them, after they'd caught their breath. "Nearly a decade ago now, when I was healthier. Caused quite a scandal, as I rode with friends – men, I mean. But my husband couldn't always go riding with me, and I enjoy riding so much. I'm very good at it. Oh, but of course, not anything like you! Your performance really was marvelous. The demonstration of the principles of motion. I have been wanting to see someone perform Mazeppa since I was a girl."

They walked on. Pierrette's nerves calmed as they approached the Marble Arch, newly moved to the north-east corner of the park that spring. There was a police station occupying a few rooms inside the Arch, and though Pierrette had no intention of involving the police in anything, it might keep Ada's pursuers at bay.

Besides, this corner was brightly lit by the gas lamps of Park Lane and Oxford Street. They dodged the wide skirts of fashionable women. A man in a shabby top hat was gesticulating to a crowd, shouting about the glories of Britain's Empire.

Now that the danger had passed, Pierrette stifled nervous laughter at what she'd done. She had picked up a lady from the audience, and deposited her in Park Lane, all while wearing her costume, which was starting to feel very chilly in the night air. Major Wallin would be beside himself. Had poor Jovita come down from her hoop?

After they passed the Marble Arch, Ada lifted one of her bird-thin hands and pointed at one of the tall, dignified brick houses. "Home. William – my husband – is out tonight, but Mother's there. She'll be frantic, of course, once she learns I am not resting in my bedroom as she thinks, but she always forgives me.

"You must come and see me, my Mazeppa." She looked Pierrette up and down in her pink maillot, and said, "But perhaps not tonight."

ASSASSIN'S CREED®:
THE MAGUS CONSPIRACY

Available now from all good bookstores!

About the Author

YAN LEISHENG has had a special interest in science fiction since an early age, but it wasn't until his thirties that he was first published. Since then, he has published twenty books, including novels, short story collections, essays, and poetry. His most famous trilogy "Heaven Prevails" has sold over 500,000 copies in Chinese.

A gripping manga based on Ubisoft's
Assassin's Creed Chronicles: China®
video game, featuring iconic
Assassin Shao Jun.

ASSASSIN'S CREED

BLADE OF SHAO JUN

Unveil a tale that will
engulf the world!

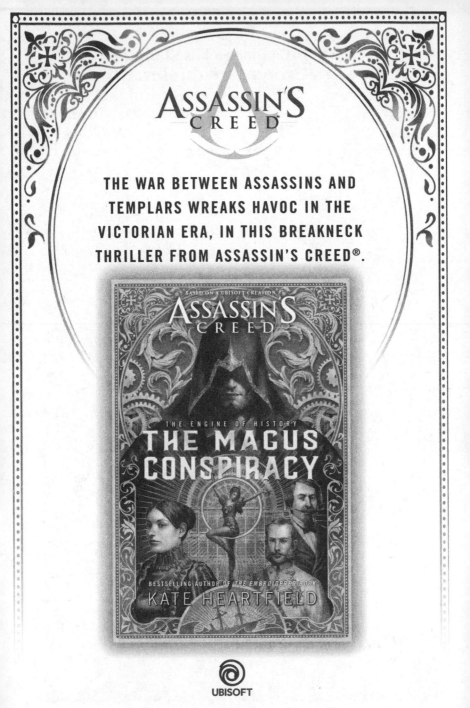

ASSASSIN'S CREED
VALHALLA

WITCH WARRIOR NIAMH INFILTRATES AN ANCIENT SECT TO DEFEAT VIKING RAIDERS IN A STUNNING ORGINAL SAGA SET IN ASSASSIN'S CREED® VALHALLA.

TOM CLANCY'S
SPLINTER·CELL®

A BRUTAL ENEMY FROM THE PAST.

AN UNSTOPPABLE CYBER-WEAPON.

A MISSION AGAINST ALL ODDS.

TOM CLANCY'S
SPLINTER·CELL
FIREWALL

NEW YORK TIMES BESTSELLING AUTHOR
JAMES SWALLOW

COMING SOON

TRAPPED BEHIND ENEMY LINES.

NO BACK-UP, NO SUPPORT.

ONLY ONE CHANCE.

TOM CLANCY'S
SPLINTER·CELL
DRAGONFIRE

NEW YORK TIMES BESTSELLING AUTHOR
JAMES SWALLOW

TOM CLANCY'S THE DIVISION

DIVE INTO THE WORLD OF THE DIVISION IN THE PULSE-POUNDING ACTION THRILLER *RECRUITED*

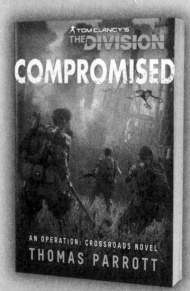

COMING SOON **FIGHT FOR HOPE, FIGHT FOR PEACE: JOIN THE DIVISION, IN *COMPROMISED***

UBISOFT

WORLD EXPANDING FICTION

Have you read them all?

ASSASSIN'S CREED®
- ☐ *The Ming Storm* by Yan Leisheng
- ☐ *The Magus Conspiracy* by Kate Heartfield
- ☑ *The Desert Threat* by Yan Leisheng

ASSASSIN'S CREED® VALHALLA
- ☐ *Geirmund's Saga* by Matthew J Kirby *(US/CAN only)*
- ☐ *Sword of the White Horse* by Elsa Sjunneson

TOM CLANCY'S THE DIVISION®
- ☐ *Recruited* by Thomas Parrott
- ☐ *Compromised* by Thomas Parrott *(coming soon)*

TOM CLANCY'S SPLINTER CELL®
- ☐ *Firewall* by James Swallow
- ☐ *Dragonfire* by James Swallow *(coming soon)*

WATCH DOGS®
- ☐ *Stars & Stripes* by Sean Grigsby & Stewart Hotston

WATCH DOGS® LEGION
- ☐ *Day Zero* by James Swallow & Josh Reynolds
- ☐ *Daybreak Legacy* by Stewart Hotston